My Lady's Trust

JULIA JUSTISS

D0034576

HARLEQUIN®

TORONTO • NEW YORK • LONDON
AMSTERDAM • PARIS • SYDNEY • HAMBURG
STOCKHOLM • ATHENS • TOKYO • MILAN • MADRID
PRAGUE • WARSAW • BUDAPEST • AUCKLAND

SAN BRUNO PUBLIC LIBRARY

If you purchased this book without a cover you should be aware
that this book is stolen property. It was reported as "unsold and
destroyed" to the publisher, and neither the author nor the
publisher has received any payment for this "stripped book."

ISBN 0-373-29191-4

MY LADY'S TRUST

Copyright © 2002 by Janet Justiss

All rights reserved. Except for use in any review, the reproduction or
utilization of this work in whole or in part in any form by any electronic,
mechanical or other means, now known or hereafter invented, including
xerography, photocopying and recording, or in any information storage
or retrieval system, is forbidden without the written permission of the
publisher, Harlequin Enterprises Limited, 225 Duncan Mill Road,
Don Mills, Ontario, Canada M3B 3K9.

All characters in this book have no existence outside the imagination of
the author and have no relation whatsoever to anyone bearing the same
name or names. They are not even distantly inspired by any individual
known or unknown to the author, and all incidents are pure invention.

This edition published by arrangement with Harlequin Books S.A.

® and TM are trademarks of the publisher. Trademarks indicated with
® are registered in the United States Patent and Trademark Office, the
Canadian Trade Marks Office and in other countries.

Visit us at www.eHarlequin.com

Printed in U.S.A.

Prologue

Soundlessly Laura crept through the dark hall. Having rehearsed—and used—the route before, she knew every carpet, chair and cupboard in the passageway, each twist of the twenty-nine steps down the servants' stair to the back door. Even were their old butler Hobbins and his wife not snoring in their room just off the corridor, the winter storm howling through the chimneys and rattling the shutters would cover the slight rustle of her movements.

Just once she halted in her stealthy passage, outside the silent nursery. Leaning toward the door, she could almost catch a whiff of baby skin, feel the softness of flannel bunting, see the bright eyes and small waving hands. A bitter bleakness pierced her heart, beside whose chill the icy needles being hurled against the windows were mild as summer rain, and her step staggered.

She bent over, gripping for support the handle of the room where a baby's gurgle no longer sounded. Nor ever would again—not flesh of her flesh.

I promise you that, Jennie, she vowed. Making good on that vow could not ease the burden of guilt she carried, but it was the last thing she would do in this house. The only thing, now, she could do.

Marshaling her strength, she straightened and made her way down the stairs, halting once more to catch her breath before attempting to work the heavy lock of the kitchen door. She was stronger now. For the past month she'd practiced walking, at first quietly in her room, more openly this past week since most of the household had departed with its master for London. She could do this.

Cautiously she unlatched the lock, then fastened her heavy cloak and drew on her warmest gloves. At her firm push the door opened noiselessly on well-oiled hinges. Ignoring the sleet that pelted her face and the shrieking wind that tore the hood from her hair, she walked into the night.

Chapter One

The crisp fall breeze, mingling the scents of falling leaves and the sharp tang of herbs, brought to Laura Martin's ear the faint sound of barking interspersed with the crack of rifle shot. The party which had galloped by her cottage earlier this morning, the squire's son throwing her a jaunty wave as they passed, must be hunting duck in the marsh nearby, she surmised.

Having cut the supply of tansy she needed for drying, Laura turned to leave the herb bed. Misfit, the squire's failure of a rabbit hound who'd refused to leave her after she healed the leg he'd caught in a poacher's trap, bumped his head against her hand, demanding attention.

"Shameless beggar," she said, smiling as she scratched behind his ears.

The dog flapped his tail and leaned into her stroking fingers. A moment later, however, he stiffened and looked up, uttering a soft whine.

"What is it?" Almost before the words left her lips she heard the rapid staccato of approaching hoofbeats. Seconds later one of the squire's grooms, mounted on a lathered horse and leading another, flashed into view.

Foreboding tightening her chest, she strode to the garden fence.

"What's wrong, Peters?" she called to the young man bringing his mount to a plunging halt.

"Your pardon, Mrs. Martin, but I beg you come at once! There were an accident—a gun gone off..." The groom stopped and swallowed hard. "Please, ma'am!"

"How badly was the person injured?"

"I don't rightly know. The young gentleman took a shot to the shoulder and there be blood everywhere. He done swooned off immediate, and—"

Her foreboding deepened. "You'd best find Dr. Winthrop. I fear gunshots are beyond—"

"I already been by the doctor's, ma'am, and he—he can't help."

"I see." Their local physician's unfortunate obsession with strong spirits all too frequently left him incapable of caring for himself or anyone else. 'Twas how she'd gained much of her limited experience, stepping in when the doctor was incapacitated. But gunshot wounds? The stark knowledge of her own inadequacy chilled her.

Truly there was no one else. "I'll come at once."

"Young master said as how I was to bring you immediate, but I don't have no lady's saddle. 'Twill take half an hour 'n more to fetch the gig."

"No matter, Peters. I can manage astride. Under the circumstances, I don't imagine anyone will notice my dispensing with proprieties. Help me fetch my bag."

She tried to set worry aside and concentrate on gathering any extra supplies she might need to augment the store already in her traveling bag. The groom carried the heavy satchel to the waiting horses and gave her a hand up. Settling her skirts as decorously as possible, she waited for him to vault into the saddle, then turned her restive horse to follow his. Spurring their mounts, they galloped back in the direction of the marsh.

As they rode, she mentally reviewed the remedies she brought. During her year-long recovery from the illness that nearly killed her, she'd observed Aunt Mary treat a variety of agues, fevers and stomach complaints—but never a gunshot. To the assortment of medicaments she always carried she'd added a powder to slow bleeding, brandy to cleanse the wound and basilica powder. Had she thought of everything?

She had no further time to worry, for around the next bend the woods gave way to marsh. A knot of men gathered at the water's edge. As she slid from the saddle, she saw at their center a still, prone figure, the pallor of his face contrasting sharply with the scarlet of the blood soaking his coat. His clothing was drenched, his boots half submerged in water whose icy bite she could already feel through the thin leather of her half-boots. The squire's son Tom held a wadded-up cloth pressed against the boy's upper chest. A cloth whose pristine whiteness was rapidly staining red.

Her nervousness coalesced in firm purpose. She must first stop the bleeding, then get the young man back to Everett Hall.

"Peters, bring more bandages from my bag, please."

At her quiet command, Tom looked up. "Thank God you're here!" His face white beneath its sprinkling of freckles, he scooted over to let her kneel beside the victim. "He's bled so badly—and…and he won't answer me. Is…is he going to die?"

"Help me," she evaded. "Lean your full weight against him, hard. Keep that cloth in place while I bind it to his shoulder. Did the shot pass straight through?"

"I don't know, ma'am. I—I didn't think to look."

Tom's eyes were huge in his pale face. "It's my fault—I wanted to hunt. If he dies—"

"Easy, now—keep the pressure firm." To steady Tom—and herself—she said, "Tell me what happened."

"I'm not sure. The dogs raised a covey, and we both fired. The next moment Kit clutched his chest, blood pouring out between his fingers. Maybe—perhaps one of our shots hit that bluff and ricocheted. He fell in the water, as you see, and we dragged him to land but feared to move him any further until help arrived."

Listening with half an ear, she worked as quickly as she could, her worried eye on the unconscious victim's gray face and blue-tinged lips. If the shot was still lodged in his body, it must be removed, but at the moment she didn't dare explore the wound. Fortunately, the chill that numbed him also slowed the bleeding. She only hoped the effect would last through the jolting necessary to take him to shelter. And that his dousing in frigid water wouldn't result in an inflammation of the lungs.

"Is he...tell me he'll be all right!"

The desperate note in Tom's voice recalled her attention. Avoiding a direct answer, she looked up to give him a brief smile. "We must get him out of the cold. Have you sent to the hall?"

"Yes. My father should be along any moment."

Indeed, as Tom spoke they heard the welcome sound of a coach approaching. Riding ahead was the squire, a short, rotund man on a piebald gray. He took one long look at the scene before him and blew out a gusty breath.

"God have mercy! What's to be done, Mrs. Martin?"

"If you would help me bind this tightly, we can move him into the carriage and back to the hall."

After securing the bandage, she directed the grooms to

carry the victim to the coach, the unconscious man groaning as they eased him against the padded squabs.

"Tom, ride on ahead and alert Mrs. Jenkins. We'll need boiling water and hot bricks and such." The squire shook his head, his nose red with cold and his eyes worried. "Go on, I'll settle with you later. There'll be a reckoning to pay for this day's work, make no mistake!"

Wordlessly his son nodded, then sprinted to his mount. After assisting Laura into the carriage beside her patient, the squire hesitated. "You'll tend him back at the hall?"

"Until more experienced help arrives, of course. But I recommend you send someone with strong coffee to sober up Dr. Winthrop, or over to the next county for their physician. I've no experience with gunshots, and to tell the truth, the young man looks very badly."

To her surprise, the squire seized her hands. "You must stay, Mrs. Martin, and do all you can! 'Tis no country doctor we'll be having! I've sent word to the lad's brother to come at once and bring his own physician. Please say you'll stay with the boy until he arrives!"

An instinctive prickle of fear skittered up from her toes and lodged at her throat. She glanced at the still figure beside her. Was there something familiar about that profile? "He is from a prominent family?" she ventured, already dreading the response.

"Younger brother of the Earl of Beaulieu."

For a moment her heart nearly stopped. "The Puzzlebreaker?" she asked weakly. "Friend to the prime minister, one of the wealthiest men in the realm?"

"Aye, he founded that daft Puzzlemaker's Club, but he's a sharp 'un, for all that. It's said Lord Riverton don't make a move without consulting him. Been visiting friends up north, with this cub set to join him next week." The squire sighed heavily. "When I consider what Lord Beaulieu may think should his brother Kit die in my care... I do swear, I rue the day my Tom met him at Oxford."

"Surely the earl could not hold you responsible."

The squire shrugged, then raised pleading eyes to hers. "I beg you to stay, Mrs. Martin. With any luck, my messenger will reach the earl within hours and bring his physician back, mayhap by nightfall. I'd not have the worthless Winthrop near him, drunk or sober, and Lord knows, my sister will be no help. Mistress Mary thought so highly of your skill—none better in the county, she swore. Will you not keep the lad alive until his kin arrive?"

And thereby encounter the Earl of Beaulieu? All her protective instincts screamed danger as the metallic taste of fear filled her mouth, seeming stronger than ever after its near two-year hiatus. Though her first impulse was to jump from the carriage, mount the borrowed horse and race back to the safe haven of her little cottage, she struggled to squelch her irrational panic.

She must fashion a measured reply. The squire would be expecting from her nothing more extreme than worry.

While she fumbled for appropriate words, the squire sat straighter. "You cannot fear I'd allow the earl to take you to task should...the worst happen. My good madam, surely you realize your well-being is of great import to me!" He leaned closer and kissed her hand awkwardly. "I only seek to do all we can for the poor lad until his brother arrives."

"I know you would ever safeguard me," she replied, and managed a smile. *You're being a nodcock,* the rational part of her brain argued. The great earl was hardly likely to recognize her as one of the unremarkable chits making her bow he'd met but twice a handful of Seasons ago. Though this task was clearly beyond her skill, she had more expertise than any other person within a day's ride, and the boy needed help now.

As she vacillated, torn between the safety of refusal and the peril of acceptance, she heard again Aunt Mary's last words *God spared you for a purpose, missy. He's given you skill—use it wisely.*

She glanced again at the boy, motionless and bloody beside her. Did not that innocent lad deserve the best possible chance to survive? Even if caring for him placed her in some risk.

But a risk much less serious than the young man's chances of dying if left untended.

"Have the coachman drive slowly. He must be jostled as little as possible," she said at last. "If the wound begins bleeding again, there will be nothing I can do."

The squire released a grateful sigh. "Thank you, ma'am. I'll keep pace by the coach. Call if you need me."

He stepped down and closed the door, leaving her in the shuttered semidarkness with a barely breathing boy whose powerful brother, Lord Beaulieu, would be upon her within hours, perhaps this very day.

What had she gotten herself into?

Hugh Mannington "Beau" Bradsleigh, Earl of Beaulieu, leaped from the saddle and tossed the reins of his spent steed to the servant who materialized out of the darkness. His bootsteps ringing out on the stone steps, he approached the flickering torches flanking the entry of Squire Everett's manor house. Before he reached the front portal, however, a tall, freckled lad he recognized as Kit's Oxford friend rushed out.

"Lord Beaulieu, thank God you're come. I'm so sorry—"

"Where is he?" At the stricken look coming over the young man's face, Beau briefly regretted his abruptness, but after a message designed to convince him Kit could die at any moment and the most exhausting gallop he'd endured in years, he had no patience for an exchange of courtesies.

A shorter, rotund man with a balding head darted into view. "This way, my lord. Squire Everett here, but we'll not stand on formality. Cook has a platter of victuals and strong ale waiting. I'll have them sent up at once."

Beau spared a brief smile for the older man who, though obviously anxious, made no attempt to delay him with excuses or explanations he at the moment had no interest in hearing. "You, sir, are both kind and perceptive." Taking a deep breath, as he followed the squire to the stairs he voiced the anxiety that had eaten at him every second of the arduous ride. "How goes it with Kit?"

The squire gave him a sidelong glance as they started up. "Not well, I'm afraid. We very nearly lost him this afternoon. When do you expect your physician?"

The tension in his chest tightened. Kit—laughing, sunny-tempered Kit, so full of the joy of life. He *could not* die—Beau would simply not permit it. "Morning at the earliest. Who tends him now? Have you a doctor here?"

"Only a jug-bitten fool I'd not trust with a lame dog. Mrs. Martin keeps vigil, a neighbor lady skilled with herbs who is often consulted by the local folk."

The image of an old crone mixing love potions for the gullible flew into his head. "An herb woman!" he said, aghast. "'Od's blood, man, that's the best you could do?"

The squire paused at the landing and looked back in dignified reproach. "'Tis not in London we be, my lord. Mrs. Martin is widow to a military man and has much experience tending the sick. She, at least, I was confident could do young Kit no harm. Indeed, she's kept him from death several times already. In here, my lord."

He should apologize to the squire later, Beau noted numbly as he paced into the chamber. But for now all his attention focused on the figure lying in the big canopied bed, his still, pale face illumined by the single candle on the bedside table.

Still and pale as a death mask. Fear like a rifle shot ricocheted through him as he half ran to his brother's side. "Kit! Kit, it's Hugh. I'm here now."

The boy on the bed made no response as Beau took his hand, rubbed it. The skin felt dry—and warm.

"He's turning feverish, I fear."

The quiet, feminine voice came from the darkness on the far side of the bed. Beau looked over at a nondescript woman in a shapeless brown dress, her head covered by a large mobcap that shadowed her face. This was what passed for medical aid here? Fear flashed anew—and anger. "What do you intend to do about it?"

"Keep him sponged down and spoon in willow bark tea. He was so chilled initially, I did not think it wise to begin cooling him from the first. I'm afraid the shot is still lodged in his chest, but I dared not remove it. When does your physician arrive?"

"Not before morning," he repeated, anxiety filling him at the echo. This kindly old biddy might do well for possets and potions, but was she to be all that stood between Kit and death until MacDonovan came?

No, he thought, setting his jaw. *He* was here, and he'd be damned if he'd let his brother die before his eyes. "Tell me what to do."

"You have ridden all day, my lord?"

"Since afternoon," he replied impatiently. "'Tis no matter."

The woman looked up at him then, the eyes of her shadowed face capturing a glow of reflected candlelight. Assessing him, he realized with a slight shock.

Before he could utter a set-down, she said, "You should rest. You'll do the young gentleman no good, once he regains consciousness, if you're bleary with fatigue."

He fixed on her the iron-eyed glare that had inspired more than one subordinate to back away in apologetic dismay. This little woman, however, simply held his gaze. Goaded, he replied, "My good madam, the boy on that bed is my brother, my blood. I assure you, had I ridden the length of England, I could do whatever is necessary."

After another audacious measuring moment, the woman nodded. "Very well. I've just mixed more willow bark tea. If you'll raise him—only slightly now, heed the shot in his chest—I'll spoon some in."

For the rest of what seemed an endless night, he followed the soft-spoken orders of the brown-garbed lady. She seemed competent enough, he supposed, ordering broths up from the kitchen, strewing acrid herbs into the water in which she had him wring out the cloths they placed on Kit's neck and brow, directing him to turn Kit periodically to keep fluid from settling in his lungs.

Certainly she was tireless. Although he'd never have admitted it, after a blur of hours his own back ached and his hands were raw from wringing cloths. Mrs. Martin, however, gave no sign of fatigue at all.

Their only altercation occurred early on, when he demanded she unwrap the bandages so he might inspect Kit's wound. The nurse adamantly refused. Such a course would engender so much movement his brother might begin bleeding again, a risk she did not wish to take. Unless his lordship had experience enough to remove the shot once the wound was bared—a highly delicate task she herself did not intend to attempt—she recommended the bindings be left intact until the physician arrived. So anxious was he to assess the damage, however, only her threat to wash her hands of all responsibility for her patient, should he insist on disturbing Kit, induced him, grudgingly, to refrain.

Despite their efforts, as the long night lightened to dawn, Kit grew increasingly restless, his dry skin hotter. When, just after sunrise, the squire ushered in Beau's physician, both he and Mrs. Martin sighed in relief.

"Thank you, Mac, for answering my call so quickly."

"Ach, and more a command than a call it was." His old schoolmate Dr. MacDonovan smiled at him. "But we'll frash over that later. Let me to the lad. The squire's told me what happened, and the sooner we get the shot out, the better. Mrs. Martin, is it? You'll assist, please."

The nurse murmured assent, and Beau found himself shouldered aside. "Go on with ye, ye great lown," his friend chided. "Fetch yerself a wee dram—ye've the look of needin' one."

"I'm staying, Mac. Let me help."

His friend spared him a glance, then sighed. "Open the drapes, laddie, and give us more light. Then bring my bag. I may be wanting it."

By the time the gruesome procedures were over Beau

was almost sorry he'd insisted on remaining. First came the shock of the jagged entry wound, the flesh angry red and swollen. Then he had to endure the torment of holding down his struggling, semiconscious brother while the physician probed the wound with long forceps to locate and remove the shot. His back was wet with sweat and his knees shaking when finally Dr. MacDonovan finished his ministrations and began to rebind his patient.

It wasn't until after that was complete, when the physician complimented Mrs. Martin on the efficacy of her previous treatment, that he remembered the woman who had silently assisted during the procedure. With the cap shadowing her lowered face, he couldn't read her expression, but her hands had remained steady, her occasional replies to the physician calm and quiet throughout. He had to appreciate her fortitude.

Having lowered his once-again mercifully unconscious brother back against the pillows, he followed as the physician led them all out of the room.

The squire waited in the hallway. "Well, Sir Doctor, how does the patient fare?" he asked anxiously.

"The shot was all of a piece, best I could tell, which is a blessing. If I've not missed a bit, and if this lady's kind offices in tending the lad until I arrived stand us in good stead, my hopes are high of his making a full recovery. But mind ye, 'tis early days yet. He mustn't be moved, and the fever's like to get much worse afor it's agleaning. It's careful tending he'll be needing. Have ye a good nurse aboot?"

The squire glanced from the doctor to Mrs. Martin and back. "Well, there's my sister, but I'm afraid her nerves are rather delicate—"

"I shall be happy to assist until his lordship can find someone," Mrs. Martin inserted, her face downcast.

"Excellent. I recommend you accept the lady's offer, Beau. At least until ye can secure the services of another such reliable nurse."

"I've already sent a message to Ellen. That is, if it will not be an inconvenience for you to house my sister and her daughter, squire?"

"An honor, my lord," the squire replied with a bow. "And yourself, as well, for as long as you wish to remain."

"Then I should be most grateful to accept your help until my sister arrives, Mrs. Martin."

After she murmured an assent, the squire turned to the physician. "If you tell me what I must do, Doctor, I'll sit with the lad while Mrs. Martin takes her rest. She's been at his side since morning yesterday and all night, too." The squire directed a pointed look at Beau, a reminder he owed the man an apology—and a humble thanks to the quiet woman who'd so skillfully nursed his brother. "Lord Beaulieu, you must be needing your rest, as well. I'll just see the lady on her way and then return to show you to your chamber."

He bowed. With a nod and a curtsey, Mrs. Martin turned to follow the squire.

Delaying his apologies to pursue a more pressing matter, Beau lingered behind. "Was that report accurate, or are you merely trying to ease the squire's anxiety?" Beau demanded as soon as the pair were out of earshot.

Dr. MacDonovan smiled and patted his arm. "God's truth, Beau. 'Tis hard on you, I know, but there's little we can do now but give him good nursing. He's strong, though—and I do my job well. I canna promise there won't be worrisome times yet, but I believe he'll pull through."

Beau released a breath he didn't realize he'd been

holding. "Thanks, Mac. For coming so quickly and—" he managed a grin "—being so good. Now, I'd best give the redoubtable Mrs. Martin a word of thanks. Probably should toss in an apology, as well—I've not been as...courteous as I suppose I might."

The doctor laughed. "Frash with her, did ye? And lost, I'll wager! A lady of much skill, Mrs. Martin. 'Tis she more than me you'd best be thanking for keeping yon Master Kit on this earth. Lay in the icy water of the marsh nigh on an hour, I'm told. The chill alone might have killed him, had he not been carefully watched." The doctor frowned. "Aye, and may catch him yet. We must have a care for those lungs. But away with ye. I can keep these weary eyes open a bit longer."

Beau gave his friend's hand a shake and started down the hall. Now that Kit was safe in Mac's care, he noticed anew the ache in his back and a bone-deep weariness dragged his steps.

He saw Mrs. Martin by the front door as he descended the last flight of stairs, apparently in some dispute with the squire, for she was shaking her head.

"Thank you, sir, but 'tis only a short walk. There's no need for a carriage."

Beau waited for the little courtesies to be observed, his eyes nearly drooping shut until he noticed the squire make Mrs. Martin an elegant leg, quite in the manner of the last century.

"No indeed, dear ma'am, you mustn't walk. I'm fair astonished such a gentle lady as yourself has not collapsed from fatigue ere now. What fortitude and skill you possess! Qualities, I might add, which nearly equal your beauty."

After that pretty speech, the squire took Mrs. Martin's hand and kissed it.

Surprise chased away his drowsiness until he remembered the squire had called Mrs. Martin a "lady," widow to a military man. An officer, apparently, since his host would hardly extend such marked gallantries to an inferior. Beau smiled, amused to discover the middle-aged squire apparently courting the nondescript nurse, and curious to watch her response.

"You honor me," said the lady in question as she gently but firmly drew back her hand.

Coy? Beau wondered. Or just not interested?

Then the nurse glanced up. Illumined as she was by the sunshine spilling into the hall, for the first time he got a clear look at her face—her young, pretty face.

In the same instant she saw him watching her. An expression almost of—alarm crossed her lovely features and she swiftly lowered her head, once again concealing her countenance behind a curtain of cap lace. What remark she made to the squire and whether or not she availed herself of the carriage, he did not hear. Before he could move his stunned lips into the speech of gratitude he'd intended to deliver, she curtsied once more and slipped out.

By the time the squire joined him on the landing his foggy brain had resumed functioning. Mumbling something resembling an apology as the man escorted him to his chamber, he let his mind play over the interesting discovery that the skillful Mrs. Martin was not only a lady, but a rather young one at that.

He recalled the brevity of her speech, even with the squire, whom she apparently knew well, and the way she skittered off when she found him watching her. More curious still. Why, he wondered as he sank thankfully into the soft feather bed, would such an eminently marriageable widow be so very retiring?

Having the widow tend his brother would give Beau
the opportunity to observe this odd conundrum more
closely. Which would be a blessing, for as his brother's
recovery—and Kit simply must recover—was likely to
be lengthy, Beau would need something to distract him
from worry. Luckily, nothing intrigued him as much as
a riddle.

Chapter Two

A few hours later Laura pulled herself reluctantly from bed and walked to the kitchen. A bright sun sparkled on the scrubbed table and Maggie, the maid of all work the squire sent over every morning to do her cleaning, had left her nuncheon and a pot of water simmering on the stove.

She'd remain just long enough for tea and to wash up before returning to her patient. The kindly Scots physician had ridden straight through, he'd told her, and would be needing relief.

She frowned as she poured water into the washbasin. It wasn't fatigue that caused the vague disquiet that nagged at her. She'd learned to survive on very little sleep while she cared for her dying "aunt Mary."

No, it was the lingering effects of working for so many hours in such close proximity to the Earl of Beaulieu—a man who exuded an almost palpable aura of power—that left her so uneasy.

He'd not recognized her, she was sure. Even when he looked her full in the face this morning, she'd read only surprise in his eyes—surprise, she assumed, that she was not the aged crone he had evidently taken her to be. An impression she, of course, had done her best to instill and one he might harbor yet if she'd not stupidly looked up.

A flash of irritation stabbed her. She'd grown too complacent of late, forgotten to keep her head demurely lowered whenever there might be strangers about.

'Twas too late to repair that lapse. However, despite discovering her to be younger than he'd expected, there was still no reason he should not, as everyone else around Merriville had done, accept her as exactly what she claimed to be, the widowed cousin of the retired governess whose cottage she had inherited.

She felt again a wave of grief for the woman who had been nurse, friend and savior. That gentle lady, sister of Laura's own governess, who had taken in a gravely ill fugitive and given her back not just life, but a new identity and the possibility of a future. Who'd become her mentor, training Laura to a skill which enabled her to support herself. And finally, the benefactor who'd willed her this cottage, safe haven in which to begin over again.

A safe haven still, she told herself firmly, squelching the swirl of unease in her stomach. She need only continue to act the woman everyone believed her to be. Young or not, a simple country gentlewoman could be of no more interest to the great earl than a pebble.

As long as she stayed in her role—no more jerking away in alarm if his eye chanced to fall upon her. She grimaced as she recalled that second blunder, more serious than the first. "The Puzzlebreaker," as the ton had dubbed him after he'd founded a gentleman's club devoted to witty repartee and clever aphorisms, was a gifted mathematician and intimate of the Prince's counselors. But as long as she said or did nothing to engage that keen intellect or pique his curiosity, she would be perfectly safe.

Be plain and dull, she told herself—dull as the dirt-brown hue she always wore, plain as the oversize and shapeless gowns she'd inherited from her benefactress.

And avoid the earl as much as possible.

Dull, dull, dull as the ache in her head from the pins that had contained her long braided locks for too many hours. With a sigh of relief, she loosed them and, tying on a long frayed apron, set about washing her hair.

Beau smiled as he surveyed the modest gig and the even more modest chestnut pulling it. How London's Four Horse Club would laugh to see him tooling such a rig.

But after a few hours' sleep took the edge off his fatigue, a deep-seated worry over Kit roused him irretrievably from slumber. A check on his brother, whose color had gone from unnatural pale to ominously flushed and whose rapid, shallow breathing was doubtless responsible for the frown now residing on Mac's tired face, had been enough to refuel his anxiety.

His physician friend looked exhausted after a ride doubtless as arduous as his own. Humbly acknowledging, at least to himself, that he'd feel better sending Mac off to bed with Mrs. Martin present to direct Kit's care, he'd offered to fetch the nurse. At least the drive in the pleasant early fall sunshine gave him something to distract himself from his gnawing anxiety.

As the squire's son promised, her cottage was easily located. He pulled the gig to a halt before it and waited, but as no one appeared to assist him, he clambered down and hunted for a post to which he could tie the chestnut. Finding none, he set off around the walled garden. Surely behind the cottage there would be some sort of barn.

Having found a shed, by its look of disuse no longer

home to horse and tackle but still sturdy, he secured the rig and headed back to the cottage. A gate to the garden stood open, from which, as he started by, a black and white spotted dog trotted out, spied him, and stiffened.

Kneeling, he held out a hand. After a watchful moment, apparently deciding Beau posed no threat, the dog relaxed and ambled over. Beau scratched the canine behind his large ears, earning himself an enthusiastic lick in the process, after which the dog collapsed in a disgraceful heap and rolled over, offering his belly.

"Some watchdog. Where's your mistress, boy?"

The dog inclined his head. When the rubbing did not resume, with an air of resignation he hopped up and loped off into the garden. Amused, Beau followed.

Behind the walls he found cultivated beds, herbs interspersed with a charming array of asters and Michelmas daisies and alternating with chevrons of turnips, onions and cabbages. Inhaling the spicy air approvingly, he was halfway across the expanse of tilled ground when a slight movement near the cottage drew his attention and he halted.

Halted, caught his breath, and then ceased to breathe.

A young woman leaned back against a bench, eyes closed, her head tilted up to a gentle sun that painted a straight nose, arched brows, high cheekbones and full lips with golden highlights. The collar of her gown lay unfastened, revealing an alluring triangle of warm skin from her arched neck downward to the top of an old worn apron, whose blockage of the view that might otherwise have been revealed below he would have fiercely resented had not the garment redeemed itself by clinging snugly to its wearer's generous curves.

The lady's hair, which she was drying in the sun,

swirled over the back of the bench and cascaded down beside her in a thick fall of burnished auburn curls.

Just then she reached up to comb her fingers through one long section, fluffing it as she progressed. The movement stretched the threadbare apron taut against her body, its thin white cloth silhouetting her breast against the dark bench, full rounded side to sun-kissed tip.

Beau's mouth grew dry, then dryer still as one curl tumbled from her shoulder, caught on the apron's edge and came to rest cupped, like a lover's hand, around the outline of that perfect breast.

She sighed, a slight exhale that parted her lips and made her look like a woman rousing to passion's whisper. His body tensed in automatic response, his mouth tingling to trace the outline of that arched throat, taste the honey promised by those lips, his fingers itching to tangle themselves in that cloud of copper silk and pull this arresting vision closer.

A vision that was, he realized with a shock that rippled all the way to his toes, the woman he'd hitherto identified as the mousy, nondescript Mrs. Martin.

He tingled in other places, as well. And had not yet regathered wits enough to decide what to do about it when the dog, whose presence he had totally forgotten, had the deplorable ill timing to seek out his mistress.

At a lick to her hand, Mrs. Martin sat up and opened eyes as piercingly blue as the clear autumn sky. Eyes that went in an instant from sleepy to shocked. With a small shriek, she leaped up and backed away.

Conscious of a sharp sense of loss, he nonetheless endeavored to set her at ease. "Please, don't be alarmed, Mrs. Martin. It's Hugh Bradsleigh—Kit's brother. I'm sorry to have startled you."

As big a plumper as he'd ever told, he knew, realizing

he'd never have been treated to this glimpse of heaven had the reclusive Mrs. Martin sensed his presence earlier. He still couldn't quite believe the silent woman who had toiled at his side all night and this enchanting siren were indeed one and the same.

"L-lord Beaulieu! You—you startled me. Misfit," she scolded the dog, who hung his head, tail drooping, "why did you not warn me we had visitors?"

Misfit. Beau grinned. Now there was an apt name. If he'd had the foresight to bring a bone, the wretched animal probably would have given him the run of the cottage.

Nonetheless, the pooch had led him to The Vision and thus Beau felt compelled to defend him. "He did inspect me rather thoroughly before he let me in."

He watched regretfully as with one hand Mrs. Martin fumbled to fasten the buttons at her collar and with the other gathered her glorious, sun-burnished hair into a knot. Though he was somewhat guilty at having startled her, he wasn't so conscience-stricken that he felt compelled to point out the dowager's cap for which, with sidelong glances as if she expected he might at any moment attack, she was quite obviously searching.

Instead he picked it up. "Your cap, Mrs. Martin." With a slow smile, he held it out, just far enough to be polite but not so close that she could reach it without approaching him.

And, ah, how he wanted her to approach. After a moment, skittish as a startled doe, she did. "Thank you, my lord. I'll take it now, if you please."

Come get it, he almost said. Biting back the words lest he frighten her off, he simply stood, waiting.

She took the few steps that separated them, then

snatched at the cap. Her hand grazed his palm as she grabbed, and for a moment, their fingers caught.

He felt the flame of contact in every nerve. And so, he realized exultantly as he watched her, did she.

Her blue eyes widened in shock, her lips once again parting slightly in surprise—an unconscious invitation. She even forgot, for a moment, to take the bonnet.

All too soon she remembered. Murmuring a disjointed thanks, she jerked it away and jammed it down on her head.

"I'll...just gather a few supplies." With that, she swiftly retreated into the interior of the cottage.

Leaving Beau gazing after her, amazed.

He sat down on the bench she'd just vacated to pull together his disordered thoughts. The *young* Mrs. Martin—she could not be more than five-and-twenty—possessed not just a pretty face, but an alluring figure. Indeed, the rush of attraction to that lush body still thrummed in his blood. An attraction that, based on her reaction to their unexpected touch, experience told him was mutual.

With his typical methodical precision, he pondered the implications of these new discoveries.

The first question posed by his now-fully-piqued curiosity was why so lovely a lady would choose to mask her beauty beneath dowager caps and ill-fitting gowns.

His second thought was of Kit—reviving a burden of worry heavy enough to extinguish the lingering embers of lust. For the immediate future all he had need of was a skillful nurse. Attraction or no, until Kit was out of danger there'd be no time to pursue other matters.

Still, that the intriguing Mrs. Martin had twice managed to distract him from his pressing anxiety was mute testament to the power of that attraction.

As he stirred restlessly, wondering how much longer it would take for her to "gather supplies," it suddenly occurred to him that having the most capable nurse in the neighborhood take up residence at the squire's manor would be much more convenient. Having that nurse be a lovely and discreet young widow with whom a mutual attraction had flared might, once his brother's condition improved, afford enticing possibilities.

Despite his worry, a ghost of desire stirred at the thought and he grinned, more cheered than he'd been since he received the dire message of his brother's injury. Kit would survive—he was in Beau's care and he must survive—but after this present crisis he would doubtless require a long convalescence. Beau had detailed his men to wrap up the investigation in the north, and must shortly return to London to assemble his report. The imperative to resolve his present case would not permit him to linger here, but he would certainly visit frequently to check on Kit.

Beau took another deep breath of herb-scented air. Now this was a charming bower to which he'd happily return.

But first, he'd have to win over the shy Mrs. Martin, which would probably also require penetrating the puzzle of why she seemed to take such pains to remain invisible.

How fortuitous, he thought, his grin widening. He did so love solving puzzles.

He reconsidered the alarm that had crossed her face when she'd seen him watching her in the squire's entry. Since his name and title were rather well known, she'd likely recognized who he was from the first, but in the sickroom she'd displayed no awe of his position or inclination to toady; indeed, rather the opposite. He smiled again at the memory of her stubbornness regarding Kit's treatment and her total lack of deference as she ordered him about.

So why the mistrustful look? Perhaps she'd been raised on warnings about the subtle seducing ways of the high nobility, and saw him as such. Though he was by no means a saint, he could recall no escapades scurrilous enough to have penetrated this deep into the hinterlands. Not in recent years, at any rate, he amended.

He must demonstrate that though the wealthy Earl of Beaulieu might sit at the councils of government and move in a society many country folk deemed immoral, he was also Hugh Bradsleigh, a man like any other, who would never lead farther than a lady would willingly follow. Somewhat to his surprise, he found the notion that the lovely Mrs. Martin might be that rare individual who could appreciate him for himself alone immensely appealing.

Disarming her wariness would be quite a challenge—the one thing, he thought, spirits rising in anticipation, he loved almost as much as solving puzzles.

Chapter Three

A few moments later Mrs. Martin returned with a large satchel. The care she took that their hands not touch as he relieved her of it reinforced his conviction that she was not indifferent to him—an encouraging sign.

Once the lady realized he meant her no harm, she would doubtless be less wary. And begin allowing herself to respond to the pull he felt crackling between them.

He paused to savor the small delight of taking Mrs. Martin's hand as he assisted her into the gig. Availing himself of this unexceptional excuse to lean close, he caught a whiff of soft perfume. Rose with a hint of lavender? Lovely, and it suited her.

How to set her at ease? he mused as he settled the satchel to one side of the seat and walked over to untie the chestnut. Questions about home and family, interspersed with teasing compliments, had usually relieved anxiety in the shier or more tongue-tied young ladies with whom he'd had occasion to converse, he recalled.

By the time he'd rounded the gig and hopped in, Mrs. Martin had repositioned the satchel between them and moved to the edge of the seat—as far from him as possible.

Suppressing a grin, he set the gig in motion. "Did you grow up in this area, Mrs. Martin?"

She slid him a sidelong glance. "No, my lord."

"It is home to your late husband's family?"

There was a minute pause. "No, my lord."

"Do you enjoy the country? Your garden is certainly lovely."

"Thank you, my lord."

"I must thank *you*, for your devoted care of my brother. We are both much in your debt."

"Not at all, my lord."

"I must apologize, as well," Beau persevered. "I fear I've not been entirely courteous. Kit and my sister are all the family I possess, and I'm very protective of them. It's distressing to know Kit was—still is—in danger."

"Naturally, my lord."

Beau stifled a rising exasperation. Could the woman not string together more than three words at a time? Even the most stuttering of young females managed better. Was she really as dull as she seemed?

He felt an irrational disappointment. *Idiot*, he chastised himself. Just because a woman possesses a certain skill—and a voluptuous body—does not mean she owns a mind of equal caliber. Besides, discretion is a more useful quality in a bedmate than conversation.

If he managed to persuade her there—an intention this one-sided conversation was doing little to strengthen. Until he recalled that sinuous fall of mahogany silk spilling about her sides and shoulders, one copper curl resting where he would wish to touch, to taste.

Interest stirred anew. Doubtless the effort would be worth the prize. Experience taught him women valued baubles, time, attention—and marriage. All he need do is discover which combination of the first three this little brown sparrow desired, and the attraction to him she was taking such pains to suppress would win out.

For a moment he allowed himself to contemplate the gloriously satisfying interludes that might thereafter ensue. And when his brother was fully healed, when he left Merriville for good, he would, as usual, be most generous.

He frowned slightly. A generosity, it occurred to him as he recalled the necessity of tying up his own horse and the total absence of servants, of which she seemed to stand in definite need. Did she truly—she a lady of gentle birth—live entirely alone in the cottage with only that unreliable mutt to safeguard her?

A well-honed protective instinct sprang up to overlay a more base desire. He glanced at her silent figure, as far away from him on the narrow bench as she could manage without falling out of the gig altogether, and smiled, a stirring of fondness in his chest.

A mutually satisfying interlude would benefit them both. He need only persevere, gently but persuasively, until Mrs. Martin realized the truth of that herself.

Would this interminable drive never end? Laura's neck ached from keeping her head angled to the side, as if in rapt contemplation of the country scenery through which she walked nearly every day. Would such action not have looked extremely peculiar, she'd have been tempted to jump from the gig and finish the journey on foot.

At last it seemed Lord Beaulieu had, mercifully, abandoned his attempt to engage her in conversation. Perhaps, if she were lucky, her monosyllabic answers to a nerve-racking series of personal questions had left an impression of such dullness that he would not choose to pursue her acquaintance any further.

She needn't find his queries alarming. Most likely the earl was merely attempting to make sure that the person he'd asked to care for his brother was entirely respectable. At least she hoped so, not daring to sneak a glance at his expression to verify that theory.

Her heart still beat a rapid tattoo, but that was to be expected after Lord Beaulieu had nearly scared her witless, suddenly appearing as if conjured out of air. Whatever had possessed Misfit to allow him to enter the garden unannounced? The animal was too shy of gunfire to make a hunting dog, for which reason the genial squire allowed the hound to stay with her, but he was usually an excellent watchman, greeting any approaching interloper, man or beast, with a volley of agitated barking.

Her cheeks warmed with embarrassment as she recalled how disheveled she must have appeared to him. She'd caught a speculative gleam in his eye at first, but sprawling like a wanton as she'd been, her hair all unpinned, she supposed she'd deserved that. Fortunately she'd also been wearing one of the oldest of Aunt Mary's gowns, possessed of no style whatever and overlarge to boot.

By the time she'd buttoned up properly and tidied her hair, that unnerving look had vanished, though she'd remained so rattled, she'd forgotten where she'd left her cap. He'd had to hand it to her, which he did politely but pointedly, as if to subtly underscore how unladylike her behavior had been.

Charleton would have been much less kind.

Then there'd been that odd rush of...fear?—when her fingers chanced to entangle his. So jolting had that touch been, she'd made sure to avoid it happening again.

To her enormous relief she spied the gateposts to

Squire Everett's manor. A few more moments and she'd
be delivered from his lordship's excruciating proximity.

They were nearly at the manor when Tom rode toward
them. A single glance at his face, tears tracking down the
dust of his cheeks, was enough to drive the discomfort
of the earl's hovering presence from her mind.

"Oh, Tom! He's not—" she began.

"No. Not yet. But the doctor was sending me for you,
Lord Beaulieu. He said you should s-see Kit n-now before…" Swallowing hard, Tom left the sentence unfin-
ished.

With a muffled curse the earl pulled up the chestnut,
tossed the reins to her and sprang from the gig. By the
time she'd controlled the startled horse and guided him
to a halt before the front entrance, the earl had vanished.

The squire's son was weeping openly as he helped her
down from the gig. "I…I'm so sorry, ma'am. I should
never… How can I ever forgive myself if—"

She patted his shoulder. "You mustn't blame yourself!
If the shot that wounded him was a ricochet, it might just
as well have been his own bullet that struck him as
yours."

Shaking his head against her reassurance, Tom took
the chestnut's reins and led both animals toward the barn.
For a moment Laura just stood there before the entry.

Should she go in and offer what help she could? But
the earl's physician was there, and much more knowl-
edgeable than she. If the boy were truly dying, his family
and friends would not want an outsider hanging about.
Perhaps she should just quietly return to her cottage.

She considered the tempting notion for a moment before rejecting it. As long as the boy lived, she must at

least offer her help. Only if the earl refused that offer might she in good conscience return home.

When she entered the sickroom a few moments later she found Lord Beaulieu bending over the boy, lips moving as if in conversation with his brother, hands clasping Kit's limp arm. Though the earl seemed oblivious to her arrival, the doctor spied her immediately and walked over.

"There's an infection beginning in his lungs, just as we feared. I've given him syrup of poppy, but weak as he is, I daren't bleed him. If you've aught of remedies to try, I should be grateful of them."

Laura scanned her memory for the treatments Aunt Mary had used when one of the squire's tenants had contracted an inflammation of the lungs the winter previous. "We might set a pot of mint steeped in boiling water by his bedside," she whispered. "The vapor seems to make breathing easier. And wrap his neck with flannel soaked in camphor."

The doctor considered a moment. "It canna hurt. An herbalist had the teaching of you, the squire said? There's much they use that works, though we're not knowing the whys and wherefores. Let's try it, for God's truth, I've done all I can for the laddie."

After that she lost track of time. When she finally slipped from the room to find the necessary, night had fallen. On her way back the squire intercepted her, begging her to let him send Maggie to the cottage for her things so that she might remain at the hall to tend the patient. Taken aback, she fumbled for an answer.

"Both Lord Beaulieu and Dr. MacDonovan asked that I add their requests to my own," he said. "The doctor admires your skill, and his lordship wishes every experienced hand available be put to his brother's care."

Though logically she knew if she were to be of continuing assistance it made much more sense for her to stay at the hall, still she resisted the notion of quitting even briefly the cottage that meant safety and comfort. A stirring at the depths of her being still whispered danger.

Don't be ridiculous, she told herself crossly. The earl was fully occupied with his brother, whose survival remained in grave doubt. He had neither time nor interest to waste on his brother's nurse.

"You will stay, won't you, Mrs. Martin?"

Since refusing so sensible a request would appear both uncharitable and extremely odd, despite her forebodings Laura had little choice. "Of course, it would be much more convenient for me to remain. If my being here will not be an imposition on you or Lady Winters?"

"It will be a blessing," the squire returned with a sigh. "My sister is in a state, what with sickness and more noble visitors about, and I've all I can do to keep the house running. 'Twould be a great comfort to me to know you were watching over the boy."

"I must stay, then." She made herself smile. "Thank you for your hospitality."

He nodded and pressed her hand before releasing it. And so she returned to the sickroom, her concern over her patient's condition underlined by the disquieting knowledge that for the indefinite future she would be residing under the same roof as the unsettling Earl of Beaulieu.

Just after dawn a week later Laura roused herself from a light doze. She glanced up quickly and was reassured to find her patient still sleeping deeply, brow free of perspiration and color pale but natural.

Another quick glance confirmed that the earl also slept,

his tall form curled on a pallet beside his brother's bed where he'd had a cot installed at the start of the crisis.

Though Lord Beaulieu had helped as much as possible, the responsibility for Kit's care had still fallen primarily on Dr. MacDonovan and herself. She'd endured an exhausting and anxiety-ridden blur of time while Kit Bradsleigh teetered on the edge between living and dying, too preoccupied with nursing him to worry about the elder brother who seldom stirred from the boy's side.

Last evening, the lad's temperature had spiked and then, for the first time since the inflammation began, dropped to normal. After having hovered for days in a restless, semiconscious haze of pain and fever, Kit woke up clear-eyed, keen-witted—and ravenous.

Laura sent for as much chicken broth as she gauged her patient could tolerate, and Dr. MacDonovan. The physician, who'd been eating a late dinner with the earl, came at once, Kit's brother on his heels. After a swift examination, to everyone's great relief the doctor declared that, though Kit was still very weak and would need a long period of rest to fully recover, his lungs were clearing and he was probably out of danger.

The squire went off immediately to fetch a bottle of his best claret while Dr. MacDonovan laughingly admonished Kit, who demanded a glass of his own. As thrilled and relieved as the others, Laura uttered a quick prayer of thanks. And then shooed the men out, telling them that since her patient needed rest and their well-deserved celebration would likely be lengthy, they should take their bottle in the salon and she would keep watch alone. Abjuring her as a downy, kindhearted lass, Dr. MacDonovan shook her hand heartily and ushered the earl out.

She heard Lord Beaulieu come back in after midnight

and gave him a nod of reassurance as he silently approached his brother's bed. He took Kit's fingers and held them a moment, as if to verify that the fever had really left, then looked back at her with a tired smile. "Thank you," he whispered, and took up his post on the cot.

The earl's valet would see to Kit's needs when he woke, and both the doctor and Lord Beaulieu would keep the boy occupied during the day. Her work here would soon be done—perhaps for good, as Lady Elspeth, sister to Kit and his lordship, was expected soon.

She could return to the safety of her cottage before the household reverted to a normal routine—and the earl had leisure to become curious about his brother's nurse.

She paused a moment by the doorway. In the hazy pastel light of dawn, the earl's stern features were relaxed, his handsome face more approachable. She felt again that inexplicable pull, as if his commanding personality called out to her even in sleep. A tiny sigh escaped her.

If events had not transpired as they had, she might risk lingering here, responding to the wordless, urgent imperative that somehow drew her to this man. And then shook her head at her own foolishness.

If events had not transpired as they had, she would never have landed in this remote rural corner of England.

Fatigue must be making her whimsical. Straightening her weary shoulders, Laura slipped from the room.

Two paces down the hallway, a touch to her back made her jump.

"Don't be alarmed, Mrs. Martin!"

She turned to see the earl behind her. "My lord?"

"I've not had the opportunity before, with you so occupied tending Kit, but I didn't want another day to go by without thanking you for your efforts. Though at times

I may have appeared…less than appreciative—'' he gave her a rueful grin ''—I want you to know mere words cannot convey the depth of my gratitude.''

She felt a flush of pleasure at his praise even as she set about denying it. ''Not at all, my lord. I did only what any person trained in the healing arts would have.''

''You've done a great deal more, as we both know. Left the familiar comfort of your own home, devoted nearly every waking hour and worked yourself nigh to exhaustion in Kit's care. Indeed, the squire's since told me were it not for your prompt and skillful action immediately after his wounding, Kit would never have survived the journey back to the hall. And before you deny it, that assessment was confirmed by Dr. MacDonovan himself.''

Since she had, as he predicted, already opened her lips to demur, she was left with nothing to say.

''I owe you debt I can never repay. I won't insult you by offering money, but were it in my power, I'd go to the ends of the earth to grant you your heart's desire.''

The quiet conviction of those words somehow compelled her to raise her downcast eyes. She found his gaze fixed on her with such intensity, her heart gave an odd lurch.

He smiled, his face lightening. ''Now what, I wonder, would such a calm and quiet lady desire most in the world?''

Freedom from fear. The thought flashed into her head on a stab of longing. She struggled to stem it, to summon up a reply blithe enough to match his teasing question. ''M-my needs are few, my lord. I'm quite content.''

The earl chuckled. ''A lady with no demands? What an extraordinary creature!''

''Not at all. Alas, I'm entirely ordinary.''

The wryness of her rejoinder faded, replaced by a curious mingling of alarm and anticipation as the earl stepped closer. While she stood motionless, breath suspended, his expression once again turned so fiercely intent she could not make herself look away.

"No, my lady," he said after a long moment. "Though you may be many things, 'ordinary' is certainly not one of them. But you'll be needing your rest." He stepped back, breaking the invisible hold. "Suffice it to say you have my eternal friendship and support. If I can ever be of service to you in any way, you have but to ask."

He made her a bow. When she continued to stand motionless, he gave her shoulder a gentle shove. "Go on now. If you expire from fatigue in the squire's hallway, Kit will never forgive me."

The unexpected contact sizzled through her. "My lord," she said faintly, and curtsied. All the way down the hall she felt his lingering gaze on her back, while the imprint of his fingers smoldered on her shoulder.

Leaving Kit Bradsleigh in the physician's charge, the next day at first light, Laura slipped from her patient's room. She turned toward the stairs to her chamber, then hesitated.

Though she was tired after her long night, a vague restlessness haunted her. Accustomed to daily exercise tending her garden, walking out to gather supplies of wild herbs or to let Misfit ramble, she felt stifled after having been confined to the squire's manor for nearly a week.

She considered taking the air in the garden, but unsure of the earl's schedule, reluctantly dismissed that notion. The intricate arrangement of alleys and shrub-shrouded pathways would make it difficult to spot someone far enough away to avoid them, and should she chance to encounter the earl, he would doubtless feel compelled to invite her to stroll with him. Though she might simply refuse, with brutal honesty she had to admit the draw of Lord Beaulieu's stimulating presence and the beauty of the fall flowers would likely prove a combination beyond her power to resist.

Why not visit the library instead? She'd become acquainted with its rich treasures two years ago when the squire had offered her a book to beguile the tedium of her long recovery. Given free rein thereafter, she'd been delighted to explore the excellent collection it contained. That decided, she headed for the front stairway.

Though Kit Bradsleigh was out of immediate danger, he remained seriously ill, and Dr. MacDonovan thought it prudent he still have care both night and day. Quite cleverly, she thought with a touch of smugness as she descended, she'd arranged with the physician to take the night watch while the doctor and Lord Beaulieu provided medical treatment and diversion during the day. She had further requested, since she would be eating at odd hours, that her meals be served in her room.

Yesterday when she'd returned to her patient, she'd discovered that Lord Beaulieu's cot had been removed from the sickroom. Naturally, with his brother on the road to recovery, the earl would resume sleeping in his own chamber. So it appeared she would not see him again during his stay, since she'd neither meet him at mealtime nor encounter him in the sickroom during her night vigil.

Her relief at avoiding his too-perceptive eye mingled with a touch of what might almost be…regret. He affected her so strangely, setting her skin tingling with a sort of prickly awareness, as if some vital essence about him telegraphed itself to her whenever he was near. She found that entirely involuntary reaction both exhilarating and frightening.

Like that touch to her shoulder, the morning he thanked her for saving his brother's life. Close her eyes, and she could almost feel it still, his fingers' imprint branded into the sensitive skin of her collarbone.

How…peculiar. And a warning to her to be doubly on her guard.

After peeping ahead to ascertain no one was in the front hallway, she scurried to the library. Safely over the threshold, she paused to breathe in the comforting, familiar scents of beeswax and leather bindings before walking to the bookcase that shelved the complete Milan set of the *Iliad* and *Odyssey*. Her self-imposed confinement would seem much more tolerable if, after her rest, she could look forward to an afternoon among the heroic cadences of Homer's poetry.

Impatient to inspect the treasure, she selected a volume and carefully smoothed open the manuscript. Just a few pages, she promised herself, and she would slip back to her room.

Within moments she was completely entranced. Eyes avidly scanning the verses, she drifted across the parquet floor, shouldered open the library door—and stepped smack into the tall, solid body of the Earl of Beaulieu.

Chapter Four

Beau was striding briskly down the hall, invigorated by his dawn ride, when a figure popped out the library door and slammed into him. The slight form rebounded backward, a book spinning from her hands.

Swiftly recovering his balance, he grabbed the maid's shoulders to keep her from falling. His automatic irritation over the girl's inattention evaporated instantly as first his fingers, then his brain registered the identity of the lady in his grip.

"Excuse me, Mrs. Martin! Are you all right?" Delighted with this excuse to touch her, he let his hands linger longer than absolutely necessary to steady her, reveling in the rose scent of her perfume.

As soon as she regained her footing, she pulled away. "Fine, thank you, my lord. And 'tis I who must apologize, for not watching where I was walking."

With regret he let her go. "Are you sure you're uninjured? I'm a rather large obstacle to collide with."

"Quite all right."

"Let me restore your book to you." As she murmured some inarticulate protest, he bent to scoop up the volume.

And froze for another instant when he read the title. The first volume of Homer's *Illiad. In Greek.*

Slowly he straightened. "*You* are reading this book?"

Something like consternation flickered in her eyes as she looked up at him. She opened her lips, then hesitated, as if she found it difficult to frame an answer to that simple question. "Y-yes, my lord," she admitted finally, and held out her hands for the volume.

He returned it. "You must be quite a scholar."

For a moment she was silent. "My father was," she said at last.

He waited, but when she didn't elaborate, he continued, "And you, also, to be reading it in Greek. As I asserted earlier, not at all an ordinary lady."

"But a tired one, so if you will excuse me—"

"Another moment, please, Mrs. Martin." He couldn't let her go, not yet, not when the only communication they'd shared for days previous or were likely, given her nursing schedule, to have in the days ahead were terse directives uttered in the sickroom. "You are looking pale. I fear you've been too long cooped up in the house. Do you ride?"

She shot him a glance before quickly lowering her gaze. "N-no, my lord."

"You must stroll in the garden this afternoon, then. The day promises to be fair and warm. No excuses, now! I shall call for you myself after your rest to ensure it. We can't have you endangering your own health."

Again, that darting glance of alarm. "That…that is exceedingly kind, my lord, but I wouldn't dream of inconveniencing you."

How could he ever disarm the wary caution so evident in those glances if she persisted in avoiding him? Determined not to let her wriggle away, he continued, "Walking with a lovely lady an 'inconvenience?' Nonsense! 'Twould be my pleasure."

"Your offer is most kind, but I—I really should return and tend my garden. Weeds grow alarmingly in a week, and I must restock my supplies."

"I should be delighted to drive you there. Perhaps you can explain something of your treatments. Dr. Mac-Donovan tells me Kit is likely to have a weakness in his lungs for some time, and may have continuing need of them."

"Possibly, but I could not allow you to abandon your work for so tedious an errand."

"I have no pressing business at the moment," Beau replied, dismissing without a qualm the two satchels of dispatches his secretary had sent from London by courier just last evening. "What time should you like to go?"

She tightened her grip on the book and inhaled sharply. His concentration faltered as he watched her dart the tip of her tongue over the pouting plumpness of her lower lip. A unexpected bolt of lust exploded deep in his gut, recalling in sharp focus that vision of her in the garden that lingered always at the edges of his consciousness— arched white throat and pebbled breasts and wild tresses calling for his touch.

Heart hammering, he wrenched his thoughts back to the present. Mrs. Martin stood a handspan away, gaze lowered, cheeks pinking, her breathing as erratic as his own. She felt it, too, this primal beat pulsing between them in the deserted hallway. And as surely as he knew his own name he *knew* eventually she must succumb to it. To him. Already he could sense in her the fluttering anxiety between acceptance and flight.

"N-no, really, I... To be frank, my lord, I should be

most uncomfortable to receive such marked attention from one so far above my station.''

She was trembling. He could feel the delicious vibrations thrum through him. How long and hard would she fight their attraction?

He did not wish to push her—too much—but he'd eagerly meet her, could she but persuade herself to advance a part of the way.

Would she? Caution said 'twas too early to rush his fences, but he couldn't seem to help himself.

''Your service to my brother makes us equals, Mrs. Martin. But given your obvious reluctance to bear me company, I fear I must have alarmed or offended you in some way. If so, I most sincerely apologize. I stand already so deeply in your debt, surely you know I would never do anything to injure you.''

She looked up then, as he'd hoped. For a fraught moment she studied him, her puzzled, questing gaze meeting his while he stayed silent, scarcely able to breathe, knowing the whole matter might be decided here and now.

Slowly she nodded. ''Yes, I do know it.''

Elation filled him, urged him to press the advantage. ''What time shall I bring the gig 'round, then?''

Energy seemed to drain from her and she sighed, as if too weary to withstand his persistence any longer. ''Four of the clock?''

''I shall be there.'' He reached toward her cheek. She stood her ground, permitting the slight glancing touch of his fingers. ''Sleep, Mrs. Martin. Until four, then.''

She nodded again and, holding the volume to her chest like a shield, turned and walked swiftly to the stairs.

Beau stood staring after her, waiting for his heartbeat to slow. He'd been attracted to her from the first, but this...compulsion—he couldn't think what in truth to call it—to claim the fair Mrs. Martin far exceeded anything he'd anticipated or previously experienced.

He shook his head, still amazed by it. Until a few days ago he'd believed that his current mistress, a lovely dancer as skilled as she was avaricious, had been more than meeting his physical needs.

Mrs. Martin roused in him a similarly intense response that was at the same time entirely different. Oh, he wanted her as he'd seen her in the garden—warm, eager, ardent—but he wanted just as fiercely to discover the story behind those skilled hands, the quiet voice that soothed his delirious brother's agitation, to penetrate within the lowered head and engage the questing mind that read Homer.

He laughed out loud. *Greek,* no less! How could he have thought her intellect dull, even for a moment?

Maybe it was the shock of Kit's close brush with death that heightened all his senses to so keen an edge. Normally he was the most analytical of men—the successful performance of his job depended upon it—but the power of whatever arced between them this morning defied analysis. This was alchemy, elemental substances bonding through some force buried deep within their respective natures, a force not to analyze, but to experience.

He intended to do so. Once Kit was out of danger, he wanted to experience every thrilling facet the unprecedented power of this mutual attraction promised.

That decided, he switched directions and headed for the breakfast room. The more he knew of Mrs. Martin, the more tools he'd possess to lure her to him—and turn his molten imaginings into reality.

Time to prime the voluble squire's conversational pump.

* * *

He was pleased to find Squire Everett already at breakfast. "Come in, come in, my lord. Fine morning for a ride, eh?"

"A wonderful morning indeed."

"M'sister won't be down this morning—female palpitations or some such, so don't stand on ceremony. Please, fill your plate. Marsden will pour your tea."

"Have you had a dish sent up to Mrs. Martin yet?" he asked casually.

"Cook will take care of that. Must see that she gets her nourishment. Thin as a wraith anyway—can't have her going into a decline."

"Indeed not. What an invaluable member of the community! Has she resided here all her life?"

"No, the last few years only. Her late aunt, Mrs. Hastings—a most genteel lady, God rest her soul—owned the cottage first. Mrs. Hastings helped her husband, a botanist he was, in his studies of herbal plants, and became something of an expert herself." The squire paused to take a bite of kidney pie and waved a finger at Beau. "So you see, my lord, 'tis no crone of a medicine woman who had the teaching of Mrs. Martin, but the wife of an Oxford don! Anyways, once the folk hereabouts learned of Mrs. Hastings's skill, they took to consulting her. And when Mrs. Martin contracted a puerile fever, her family sent her to her aunt. Nearly died, Mrs. Martin did, and took the better part of a year to recover."

"I'm sure her neighbors are most grateful she did."

"God's truth, that!" The squire motioned the footman to pour him another cup. "Given the, ah, weakness of the local sawbones, there's a number of folk who'd be in bad frame indeed, were it not for Mrs. Martin."

"My own brother included."

The squire nodded. "Glad to know you realize that!"

"Her husband was a military man, you said. In what regiment?"

The squire stopped buttering his toast and looked up. "Can't say as I know. Does it matter?"

Back off, Beau. "Not really. I'm trying to ascertain how I might best reimburse her for the time and skill she's expended for my family. She would not accept payment in coin, I expect, but I should like to offer some gesture of appreciation. Is she perchance a reader?"

The squire chuckled. "My, yes! Quite a little bluestocking. Why, when she was laid up recuperating from her illness, I swear she must have read every musty tome in my library twice through. Not that I grudged her the loan of them, of course. Nay, I was glad to see them off the shelf for better reason than to make way for Hattie's feather duster." The squire put down his fork, suddenly serious. "Mustn't think she's one of them annoying, opinionated females who are always trying to tell a body what to do. Not a bit of it! Our Mrs. Martin's quiet and deferential, a real lady."

"So she has shown herself, under the most trying circumstances," Beau agreed, noting the squire's slight stress on the possessive "our." "The rest of her family is not from this county?"

"No. Now that I think on it, I'm not sure where her parents live—nor her husband's people." The squire shrugged. "Never seemed important. She's quality, as one can tell by looking at her, and that's all that matters."

"Of course." Beau paused, choosing his words with care. "It does seem to me somewhat—odd, though, that she should be living alone, without any relations to accompany her. I must confess I was shocked when I went to fetch her and found not a single servant. I cannot help but think she stands in need of better protection."

"Protection?" The squire stiffened and threw him a suspicious glance. "She's well protected now, sir. I'd have a servant at the cottage full-time, if that's what you're hinting, but she'll not hear of it. And my grooms have standing orders to keep a close eye on the place."

Beau returned a bland smile. "That's not the same as having her safe within one's household. Perhaps I should speak to my sister—"

"No need for that!" the squire interrupted, his glance turning frostier. "She'd not stir from Merriville—likes to feel useful, she tells me. In any event, I've plans for her eventual protection—quite legitimate plans! No need to disturb your lady sister—Mrs. Martin will be well cared for, I assure you." Pushing his chair back, the squire rose. "I'll just go check on that breakfast plate."

Giving Beau another sharp look, the squire paced out.

Beau savored the rich scent of his tea and smiled. So, as he'd suspected, the squire had "legitimate" plans in regard to Mrs. Martin. But though a match of such unequal age would not be unusual, often resulting in affection on both sides, he was certain the lady did not in any way reciprocate the squire's tender regard.

Thanks be to God.

To his eye, Mrs. Martin's reaction to the squire's gallantry indicated disinterest cloaked in polite avoidance rather than coquetry. Nor, given the care she took to mask her beauty, did it appear she sought to attract any of the eligible gentlemen hereabouts.

Twofold thanks to heaven.

Why a vulnerable lady in such a precarious financial position would not wish to ensnare the affections of a potential suitor puzzled him. Solving that mystery was the key, he suspected, to unfettering the attraction between himself and Mrs. Martin.

Fortunately, uncovering people's emotions and intent was a skill he'd perfected when still a lad, fascinated by puzzles of all sorts. While mastering chess, he'd discovered to his amusement that he could often learn as much about his adversary's strategy from watching the reactions of face and body as by following the play. A sudden widening of the eyes, a quick indrawn breath, the alerting of the body and tensing of shoulders might indicate an opportunity discovered, or a check about to be set. Intrigued, Beau began to actively track such reactions. By the time he left Eton for Oxford he was able to pick up much more subtle signs.

Which allowed him to enjoy a quite profitable career at cards while at university. In addition, his ability to sense out which of two boxers would triumph, which jockey would bring home the winning horse, or which of two gentlemen would win a bet had led friends—and opponents—to wait on his choices and seldom wager against him.

And later led him to the secret career he now pursued, assisting Lord Riverton, an older Oxford classmate and now a cabinet member, in rooting out governmental corruption.

Given the strength of his need to disarm the wariness of Mrs. Martin, he gave thanks both for his skill and the invaluable contacts he'd accumulated over the years.

The news of Kit's accident had pulled Beau from a house party, where the number of congenial friends present had sweetened the business of observing a high-ranking government official suspected of embezzlement. His agents were at work amassing invoices and shipping figures—hence the satchels arriving daily by courier. The accumulating evidence, observation and instinct all told him the suspect he'd been watching was indeed the architect of the scheme.

Though he'd put all thought of miscreants aside while Kit's life hung in the balance, once he was assured his brother was truly out of danger and Ellie arrived to oversee Kit's care, duty compelled him to return to London and finish his assignment. Still, he could spare a few more days to recover from the shock of nearly losing a sibling—and to figure out how best to win the trust of the cautious Mrs. Martin. For when he returned to check on his convalescing brother, he intended for her to welcome him back with all the fire he knew she possessed.

As he drained his cup and took the stairs to Kit's room, Beau considered various explanations for Mrs. Martin's atypical behavior. Perhaps the lady avoided gentlemen and garbed herself in gowns that camouflaged her beauty because her heart still belonged to her late husband. If she didn't avoid men out of heartache, she might do so from distaste, though he'd not noticed in her interactions with Mac, the squire, or his brother anything to indicate a dislike for men in general. Or perhaps she brooded over some disappointment in love.

The powerful physical connection that flared between them did not support any of those theories. Besides, he sensed in her not aversion, disdain, or the despair of lingering grief, but...a wary watchfulness.

The hallmark of someone with secrets to hide.

He stopped dead, arrested by the conclusion. He might be wrong—occasionally he was—but he didn't think so.

He continued his analysis, excitement accelerating the pace. Mrs. Martin apparently moved easily among—indeed, was sought out by—the community in and around Merriville, so she didn't avoid all society.

Mrs. Martin the widowed healer met society, he

amended. Mrs. Martin the woman hid behind shapeless gowns and voluminous caps. What could a lovely lady of gentle birth feel so obliged to conceal that she tried to make her person virtually invisible?

Beau couldn't imagine. But with urgency thrumming in his blood and the goad of an imminent departure, he intended to bend every effort to find out.

Chapter Five

Her palms damp with nervousness on the wicker basket she carried, at precisely four o'clock Laura Martin walked into the entrance hallway to meet the Earl of Beaulieu.

Despite her exhaustion this morning, she'd lain awake wondering if there might have been some way she could have avoided this excursion. Before falling into a leaden sleep, she'd concluded there was none, save a blunt refusal that would have been as ungracious, given the concern the earl expressed about her well-being, as it was insulting.

She'd blundered badly again, being caught with that volume of Homer. No chance now of Lord Beaulieu believing her to be dull-witted. But a scholarly lady could still be a recluse of little social skill—indeed, before her marriage had she not been just such a girl? As long as she kept conversation to minimum and behaved with an awkwardness that, given the state of her nerves, she would not have to feign, the outing might pass off well enough.

But as she stepped out under the entry archway to await the approaching gig, Laura couldn't help but feel a surge of gladness. The afternoon was as fair as the earl had promised, gilded with the special light that only occurs in late autumn when balmy breezes, teasing reminders of the summer just past, seduce the mind into forgetting the cold threat of winter to come. The sun-warmed herbs in her garden would greet her with a bouquet of piquant scents, the beds of mums and asters with a painter's palette of russets, oranges, golds, lavenders and pinks.

After having been trapped indoors for nearly a week, she simply would not let the exasperating, unnerving seesaw of reaction the earl seemed always to evoke in her spoil her enjoyment of this perfect afternoon.

Given the paucity of her experience with men, it had taken her time to realize, with some chagrin, that at least part of the uneasy mix was an entirely carnal attraction. Once long ago, when young Lord Andrew Harper took her walking in her mother's garden, she'd experienced the same quivery awareness and agitation. Acutely conscious of the muscled masculine form beneath Lord Andrew's tight-fitting coat and buff breeches, she'd both longed for and been terrified that he might kiss her.

He hadn't, though he'd looked into her eyes with the same searing intensity as the earl. Soon after that walk, her father informed her he'd accepted the distinguished and much older Lord Charleton's offer for her hand, putting an end to titillating interludes in the garden.

Could the earl desire her, too? A flattering thought, though ludicrous. If the Earl of Beaulieu did find his brother's dowdy nurse attractive, it would only be because gentlemen, as she knew well, were not particularly discriminating in their passions. Any minimally satisfactory female would do until a more appealing prospect happened along, and there were surely few prospects in Merriville.

She was still smiling at the notion of the Lord Beaulieu ogling the village baker's buxom daughter when the earl pulled up in the gig.

Sunlight glistened in the burnished ebony of his dark hair and warmed the brown eyes to amber flame. *Apollo cast in bronze,* she thought, as a now-familiar slash of awareness stabbed her belly and quivered down her legs. She didn't realize she was standing motionless, simply staring at him, until the earl addressed her.

"Should I call someone to assist you up? I'm afraid the horse is so fresh, I cannot leave him."

"No, I can manage," she replied, cheeks warming. *The cat looking at the king,* pathetic as the old nursery rhyme.

Transferring the reins to one hand but keeping his eyes on the restive chestnut, Lord Beaulieu leaned over to steady her elbow as she climbed in, his touch light and impersonal. Nonetheless, tension simmered between them as she took her seat.

"Is the day not truly as splendid as I promised?" he asked, and turned to give her a brilliant smile so full of comradely enjoyment she had to smile back.

"Indeed it is. Thank you for offering to drive me."

"Let's be off, then. Do you need to gather wild herbs as we go, or just those in your garden?"

"I need only garden-grown medicinals."

"Nonetheless, if you spy anything on the way that you can use, let me know. This fine animal isn't capable of blazing speed, so it will be no trouble to bring him to a halt. Squire Everett told me your uncle was a botanist, and you came to Merriville to be treated by your aunt. Had you worked with herbs before then?"

Laura tensed. "No."

But his tone was easy, almost teasing as he continued. "I understand you were quite ill. A lady whose mind is active enough to acquire Greek must have found the forced inactivity of convalescence irksome. Learning about herbs would have blunted the frustration, I should guess."

She glanced at him, surprised at his perspicacity. "Yes, it did."

"A fascinating art, the business of healing. From time immemorial men have attempted to understand it, sometimes with appalling results. Imagine, recommending the ingestion of black powder and lead to relieve stomach distress!"

She laughed. "Barbarous indeed."

"Did your aunt start treating illness at your uncle's behest? Or out of her own concern?"

Laura paused, uncertain how to frame a monosyllabic answer—or whether, in truth, she needed to do so. Unlike the unnervingly probing inquiry he'd subjected her about her family the last time he drove her, these questions were less personal.

Perhaps, given his brother's illness, Lord Beaulieu had developed a genuine interest in the practical use of herbs. What harm if she replied at more length on this relatively safe topic?

Cautiously, tracking his reaction with quick, cautious glances, she began, "My uncle studied the makeup of plants and how the elements in them affect healing. He believed, and my aunt practiced, that only natural materials, especially such long-utilized botanicals as willow bark, foxglove, rosemary, and the like be used to treat the sick, and then in small doses. 'Tis best to intervene as little as possible, let the body's natural strength heal itself.''

''That sounds wise. Do we pass any beneficial wild herbs on our route?''

''Several, though they are not at the peak moment for harvesting now.''

''Point them out, if you would.''

And so during the remainder of the drive, she indicated stands of willow and horehound, pockets of tansy, goldenseal and echinacea. At his prompting, she added details of the teas, infusions and poultices one could make from them.

Having the earl's intense, probing mind focused on treatments rather than the individual describing them was an immense relief. Though a strong awareness of him as a man still bubbled at the edges of consciousness, by the time they reached her cottage Laura had relaxed to a degree she wouldn't previously have believed possible in his lordship's company.

As soon as Lord Beaulieu handed her down from the gig, which he did with business-like efficiency that further reassured her, Misfit bounded up. Whining with joy, tail wagging at manic speed, he blocked her path and insinuated his head under her fingers. Perforce halted, Laura laughed and scratched hard along the knobby bones at his tail while the dog groaned with delight.

The earl laughed, as well. ''I believe he missed you.''

''He becomes distressed if I'm away for long.''

''Don't like being left alone, do you, old boy?'' Lord Beaulieu reached over to rub his long fingers behind the dog's ears. ''Misses his fellows, too, I'll wager. Why doesn't the squire take him out with his pack?''

''Having been caught in a poacher's trap as a pup, he

shies so at the sound of gunfire he's useless as a hunting dog. After I healed him, the squire let me keep him."

"As your guardian?" the earl guessed.

She shrugged. "Something like, I suppose. Please, do go in. I'm afraid I haven't much to offer, but there will be cool water in the kitchen."

"Knowing you'd likely not have anything in the house, I had the squire's cook prepare us a basket of refreshments. I'll fetch it when you're ready."

That so wealthy a gentleman, who doubtless had his every need anticipated by a small army of servants at every one of his numerous establishments, should have noted and planned for that small detail impressed her. "Thank you. Should you like to wait in the parlor while I tend the garden? I have a set of the studies my uncle published. You might find them interesting."

"I'm sure I should, but I can't imagine remaining indoors on so glorious a day. Let me help you."

The idea of the impeccable earl down on his knees pulling weeds was too ludicrous to resist. Stifling a grin, she recommended that if he preferred to stay outside, he might seat himself on the old willow bench on the porch.

The same one, she recalled with a jolting flash of memory, on which he'd discovered her drying her hair that afternoon.

If he remembered the incident, too, he gave no sign. Thanking her, he inclined his long form on the bench and sat watching her.

At bit uncomfortable under his scrutiny, she donned her faded apron and a tattered straw bonnet. But after a few moments she fell into the familiar, satisfying routine, wholly absorbed in freeing the beds of weeds and snipping the leaves, stems and branches she needed.

A short time later he materialized at her side, startling

her. To her surprise and amusement, there he remained, questioning her about each plant she weeded out or clipped to save, holding the trug for her to deposit the harvested bounty, and twice, over her laughing protests, carrying off a load of weeds.

After she'd finished, the earl fetched the picnic basket. Once more claiming it was too lovely to go indoors, he insisted on seating her beside him on the willow bench and unpacking the refreshments there.

Having abandoned them during the dull weeding process to sniff out rabbits or other pernicious vermin, at the first scent of food Misfit ambled back, waiting at Laura's feet with polite, rapt attention for the occasional tidbit.

The golden afternoon dimmed to the gray of approaching dusk and the mild air sharpened. As if sensing his mistress would soon depart, Misfit trotted off and brought back a fallen tree limb, then looked up at Laura with tail wagging, an irresistible appeal in his eyes.

"All right, but only for a few moments," Laura told him. With a joyful bark, Misfit dropped the limb and danced on his paws, awaiting her throw.

She lobbed it to the far wall, watching with a smile as the dog raced after, a dark streak of motion in the fading daylight. He bounded back, did a little pirouette before her, and dropped the stick once more.

Lord Beaulieu snatched it before she could, and after a grimace at its condition, threw it again, clear over the fence and into the brush beyond. The hound rushed to the wooden barrier and then out the gate.

"He'll love that," Laura said. "'Tis a shame he cannot hunt, for he dearly loves to retrieve. Keeps my vegetables safe, and provides hares for the stew pot several times a week."

The earl gave his slimy hands a rueful glance. "He makes a rather messy business of it."

"So he does. Thank heavens you were not wearing your gloves—they'd be ruined!" Laura rummaged in her basket for a rag. "Here, let me wipe them."

He held out his hands. Without thinking, Laura grasped his wrist. Which, she immediately realized, was a mistake.

The warm touch of his skin sent a shock through her, while below the cuff of his shirt she felt his pulse beat strongly against her fingertips. Without conscious volition she raised her eyes to his.

He stared back. The air seemed suddenly sucked out of the afternoon sky, and she had trouble breathing.

She should look down, wipe his hands, step away. But she didn't seem able to move, her body invaded by a heated connectedness that seem to bind her to him by far more than the simple grasp of his wrist.

Finally, with a ragged intake of breath she tore her gaze free and wiped his dog-slobbered hands with quick jerky motions. After achieving the barest minimum of cleanliness, she released his wrist and shoved it away.

Still shaky, she stepped back—and tripped over Misfit, who chose that moment to bound up to her, stick in mouth. Not wanting to step on the dog, she hopped sideways and lost her balance altogether.

An instant later she hit the ground in an undignified tangle of skirt and limbs, face up to the startled earl and the star-dusted sky. Her cheeks flamed with humiliation, but before she could speak, Misfit, delighted she'd apparently decided to join him at his level, put both paws on her chest and leaned over to lick her face.

"Stop...Misfit...down!" she attempted to command between swipes by his long pink tongue, all the while trying unsuccessfully to wriggle out from under his weight. After a moment the absurdity of her position overwhelmed embarrassment. Leaning her head back under a continuing assault of doggy kisses, she dissolved into laughter.

He ought to shoo the dog away, help her up. Instead Beau stood frozen, watching the arched column of long white throat, the chest quivering with amusement. All afternoon he'd been haunted by memories of her on the bench where he'd surprised her sun-drying her hair, where today she'd invited him to linger, where, separated only by a picnic basket, they'd eaten the cold meat and cheese and bread, sipped the wine the squire's cook had packed. Which he'd eaten and drunk without tasting anything because it was her slender body, her wine-sweet lips he wanted to devour.

And now, while that ungrateful mutt dribbled slobber on her face, all he could think of was brushing the dog aside so he might kiss that throat, cup his hands over the breasts now prisoned by muddy paws, move over her and into her. It required another full minute and all the strength of mind he could muster to beat back the pulsing desire to gather her in his arms and carry her into the cottage.

But he was master of his appetites, and she was not ready for that. He called once more on the iron self-discipline upon which he prided himself, under whose guiding check he'd operated all afternoon, keeping the conversation carefully neutral, masking the desire she aroused in him with every small movement—the way she touched the tip of her tongue to her top lip when in contemplation, the subtle sway of her hips as she walked, even the tilt of her head as she gazed up at him inquiringly, like a little brown sparrow.

How unobservant people were, he marveled as he watched her tussle with her dog. How could any man look at Mrs. Martin, really look at her, and see only the drab exterior, miss the translucence of skin, the smoky fire of her hair beneath the ubiquitous cap, the sparkling brilliance of mind so evident once he finally got her into conversation. Dismissing the sparrow as dull and familiar without noting the intricacy and subtle shadings of color and pattern. Even the squire, though he'd not been totally blind, had perceived but little of her subtle allure, else she'd not still be a widow.

He was fiercely glad of that blindness, however. For she was his sparrow—*his.* The strength of that sudden conviction startled him, but it emanated from somewhere so deep within him he didn't bother to question it.

It would be a novel experience, using his skills to entice a lady. He'd not previously done so, being too circumspect to dally with married women of his own class and too protective of his bachelor state to pay singular attention to a maiden. The strength of his wealth and title alone, he considered cynically, had always been more than enough to garner him the favor of any lesser-born female who caught his eye.

But he would use them now, his vaunted skills, to lure this little brown sparrow and tame her to his hand.

Mrs. Martin, with her long white throat and deliciously heaving chest and frothy petticoats thrown back to reveal shapely ankles, represented temptation strong enough to break the resolve of a saint. Not being one, he'd best bring to an end the torturous pleasure of watching her. Thank heavens she was too modest to let her glances stray below his waistcoat, else she'd have clearly defined evidence of his desire the sternest of will could not conceal.

Ruthlessly he disciplined his thoughts, reassuring himself of the intimacy to come by recalling that timeless, breathless interval when she captured his wrist and his gaze. So strong was the sense of connection that he knew, he *knew,* she sensed and reciprocated the same powerful emotions that were roiling through him. However, though her agitation immediately after spoke of the depth of her attraction, her care to quickly move away told him she wasn't ready quite yet to succumb to the force that sparked so readily between them.

But she would be. Soon. And having made such progress today in setting her at ease, he'd not jeopardize her willing acquiescence by rushing his fences now, like an untried schoolboy.

"Misfit, heel!" he commanded. When, with a droop of tail, the dog reluctantly complied, Beau held out a hand. "Mrs. Martin, shall we retrieve you from Misfit's pack?"

At his teasing comment, she froze. The unselfconscious delight drained from her face and, ignoring his outstretched hand, she scrambled to her feet, brushing at the mud the dog had left on her apron.

"L-lord Beaulieu, excuse me! That was undignified."

"What need has one of dignity on so lovely a day?"

Her glance shot to his face and probed it, as if looking for evidence of mockery or disapproval. He held her gaze, his amusement fading.

Abruptly she lowered her chin, took a step away and grabbed her basket. "We've lingered far too long. 'Twill take but a moment to pack up the herbs. If you would be so kind, my lord, would you make sure the gig is ready?"

Somehow in an instant, the easy mood that had gilded the golden afternoon had shattered, leaving in its place a chill that had nothing to do with the evening's approach. Beau was at a loss to explain why it happened, or to figure out how to recapture their warm intimacy. Dismay and anger and heated frustration seized him.

He knew instinctively that pressing her to stay, teasing her further, would only deepen her wariness.

After a moment in which, his mind still a swirl of protest, he could summon no logical reason to stall their departure, he replied, ''Of course, madam.'' And bowed, though she'd already turned away, retreated to her workbench, putting even more distance between them.

After watching her for another moment, Beau headed for the shed. Analyze, analyze, he told himself as, teeth gritted, he stalked over to prepare the gig. He hadn't even touched her hand to help her up, so it couldn't have been his barely repressed desire that frightened her off. What was it she had apologized for—a loss of dignity?

Dignity—a stifling word, that. Had some repressive individual—a stern governess, a cold mama, a disapproving father—or husband—stolen from her the ability to express joy openly? So that the keen zest for life, the unfettered laughter he'd just witnessed, emerged only in unguarded moments and was viewed as a lapse of propriety to be immediately regretted?

His anger shifted, redirecting itself against whomever had required his Sparrow to restrain her innocent delight in life. He'd like to teach the fellow the propriety to be found at the end of a clenched fist.

He felt again that surge of fierce protectiveness. Mrs. Martin had an enchanting laugh, and he meant to hear it, often. He'd have her indulging—and sharing with him— all the passionate responses she so diligently suppressed.

I'll make it so good for you, for us, he vowed as he speedily checked over the chestnut. *I'll give you freedom from want and restraint, cherish your body, revel in that questing, active mind. You need only let me.*

But his frustration revived on the drive back, which mirrored in unwelcome parallel the first time he'd driven her from the cottage to the hall. Mrs. Martin perched on the edge of the seat, as far from him as possible, replying to his every conversational opening an unvarying series of "yeses," "nos" or "I don't know, my lords."

How could she sit there so composed and distant, virtually ignoring him, when his body hummed with suppressed desire, his mind with the fervent need to probe her thoughts, know and explore and nurture her?

By the time he drew rein before the squire's entry hall, irritation at the unexpected setback drove him to be just a bit less cautious.

And so, after a groom came to the chestnut's head and Mrs. Martin turned to climb down from the carriage, he stayed her with a touch to the shoulder. Enough of impersonal, nonthreatening courtesy.

Beau took her hand and slowly, deliberately, raised it. "I enjoyed this afternoon very much, Mrs. Martin."

He moved his mouth across her knuckles, the barest touch of lip and warm breath. Then, while her eyes flared open and her gaze jerked up, he turned her hand over and applied the glancing, shock-spitting caress of his lips down her slender fingers to her callused palm. He had to call once again on his famous self-control to stifle the near-overwhelming impulse to sink his teeth into the tempting plumpness beneath her thumb where the palm narrowed to the soft, rose-scented skin of her wrist.

He released her then, pulses hammering, astounded that a simple brush with his lips could instantly rekindle desire to urgent fever pitch. He glanced down at her.

Lips slightly parted, eyes locked on him, she stood

motionless, oblivious of the footman waiting to hand her down, looking awestruck as if she, too, could not credit the strength of what just passed between them. Her hand was still outstretched where he'd released it, fingers splayed and trembling.

Oh, yes, she felt *that*. Satisfaction surged through him, his only compensation for being forced to restrain himself from claiming her on the spot.

No, Mrs. Martin, he told her silently as he bowed in farewell. *This unnameable force between us cannot be ignored, try you ever so coolly to deny it. Sooner or later, all the secrets and passion you are at such pains to hide will be mine.*

Chapter Six

Her body and mind still spellbound by the earl's simple gesture, not until the squire offered a bluff greeting did Laura notice her host striding out.

"Come in, come in, my lord, Mrs. Martin! We've guests for you to meet. Lady Elspeth and her daughter, Lady Catherine, have just arrived."

Another stranger. Rattled as she felt at the moment, Laura was tempted to avoid the introduction. However, she swiftly realized that if she excused herself now, she might be pressed to join the party in the drawing room later. Better to brush through this quickly and avoid a more protracted conversation over biscuits and tea.

The arrival of his lordship's sister, however, meant she would soon be able to return home. An unexpected ambivalence dampened the surge of relief she'd anticipated at that reprieve.

Swallowing her protests over windblown hair and grubby gown, she followed the squire to the south parlor.

She refused to glance at Lord Beaulieu during the short walk. Drat, how the man unsettled her! Just when she'd thought they'd developed a comfortable rapport, nurse to patient's elder brother, he had to intrude again upon her senses with his tantalizing, dangerous appeal.

That so small a gesture as his lips brushing her palm could evoke so agitated a response only underscored she was a fool to believe she could remain a detached acquaintance. His very presence stirred both memories she'd rather suppress and longings she could scarcely put a name to.

She'd do better to follow her original plan of avoiding him.

By the time she reached that conclusion, the squire had ushered them into the parlor. A beautiful, raven-haired lady with the earl's dark eyes rose as they entered.

"Beau!" She held out her arms.

The earl strode over to envelop his sister in a hug. "How glad I am to see you, Ellie! But you're so pale. A difficult journey? Or did this scamp worry you to death?"

He turned to catch a child who hurtled into the room at him. "Uncle Beau! Do not tease Mama! She's been sick, so I've been ever so good. Did Uncle Kit really get his arm—ooh!" The rest of her sentence ended in a squeal as Beau tossed her into the air.

Laura looked at the small face, rosy-cheeked with excitement, the plump arms clasped about Lord Beaulieu's neck, and a painful contraction squeezed her chest. *My Jennie,* she thought, helpless to stop the wave of grief that swept over her.

By the time Lord Beaulieu deposited the girl on the sofa, she'd managed to form her lips into a smile.

"Stay still, imp!" his lordship ordered, and turned to the ladies. "Ellie, I have the honor to present Mrs. Martin, the lady whose skillful hands kept our graceless brother from a premature demise. Mrs. Martin, this is my sister, Lady Elspeth, and her daughter, Lady Catherine."

Laura rose from her curtsey to find his lordship's sister gesturing to her. "Come, Mrs. Martin, sit beside me. How can I ever thank you for saving Kit?"

"His lordship's physician deserves the credit, my lady. I merely kept watch," Laura said, reluctantly taking the seat indicated.

"'Twas much more than that, I'm told! But I must apologize for taking so long to arrive. As Catherine mentioned, I haven't been…well, and was forced to take the journey in much shorter stages than I should have liked."

The earl's face clouded. "What is it, Ellie?"

She patted his hand. "Nothing alarming, so you may lose that worried look! Though I fear I shall not be as much help to you as I'd hoped. I'm…I'm breeding again, you see." A smile of rapturous delight lit her face.

Lord Beaulieu leaned over to kiss her. "I know how happy that makes you. But after the difficulties you've had since Catherine's birth, was it wise to travel? I'm delighted to see you, of course, but I'm also astounded, given your condition, that Wentworth allowed you to come."

Lady Elspeth's smile turned impish. "He didn't. He was in London preparing for another tiresome diplomatic mission when your message arrived. I expect he'll be furious when he gets my note, but…oh, Beau, useless as I may be, I couldn't bear to remain away with Kit so ill!"

She turned appealing eyes to Laura. "We're hopelessly clannish, Mrs. Martin. And so, having barely met you, I must beg a favor. I've suffered two…disappointments since Catherine, and much as I want to care for Kit I know I must rest and conserve my strength. Can I prevail upon you to remain until Dr. Mac feels he no longer needs constant nursing?"

A whirlwind of surprise, consternation, fear—and a guilty gladness disordered Laura's thoughts. From the confusion, only one conclusion surfaced clearly. As a healer, she could not abandon her patient until her services were no longer needed. *She would not be leaving*.

She curtsied once more. "My hearty congratulations at your good news, my lady. Of course, if Dr. Mac-Donovan, his lordship, and you all think it best, I shall remain."

"I'm sure the doctor will add his pleas to Ellie's," Lord Beaulieu said. "You know how much I myself value your skill, Mrs. Martin."

The warmth of his tone, the compelling gaze he focused briefly on her before turning to the child pulling impatiently at his coat sleeve, left her stomach churning even as the protective part of her brain warned that remaining was a very bad idea.

"I want to see Uncle Kit! I want to see his shotted arm. You have the bullet?"

"Catherine, please!" the child's mother protested, but Lord Beaulieu merely laughed. "Bloodthirsty chit. If the doctor says Kit is up to the visit, you may see him. But no probing his wounds! It will hurt him too much, poppet."

The girl's bright eyes dimmed briefly, but she nodded. "I won't hurt Uncle Kit. Take me now?"

"If you'll permit, I should withdraw and rest," Laura inserted quickly and rose to her feet. "Lady Elspeth, Lady Catherine, a pleasure to meet you. My lord." She curtsied, eager to quit the room before he could protest.

"I must rest, as well," Lady Elspeth said. "Indeed, I only returned to the parlor after our arrival because I wished to meet you, Mrs. Martin, at the first possible instant. Shall you be down for tea? I should very much like to become better acquainted.''

Not if I can help it, Laura thought. ''I'm afraid not, ma'am. I must rest if I am to watch through the night.''

''Of course. Perhaps you can visit with me tomorrow? I have not yet begun to thank you! And as my brothers will warn you, once I determine upon something, I'm most horribly persistent.'' The engaging smile which accompanied those dire words belied their threat.

''As you wish, my lady. Good day. And thank you again, my lord, for driving me to the garden.''

That summary of their afternoon together should put the interlude in proper perspective, Laura thought as she escaped from the salon.

''Beau, escort me to my chamber, please?''

''Ride me on your shoulder, Uncle Beau!''

Grinning, Beau bowed. ''As my ladies command.'' After inducing a series of giggles by throwing Catherine up to her post, he offered Ellie an arm. ''Are you truly 'fine'? Wentworth would never forgive me were something to happen to you while under my care. Nor should I forgive myself.''

''You know I want this too badly to take any risks. It nearly drove me mad to progress so slowly, but I forced myself to call a halt as soon as I tired or,'' she added with a rueful grimace, ''when the motion of the carriage overcame me.''

''Mama casts up her accounts,'' Catherine informed him. ''Mostly every day. It's nasty.'' She wrinkled her small straight nose.

''Nasty indeed,'' her mama agreed with a sigh. ''I shall be just as comfortable here as at home, and easier of mind, since I can see myself how Kit progresses. So if…something should happen, you cannot be blaming yourself.''

Beau grimaced. "Is it so obvious?"

Lady Elspeth squeezed the arm she held. "Mac told me you had a cot placed so near Kit's bed, his every restless breath woke you. And that you scarcely slept or left his side the whole first week, as if you would hold him to life by strength of will alone.'' She paused, then added softly, "You cannot keep us from all harm, Beau."

The sound of a horse's scream, the smash of impact and shriek of shattering wood echoed out of memory. Forcefully he shut them out. "You are my charge, Ellie."

"I pray daily that all will go well, but what happens is in other hands. You might do well to remember that."

Beau nodded at the rebuke. "I shall, Madam Confessor. Now, scamp—" he eased his niece down "—here's Mary to take you to the nursery.''

The girl clung to his arm. "Please, don't make me go! I want to ride with you!"

"It's too late today for a ride, poppet. But if you're a good girl and go without teasing your mama, I'll come up later and have tea with you."

The small hands at his shirt cuff stilled. "With rasp'ry jam and macaroons?"

He nodded solemnly. "Devon cream, too."

Lady Catherine sighed deeply. "And a ride tomorrow?"

"If the weather is fine."

"And I get to see Uncle Kit?"

"If the doctor says you may."

The pointed chin nodded agreement. With quaint dignity she dipped him a perfect curtsey, back straight, skirts spread gracefully. "As you wish, Uncle Beau. Good day, Mama. I shall go with you now, Mary.''

Hiding a smile, the maid took the hand Lady Catherine offered. "Very good, miss."

Her mother stood looking after her, affection and despair mingled in her face. "She's such a scamp! One moment she's climbing trees, her petticoats in tatters, and the next she makes a curtsey that would not cause a blush at the queen's drawing room."

"Ah, the hearts she will break," Beau said with a chuckle. "I shall have to have all my unmarried friends transported the year she debuts."

"Thank heavens that won't be for a decade! Now, come sit with me a moment."

"Should you not better rest?"

Elspeth slanted him a knowing look. "As the lady managed to slip away, you must come in yourself and tell me all about Mrs. Martin."

Since his sister possessed an intuition superior to his own and powers of observation only scarcely less acute, Beau knew he'd not be able to avoid her questions without raising suspicion. Better to answer directly—but with care. He wanted no well-meaning "assistance" in the delicate matter of Mrs. Martin.

"She's been a godsend," he admitted as they took their seats. "Her quick action saved Kit's life the day he was wounded, as I'm sure Mac's informed you. She's been the mainstay of caring for him through this difficult first week. Her remedies were most effective with fever, and the infusions seemed to calm Kit's restlessness."

"She's a widow, the squire told me."

"Yes."

"And lives here alone, without other family?"

"Her aunt, who bequeathed her their cottage, died only recently, I understand."

"She's not nearly the old crone I was imagining."

Beau smiled. "No."

"In her mid-twenties, I would say. Hideous gown, which totally disguises her form, but her complexion is lovely and that auburn hair, what little I could see beneath that awful cap, is striking." She paused.

Grinning inwardly, Beau schooled his face to polite interest. "Yes, I agree. She is rather younger than I'd expected and quite attractive. As you'll doubtless see, our host has strong proclivities in that direction."

"Indeed!"

"It would not be so unusual a match."

Elspeth studied him a long moment. He maintained a face of bland innocence. "Perhaps he would do, if there are no younger contenders to hand. Or perhaps—she is of gentle birth, the squire said—I shall take her to London with me next season. So young and lovely a widow should have more choice in settling her future than is available in this country outpost."

"Is it so essential that she remarry?"

Elspeth gave him an exasperated look. "Certainly! What else is a woman to do? If what you say is true, she has no family to assist her. Who is to protect her if she falls ill or someone threatens her? Besides, she has no children, and she's certainly young enough to hope for some. No woman would wish to be deprived of that joy."

The bittersweetness in her voice made his chest ache. Poor Ellie had suffered much for her babes. To lighten her mood he replied, "Does Mrs. Martin have any say in this?"

Elspeth blushed. "Of course. But our family owes her an enormous debt, you must allow. I'm merely considering how we might best go about repaying it."

"Perhaps Mrs. Martin has plans of her own which will

obviate your needing to intervene on her behalf.'' *Or mayhap someone else does,* he added mentally.

''Perhaps. But if not…I shall certainly do my possible. Now I really must rest. Don't let my minx of a daughter tire you out. She can be exhausting!''

Beau leaned to kiss his sister's cheek. ''I'm glad you're here, Ellie. I've missed you.''

She gave him a quick hug. ''And I you, big brother.''

Beau's smile faded as soon as he exited his sister's chamber. Having the determined Elspeth play match-maker for Mrs. Martin was a complication he certainly didn't need. The mere idea of that lady giving herself to any other man, even in marriage, roused in him imme-diate and violent objections, though he would hardly voice them to Ellie.

For one, Mrs. Martin responded to *him* as she did to no other man in Merriville. True, he was hardly a dis-interested observer any longer, but in his most profes-sional assessment she'd displayed no such attraction to the squire, nor had her behavior indicated she harbored marital intentions.

Remarriage was certainly one remedy to her current insecurity, the most conventional remedy, but not the only one. He had the power and resources to make her permanently safer and more comfortable than any pro-spective husband Ellie could bring up to snuff, particu-larly the aging and only modestly well-to-do squire.

And Beau would make her happier. As lovers, partners and friends, they would please each other. He would stake his last shilling on it.

When—if—eventually they parted, Mrs. Martin would still have the option of remarriage. Only by then, their liaison would have left her socially and financially secure enough to take such a step out of desire, not necessity.

The vague discomfort occasioned by the very idea of Ellie marrying off Mrs. Martin faded, and Beau's mood brightened. He *was* delighted to have his sister here—he much preferred having all his family about. Especially since—a double blessing—Ellie's condition meant that her arrival no longer signaled the departure of Mrs. Martin.

Ellie would certainly attempt to befriend the widow, who was more likely to confide in his sister than in him. Through cautious questioning of his sibling, he'd probably discover more of Mrs. Martin's circumstances. Even better, Ellie might be able to coax her to join them at dinner or for tea. His spirits quickened at the thought of spending more time with her, even in company.

Of course, if Ellie did get her matrimonial plans in train, it would be the lady's choice whether she preferred a discrete and long-term liaison with Beau, or marriage to some beau of Ellie's choosing.

He'd just have to make sure her choice fell on him.

Later that evening another caller joined them. The vicar, Reverend Eric Blackthorne, had stopped by daily with prayers and encouragement during the crisis. Upon learning Lady Elspeth had arrived, he felt obliged to come by at once and pay his regards, he informed Beau's sister as they sipped tea, his own mama having been a good friend of her mother, the late Lady Beaulieu.

In virtually the next breath, Mr. Blackthorne requested that Mrs. Martin be bid to join them. Perhaps prompted by his recent conversation with Ellie, Beau was suddenly struck by suspicions he had not previously entertained concerning the reverend.

Beau's initial satisfaction when the footman returned to report Mrs. Martin begged their pardon for declining the invitation, as she was already on her way to relieve Dr. MacDonovan, turned to irritation when the reverend announced he would visit them both in Kit's chamber.

Best to determine the nature of this unexpected complication immediately, Beau decided. With brisk efficiency he eluded the squire and Ellie in the salon and insinuated himself into the sickroom call.

"Your mother, Mrs. Blackthorne, was a friend of my mama's?" Beau asked as the two men took the stairs.

"My mother, Lady Islington, was her friend," the vicar corrected. "My father is Viscount Islington."

Blackthorne of Islington. Of course. Annoyed with himself for not picking up the family connection upon their first introduction, Beau continued, "Richard, Baron Islington, is your brother? We were college mates."

The reverend slanted him a glance. "My *eldest* brother, yes."

Netted at that dig about his age, Beau nodded. So the vicar wasn't a country nobody, but scion of an important family. A detail that would surely be noted by his scheming sister.

"Do you intend to stay much longer, my lord?" the vicar asked. "I understand Kit is quite improved."

Beau's instinctive wariness deepened. Wanted him out of the way, did the vicar?

"That depends on Kit. Of course, I have pressing business in London, but I cannot depart until I am sure my brother is well and truly out of danger."

The vicar nodded in turn and the two men continued to the sickroom without further conversation, frosty awareness settling between them. During their previous meetings Beau had been too preoccupied by worry over Kit to take much notice of the vicar. It now appeared the man cherished as little enthusiasm for his presence here as Beau felt at this moment for the clergyman. An unsettling realization.

The frostiness, on Beau's part, grew chillier as he analyzed the vicar's behavior toward Mrs. Martin. The reverend was too well bred to single her out, instead conversing easily with Mac, encouraging Kit, and exchanging no more than a few polite sentences with Mrs. Martin.

Even so, Beau had no trouble determining from the warmth of the vicar's tone toward her, the glances that periodically strayed to the lady's downcast face even as he conversed with the doctor and Kit, that the reverend held Mrs. Martin in more than a pastoral regard.

Mac left to seek his dinner, the other two men walking with him. But when the vicar halted at the doorway, Beau stopped, as well. With Kit having dozed off again, Beau would be damned if he'd give the insolent fellow the opportunity for a private chat with Mrs. Martin.

Clearly as irritated by Beau's persistent presence as Beau was by his, the vicar said, "You'll wish to dine with the doctor. Please, my lord, feel free to do so. There is no impropriety in *my* remaining here with Mrs. Martin."

Was that a subtle rebuke? Beau's temper stirred. "I know you would never overstep the bounds of your calling," he replied. "But having lived for a week in constant anxiety over Kit, it still soothes me to be near him."

Counter that, he thought, watching the vicar struggle for another argument to urge Beau's departure. Obviously failing, Mr. Blackthorne replied, "As you wish, my lord." Walking to the chair where the widow sat beside her dozing patient, he said in low tones, "How are you, Mrs. Martin? I trust you are watching after your own health."

She did not look up, nor was there a shade of flirta-
tiousness in her tone. "I am well, thank you, sir."

"In any case, with Lady Elspeth here, you should now
be able to return home."

Before she could reply, Beau intruded into the conversation. "My sister is in a delicate condition and must
conserve her strength. Mrs. Martin has consented to remain here and continue to nurse Kit in her stead."

Barely concealed annoyance colored the brief glance
the vicar shot to the earl. "Indeed."

"A true compassionate, Christian lady is our Mrs.
Martin," Beau said, nodding to her. "All of us at Everett
Hall value her highly, Reverend Blackthorne."

"So I should hope. Though I must confess, having you
remain under such…crowded conditions does trouble me,
Mrs. Martin. Should you choose to return to your cottage,
I would be happy to insure that you are escorted to the
hall as required."

"A kind offer, Mr. Blackthorne, but unnecessary,"
Beau again answered. "Mrs. Martin would never slight
the squire by inferring that his hospitality is less than
adequate. And it is more convenient having her close."

The vicar looked him full in the face. "I'm sure it is—
for you. 'Tis the *lady's* well-being that concerns me."

"The squire's accommodations are quite satisfactory,
Mr. Blackthorne, though you are kind to be concerned,"
Mrs. Martin broke in at last, a hint of exasperation in her
tone. "If I require assistance, I shall certainly let you
know. But now, gentlemen, your discussion seems to be
disturbing Mr. Bradsleigh. Why don't you continue it
elsewhere and visit him again later."

"As you wish, Mrs. Martin," Beau replied, amused
and impressed. She'd just managed to banish the vicar—
and himself, as well, unfortunately—with both tact and

dispatch. "Mr. Blackthorne, I believe we've been dismissed."

His only consolation was that the lady seemed no more encouraging of the vicar than she was of the squire.

After the obligatory exchange of compliments, the two men left. Falling into step beside the vicar, Beau said, "You need not worry about Mrs. Martin. I shall personally insure she takes proper care of herself."

"That is precisely what worries me, my lord."

Beau halted and pinned the vicar with an icy glare that had daunted many a subordinate. "You will explain that remark, please."

The vicar, to Beau's grudgingly accorded credit, did not flinch. "I am concerned with the welfare of all my parishioners, Lord Beaulieu. You are a stranger, and may not understand the...harm you could do Mrs. Martin, however unintentionally, if it becomes known she is much in your company. Folk here do not approve of loose London ways."

By gad, was the vicar maligning his honor by suggesting he'd give Mrs. Martin a slip on the shoulder under the very nose of the injured brother whose life she'd just saved? Had it been anyone other than a man of the cloth, Beau would have called him out on the spot.

Instead, controlling his outrage with an effort, Beau replied, "You overstep yourself, sir. I am fully conscious of the magnitude of the service Mrs. Martin has done my family. I would never cause her harm."

The vicar held his ground. "I should hope not. But you should be aware, sir, that Mrs. Martin is not as defenseless as she might appear."

"No, she is not," Beau shot back. "She has the full protection of the Bradsleigh family. See that you remember that.'' Having reached the entry landing, Beau made a stiff bow. "I will rejoin them now. Your servant, sir."

"My lord." Face impassive, the vicar nodded and walked back toward the entry.

Beau watched him depart, struggling to master his anger. As if Beau would force his attentions on any lady, much less one to whom he owed such a debt of gratitude! Still, he noted, the vicar could have done nothing more revealing of his feelings toward Mrs. Martin than practically accuse Beau of intending to seduce her.

Given the judgment-impairing effects of such partiality—effects Beau had suffered himself—he would attempt to excuse the vicar's insulting innuendo.

That Beau entertained hopes of winning the lady's favor he would not deny. And though those hopes might not veer toward matrimony, Mrs. Martin was not a young virgin whose reputation could be ruined by a discreet affair.

Except…the vicar might be correct in asserting the rural folk of this neighborhood might take a less enlightened view of such a relationship. Perhaps Elspeth's idea of relocating Mrs. Martin had merit.

A circumspect liaison conducted elsewhere would, if anything, enhance her stature. In addition to the financial protection he was eager to offer, she'd meet prominent individuals whose influence could ease her way the rest of her life, as well as becoming acquainted with all the gentlemen of birth and status Ellie could hope for.

Should they later part company, most of these gentlemen would not consider her relationship with Beau disqualified her as a possible wife. Indeed, though her birth seemed merely respectable and her current position was less than modest, he wouldn't rule out the possibility of wedding Laura Martin himself. Especially since he found the notion of her going to any other man extremely distasteful.

The spark of an idea caught fire in his heart and head. Beau had already absented himself from his work about as long as he could afford. Returning to visit Mrs. Martin at this remote area on a regular basis might well be difficult. Having her established somewhere close enough for daily visits would be much more satisfactory—so satisfying, in fact, that Beau could almost forgive the vicar his temerity in broaching the issue.

That decided it. As soon as Kit had sufficiently recovered, Beau would have to persuade her to come to London.

Chapter Seven

By the next afternoon Beau was once again out of charity with the vicar. Apparently the reverend had spread word of Ellie's arrival and Kit's improvement throughout the county, for beginning that morning they'd had a steady stream of callers. Having been interrupted three times already while trying to assimilate the contents of the satchel his courier had delivered at dawn, Beau nearly told the apologetic footman who'd just appeared once again to convey his regrets.

Then, knowing his kindhearted sister would never be so uncivil as to refuse to receive the local gentry, and realizing the task of entertaining the curious would fall on her delicate shoulders should he shirk a duty he was finding particularly irksome today, he relented.

With a sigh he set his papers aside and followed the footman to the parlor. The striking blonde seated beside his sister surprised him out of his irritation.

The lady rose and followed him to the window where, after bowing a greeting, he'd gone to join the squire. "Lord Beaulieu, what a pleasure to see you again!"

She held out her hand. Compelled by courtesy, he accepted it, his initial appreciation of her striking beauty dimming. *Forward baggage.*

"You'll remember me from Lord Greave's house party last fall at Wimberley. Lady Ardith Asquith."

As usual, the business reasons behind his attendance at that event had limited his time among the female guests. He scoured his memory, finally coming up with a flashy blonde accompanying an elderly peer.

His eyes narrowed as he swiftly assessed the daringly low-cut gown, the guinea-bright curls, the perfect skin, pouting lips—and bright, hard eyes. *A self-absorbed beauty.*

"Yes, I remember, Lady Ardith," he said, bringing her fingers to his lips for the obligatory salute. "And how is your husband, Lord Asquith?"

She flapped long painted lashes and gave him an overly familiar smile whose hint of shared intimacy he immediately resented. "Preoccupied as usual, my lord. Poor me—I so often have to find my own… amusements."

He knew he wasn't imagining the barely veiled innuendo, and his assessment of her character dropped lower. So Lady Ardith enjoyed collecting titled lover pelts, did she? He determined on the instant to discourage the connection.

But when he tried to reclaim his hand, she clutched it, causing him to automatically glance at his fingers— straight at the lavish breasts just below them, revealed to any downward-gazing eye all the way to the taunting pink edge of the nipples. A quick sideways glance confirmed the squire's gaze was riveted on the view.

He looked back up to catch his sister's amused but sympathetic eye. "Lady Ardith tells me her husband owns property in the neighborhood," Elspeth said, "and they often spend a few weeks here when not occupied in London.''

''On those occasions when Lady Ardith—and Lord Asquith, of course—choose to honor us, their company is always a valued addition to our society,'' the squire said.

Lady Ardith leaned further forward as she squeezed the squire's hand. ''Dear Squire Everett! How could I not attend your gatherings as often as possible when I know such a gallant gentleman awaits me?''

The squire paused, apparently too distracted for speech while he struggled between the propriety of raising his eyes to her face and the titillation of visually fondling the display beneath his nose.

Beau watched a knowing smile curve the corners of Lady Ardith's lips and his disdain increased. He'd bet the price of her elegant gown that, even bored to flinders in what she no doubt considered a rustic outpost, Lady Ardith would never consider adding the middle-aged, balding squire to her list of indoor sportsmen. Yet she seemed driven, as beautiful females often were, to captivate every male who crossed her path, whether she valued his regard or not.

Attracting a man of Beau's wealth and rank likely *would* interest her, he thought cynically. Since he had no desire whatsoever to help Lady Ardith beguile the tedium of her country sojourn, he'd end this game at once.

While she toyed with the squire, Beau crossed the room and usurped her seat beside his sister. Lady Ardith's self-satisfied smile wavered briefly when she discovered his move, but brightened again after the squire led her by the hand to a chair beside his own.

''Squire Everett, you must give a ball in honor of Lord Beaulieu and Lady Elspeth!'' the lady exclaimed. ''I should do so myself, but since we open the house here for such short periods, we do not maintain sufficient staff.''

A pinch-penny, as well, Beau thought, disgusted. ''With my brother's health so uncertain, I do not believe we could consider a ball. And at present, Lady Elspeth's health is too…delicate for dancing,'' he replied.

''His lordship's got the right of it,'' the squire agreed. ''With young master Kit still so ill, 'twould not be fitting to disport ourselves at a ball.''

''You are right of course, my lord. A dinner, then,'' Lady Ardith persisted. ''Something rather more quiet, with just the first families of the neighborhood in attendance. That would not tax Lady Elspeth's strength, for she could retire early. I should be happy to preside over the tea tray for you, Squire Everett.''

''His sister, Lady Winters, could do so,'' Beau said.

His repressive tone didn't seem to dampen the lady's pretensions a bit. ''Ah, dear Lady Winters? Is she visiting you currently? I thought she'd removed to Bath.''

''No, surely you remember, Lady Ardith, she returned here when her husband died two years ago,'' the squire said.

Lady Ardith trilled a laugh. ''Oh, yes, how silly of me.'' She waved a hand, dismissing Lady Winters. ''I fear I have no head at all for dates and figures.''

''A dinner would be lovely,'' Elspeth intervened, wary of the growing irritation she no doubt perceived in Beau's expression. ''Assuming Kit continues to improve, Dr. MacDonovan will want to depart by the week's end. Before he goes, we should like to do something to honor him. And Mrs. Martin, of course.''

''Aye, it could be a tribute to both our angels of mercy,'' the squire concurred.

Beau opened his lips to squash the idea. He had no intention of providing both the forum and the target for Lady Ardith's next hunt.

But then he reconsidered. With a little arranging he could pawn that lady off on Mac and the vicar—and arrange to have himself seated near Mrs. Martin.

Mrs. Martin, her auburn hair freed from the ubiquitous cap, her form garbed in something more becoming than the awful brown sacks she habitually wore. His Sparrow in evening dress.

To savor that vision would be worth fending off a dozen Lady Ardiths.

"A capital idea, Squire Everett," he said. "The doctor and Mrs. Martin deserve our most warmest gratitude."

Lady Ardith's look of triumph faded. "Mrs. Martin? That local—*herb woman*—was allowed to tend your brother!"

"She saved his life, as the doctor will testify," Beau said, "and deserves the highest commendation."

"Your desire to acknowledge her is most kind, my lord, but…at a dinner?" Lady Ardith interjected. "Such a lowly personage would doubtless be most uncomfortable to be seated at a social gathering among her betters."

"Nonsense," the squire returned. "Mrs. Martin's gentry-born—her late husband was an army officer—and has dined with us on several occasions."

Better and better, Beau thought, his enthusiasm for the dinner party growing. Since Mrs. Martin had apparently already appeared at neighborhood social gatherings, she would not be able to escape with that excuse.

"It's settled then," Beau said. "On Friday, shall we say? Dr. MacDonovan told me this morning he hopes by then to declare Kit finally out of danger."

"Squire Everett, will arranging a dinner party on such short notice be too much for your sister?" Elspeth asked.

"Not a bit," Squire Everett replied cheerfully, obviously taken with the idea. "If she falls prey to the vapors, Mrs. Martin can help out. She's assisted Emily before. A lady of many talents, our Mrs. Martin."

"So it appears," Beau murmured.

Lady Ardith continued to haggle over the wisdom of including an unattached lady in the gathering, but convinced the squire would go through with the plan whether Lady Ardith chose to attend or not, Beau let the conversation fade to a babble while he set about reviewing the pleasing implications.

This dinner might be just the thing to breach Mrs. Martin's reserve for good. If she appeared at the party to receive the admiration and respect he knew her loveliness would generate, perhaps that acclaim would cause some of her nervous reticence to fade. Even better, he'd be able to pay her gentle, persistent attention in a forum where such behavior was entirely appropriate, nothing to inspire alarm. Once she grew less wary and more comfortable around him, he'd finally be able to get close enough to demonstrate his genuine respect and concern.

Surely then she would come to trust him—and heed the call that impelled her to come to him.

The next afternoon, in a pretty note begging her pardon for the inconvenience, Lord Beaulieu's sister asked Laura to join her in the sitting room attached to her chamber, as she found herself too weary after her journey to come downstairs. Bowing to the inevitable, Laura steeled herself for the interview.

As Lady Elspeth was several years older, she had already come out, married, and left London to raise a family by the time Laura made her debut. So there was no chance whatsoever, Laura told herself, trying to squelch her ever-present anxiety, that Lord Beaulieu's sister might recognize her.

Deliberately garbing herself in the ugliest of Aunt Mary's gowns and the most voluminous of the lace dowager caps, Laura forced her face into a mask of serenity and knocked at the door of Lady Elspeth's sitting room.

But as she entered, a small figure bounded up. "Did you nurse Uncle Kit and keep the angels from taking him to heaven?" she demanded.

"Catherine!" her mother protested from her reclining position upon the sofa. "You mustn't pounce upon people like that. Greet Mrs. Martin properly, if you please."

With a sigh the girl straightened, then dipped a curtsey. "Good day, Mrs. Martin. I trust you are well?"

The speech was so clearly parroted—and practiced— Laura had to smile. "Good day to you, Lady Catherine. I am quite well, thank you. And you?"

"Very well, but Mama's not. That's why she's so cross. Uncle Beau said you kept the angels from taking Uncle Kit. I'm so glad! He's ever so much fun, and I'm not finished with him yet."

The vision of angels tussling over Kit Bradsleigh's bed tickled Laura's whimsy, and some of her nervousness fled. She took the hand Lady Catherine held out and walked with her to the sofa.

"Perhaps God wasn't ready for him yet," Laura said. *Unlike my Jennie.* A dull ache permeated her at the unbidden thought, and wearily she suppressed it. "But Dr. MacDonovan did most of the work, you know."

The little girl looked thoughtful, then nodded. "Angels would surely leave Dr. Mac alone. He talks too loud and he makes you drink nasty medicine." She gestured to Lady Elspeth. "I think that's why mama is sick."

"Don't be impertinent, Catherine," her mama reproved with a frown. "If you cannot confine your conversation to more proper subjects I shall send you back to the nursery."

The small face grew instantly contrite. "I'll be good, Mama. Please let me stay. Uncle Beau said we can't ride for hours yet and Mary doesn't know any games, and the books Uncle Beau left are full of big words."

Lady Elspeth, looking in truth very pale and weary, sighed and leaned over to ruffle her daughter's hair. "I'm sorry, pet. Mrs. Martin, I'm afraid Catherine's nurse came down with a putrid sore throat this morning and has taken to her bed. I can't seem to summon the energy to go out, which leaves poor Catherine stranded in the nursery with only Mary for company. She's a kind girl, but not at all used to dealing with children."

Laura felt an instant sympathy for the spirited, active little girl forced to remain cooped up indoors. "Should you like to take a walk, Lady Catherine? The gardens are still pretty with the late roses blooming. That is, if you would permit, Lady Elspeth."

Lady Catherine's face lit. "Oh please, Mama, may I?"

"Are you sure, Mrs. Martin? I wouldn't like her to tease you, and she can be quite—energetic."

"I would love to! I used to tend my older sister's girls when their governess was—" Alarmed, Laura caught herself before she blundered into revealing more details. "Occupied," she finished, hoping Lady Elspeth hadn't noticed her sudden dismay. "I do enjoy children."

"Then I should be grateful. Mind, Catherine, that you let us drink our tea in peace."

"Yes, Mama." Lady Catherine looked up to give

Laura a beaming smile. "You're nice, just like Uncle Beau said. I like you, even if you do wear such ugly gowns."

Lady Elspeth's eyes widened and she straightened, as if to make a grab for her lamentably plain-spoken child. But as she leaned forward, her face grew paler still. Clutching a handkerchief to her mouth, she struggled from her seat and seized a nearby chamberpot.

"Ugh," Catherine said over the ensuing sound of her mother's retching. "I hate Mama being sick. Uncle Beau says soon she'll be better, but she's been sick ever so long." The small chin wavered. "It scares me," she admitted, tears forming in her eyes.

Laura had intended to keep this meeting as brief as possible. But she couldn't bring herself to leave a frightened little girl in need of comfort, or depart without attempting to help alleviate the distress of her suffering mother.

She hugged Catherine, who came into her arms with no resistance, her body trembling. "Your uncle Beau is right, Catherine. Your mama won't be sick for too much longer." Not knowing what the child had been told, she decided not to explain further. "I've nursed lots of people, and I can tell when someone is very ill and when they're about to get better. Your mama will get better."

"You're sure?" The child looked up at her, anxious eyes huge in her troubled face.

"Cross my heart," Laura promised.

The girl sighed. "If you could keep the angels from taking Uncle Kit, I suppose you can keep them from Mama."

"Why don't you go back to the nursery and find your cloak and some heavy shoes. Then you'll be ready to walk when your mama and I finish tea."

The child nodded. "She won't drink any, though. She doesn't drink anything at tea now, and we don't have the pretty pink cakes anymore 'cause she says the smell makes her ill."

"How disappointing," Laura said. "You know, if we meet Squire Everett on our walk and you ask him nicely, I wager he'd have his cook bake some pretty pink cakes. You could share them with your uncle Beau in the nursery, where the smell wouldn't bother your mama."

The small face brightened. "He would? I shall ask today!" The child leaped up and hugged her. "You must have some cakes, too. Oh, I do like you! I'm sorry I said your gown was ugly. Though truly it is."

Grinning, Laura bent down until her lips were close to the girl's ear. "I know," she whispered, and winked.

With a giggle, the little girl skipped out. Laura turned to the mother, who was now wiping her face and trying to gather the remnants of her dignity.

"M-Mrs. Martin, I do apolo—"

"Please, Lady Elspeth, there's no need! I'm a nurse, you will recall. Come, sit down and try to get comfortable. Has your physician given you any remedies to help alleviate the sickness?"

Wearily Lady Elspeth settled against the cushions. "He said an overheating of the blood causes it, and ordered Nurse to mix up some vile concoction that was supposed to cool the humors, but I couldn't keep it down. Nor would I let him bleed me, as he urged and Wentworth pleaded. I—I'm already so weak, I cannot see how bleeding would help."

Laura nodded. "My uncle found, after much study, that bleeding does tend to weaken the patient. He recommended more gentle means—teas blended with chamomile and peppermint to soothe the stomach, and lozenges composed of sugar, ginger root, and lavender to suck on when the queasy feeling strikes. I—I have a stock made up and could obtain some for you, if you should like to try.''

''Just now I'm willing to try anything short of a pistol bullet to the head,'' Lady Elspeth replied grimly.

''I shall make up a tea at once. Here, recline with this pillow to your back. A cloth dipped in cooled rosewater applied to your temples may help, as well. I'll fetch one. Try it while I brew the tea.''

''You truly *are* an angel of mercy, Mrs. Martin,'' Lady Elspeth sighed as she settled back. ''But I did so want to chat with you.''

''Later. First, you must rest and rally your strength.'' Laura paused. ''By the way, does your daughter know the nature of your illness?''

Lady Elspeth opened one eye. ''No. I thought it best not to tell her. For years she's begged me for a baby brother or sister. I feared if…if this ended as the previous two have, she'd be disappointed—and upset. When her dog died last summer, she was distraught for days.''

''She's upset now, worrying about her mama,'' Laura said gently. ''''Tis your choice, my lady, but if it were me I'd tell her what afflicts you is normal and shall soon pass. Children that young do not understand how babies arrive. If you tell her only that a new sibling is a happy possibility, she would probably be no more than mildly disappointed should your hopes…not be realized.''

''She worries?'' Lady Elspeth said. ''Ah, my poor babe. I suppose I've been too ill and cross to notice. Perhaps you are right, Mrs. Martin.'' She forced a tired smile. ''A wise angel as well as a guardian one.''

''Rest now and I'll fetch your tea. We'll talk later.'' *Much later, if I have any say in it,* Laura thought.

She'd brushed through that well enough, and the idea of walking in the garden with Lady Catherine—someone with whom she needn't be always on her guard—was enormously appealing. Perhaps she'd slip invisibly through the last few days of tending Kit Bradsleigh and reach home safely after all.

Chapter Eight

Feet clothed in sturdy walking boots and hands encumbered by a linen cloth filled with jam tarts fresh from the oven, two days later Laura entered the garden.

Though she still spent much of her time alone, keeping vigil over Kit Bradsleigh at night and dining in her room, she now had these afternoon outings with Lady Catherine to look forward to. Dr. MacDonovan had informed her this morning that, unless their patient took a sudden turn for the worse, he expected to leave at week's end. By then, Kit Bradsleigh would no longer need round-the-clock care.

Which meant surely Kit's older brother would be leaving soon, as well. A departure which she viewed with increasingly mixed feelings.

Removed from his too perceptive scrutiny, she'd be safe once more. And if life without the surge of mingled elation and alarm he sparked in her whenever he appeared would be less energizing, she'd do well to remember why she'd previously rejoiced at a life of dull monotony.

She'd also be able to return home, though she'd still

spend much time at Everett Hall tending the recuperating invalid. And visiting her new friend Lady Elspeth.

Laura shook her head ruefully. Lady Elspeth insisted Laura called her "Ellie," claiming she could not remain on formal terms with the woman who'd saved her brother's life and the practitioner whose treatments had considerably eased her own misery. She treated Laura with such beguiling warmth that, having been so long deprived of the companionship of a woman her own age, Laura had great trouble maintaining any reserve.

Catching sight of Lady Catherine, whose nurse, though recovered from her ailment, was happy to let Laura walk her energetic charge about the garden, Laura waved.

She loved spending time with Catherine, despite the ever-present ache of regret for what might have been and now would never be. She'd grown up the youngest child of a large family. When her elder siblings returned to visit with their offspring, it was only natural that the aunt, hardly older than her nieces and nephews, should join them in the nursery. Only natural, as well, that with only adult companions most of her days, she reveled in their company.

Better even than the warm memories Catherine's chatty escort revived, or Laura's freedom when with the child to relax the constant guard she otherwise maintained, was the precious ability to wander the grounds as long as she liked, protected by Catherine's small hand in hers from having to worry about encountering the earl alone.

In fact, Laura and her charge had met "Uncle Beau" every single afternoon. Always delighted to see the earl—who seemed to take equal delight in his niece, Laura noted with approval—Catherine had no qualms about monopolizing Lord Beaulieu's time and attention.

Laura was able to observe him and indulge in the heady thrill of his company, freed of the stomach-clenching anxiety that normally afflicted her in his presence.

Since Catherine had confided her uncle planned to meet her after their walk to take her riding, Laura was not surprised when, soon after she and Catherine seated themselves on their favorite bench beside a fragrant hedge of late-blooming damask roses, Lord Beaulieu approached.

Awareness of him flashed over her nerves like a wind-driven ripple across a lake's calm surface.

"I saved you a tart!" Catherine cried, running over to offer him the crumbling remains of a pastry.

Ignoring the grubbiness of the jam-stained fingers, the earl accepted the treat. "Kind of you, princess. And I must thank the little wizard who coaxes the squire's cook to come up with these delicacies for tea every day."

"Not me," Catherine pointed out with scrupulous fairness, munching the last bit of her tart. "Laura does. Cook likes her. I do, too. Don't you, Uncle Beau?"

The earl turned his smiling face toward Laura—and caught her staring. She felt the warmth of embarrassment flood her cheeks and tried to look away, but his smile fading to something deeper, more intimate, he held her gaze...one minute, two. "Very much indeed," he said softly before turning his attention back to his niece.

While her cheeks burned hotter and fluttery wings beat within her stomach, Catherine continued, "Uncle Beau, I have a secret! Only Mama said I could tell you and Laura, so it's all right to share, isn't it?"

"If she said you could, poppet." The earl flashed Laura a brief but oddly intense look. "I love secrets, and I *never* tell anyone."

Lady Catherine's eyes gleamed with excitement as she

grabbed her uncle's coat sleeves. "It's wonderful, and you'll never guess. Mama said next Easter, I might get a new brother or sister!"

So Lady Elspeth had confessed, Laura thought, pleased.

"That's indeed wonderful news," Lord Beaulieu said. "Which should you prefer—a sister or a brother?"

"I don't suppose it matters. I'm ever so much older, it shall have to mind me. Mama says getting a baby is a curious sort of game. Playing it makes her sick sometimes, but if she wins, she gets to keep a baby. But not everyone wins, so I should not be disappointed if we don't get a baby after all." Lady Catherine wrinkled her brow. "It's a very odd sort of game, don't you think?"

Lord Beaulieu laughed. "I wonder what your papa would say to that?"

"Well, I much prefer ball and spillikins, but Mama says I can't play the game anyway until I'm a lady, and married. If we should get a boy, he can ride and play catch with me. And if it's a girl, I shall give her my old dolls and my dresses when I outgrow them. But only pretty ones. Not ugly ones like Laura's aunt Mary gave her."

Laura stifled a gasp, and Lord Beaulieu caught his breath. "That was very rude, brat!" he said after a moment. "Apologize to Mrs. Martin at once!"

A little daunted, Catherine raised pleading eyes to her uncle. "It's all right, Uncle Beau. Laura knows they're ugly—she told me so herself, didn't you, Laura?"

Her cheeks pinking, Laura merely nodded, carefully avoiding the earl's gaze.

"See?" Catherine turned back to her uncle. "Laura told me she wears the dresses even though they're ugly because her aunt Mary gave them to her, and she loved

Aunt Mary. But I shall give my sister only pretty ones, so she'll love me even better.''

"How could she resist?" Lord Beaulieu said, with a rueful glance at Laura.

Focusing her attention on Lady Catherine, Laura said, "I expect your uncle came to tell you the horses are ready. Since we've finished our snack, you'd best be off before it's too late to ride."

"Can you not ride with us?" the child asked.

Laura hesitated. "I—I have no horse."

"Uncle Beau can get you one. He knows all about horses. He brought me the wonderfulest pony."

"Another time, perhaps. You mustn't keep your mounts waiting, so off with you now."

"Go to the stables, and make sure Manson had your pony ready," Lord Beaulieu said. "I'll be right along."

"Can we race today?"

The earl rolled his eyes. "Perhaps—it depends on how wet the fields are. I make no promises!"

Lady Catherine angled her chin up and grinned at him, a mixture of precocious coquette and childish charm. "Bet I'll beat you." Evading the earl's mock punch with a giggle, she scurried off down the path.

The earl sighed and turned to Laura. Knowing their chaperone was even this moment racing out of sight, all her nerves alerted.

"I must apologize once again for my niece. She has a deplorable tendency to say exactly what she thinks."

"I'm not offended, truly." She attempted a smile, a difficult matter when her lips wanted to tremble and her heart was beating so hard she felt dizzy. "Children usually do speak the truth as they see it, even when it might be better sugar-coated."

At that he turned his face to once again snare her with

a searing gaze that would not allow her to look away.
"'Tis always wise to tell the truth. Especially when those
who hear it are friends who seek only our good."

Laura's breath caught in her throat and her lips went
dry. He was speaking of much more than hand-me-down
gowns, and they both knew it.

Trust him, a small voice deep within her whispered.
He will be that sort of friend.

But the legacy of fear and a now-ingrained compulsion
for concealment drowned out the voice. "No, my lord,"
she said, her voice barely louder than a whisper. "'Tis
not always wise. Enjoy your ride."

Pivoting on her heel, she made herself walk back to
the house, calm and unhurried. Feeling with every step
the weight of his thoughtful gaze heavy upon her back.

Chest tight and mind seething with frustration, Beau
watched Mrs. Martin escape to the house. In her expressive face, her guileless eyes, he'd read how very close
he'd come to breaking through that wall of silent reserve.
So close he could feel the acquiescence trembling on her
lips, and now tasted the bitter sense of loss.

Still, the very fact that he had come so close was cause
to hope that very soon the remnants of her reserve would
crumble.

He could assemble all the small clues she'd let drop,
add them to the information he'd extracted from the
squire, set his team to work on it, and probably within a
fortnight be able to reconstruct the whole of her life up
to now. He could, but he didn't want to.

With a determination that grew daily more intense, he
wanted Mrs. Martin to come to *him,* confide in him, trust
him of her own free will.

He really ought to be making plans to leave. The in-

formation in the latest dispatches confirmed the careful
theories he'd previously constructed, and if events continued in the same manner, he'd soon have enough evidence to complete the dossier and turn it over to Lord
Riverton. Perhaps he ought to do that immediately and
then return, free to devote as much time as necessary to
finish winning over his Sparrow. He could then leave
Merriville for good—with Laura Martin.

Still, the dinner party Friday night might allow him
close enough to finally gain her trust. Tonight before Mrs.
Martin went in to tend Kit, the squire would tender the
invitation. Beau had primed both his sister and his brother
Kit to press her to accept. He wasn't above enlisting
Catherine, as well, if necessary.

He already had his niece to thank for one piece of
information that, if handled correctly—and he was a master of handling information—should insure Mrs. Martin
appeared at the party garbed in evening attire far more
attractive than the hideous gowns she normally wore.

Yes, his niece—who was doubtless at this moment be-
deviling the grooms while she waited impatiently for her
uncle to arrive.

Beau took one more look at the door through which
Mrs. Martin, with a calm belied by the agitation he'd read
in those stark blue eyes, had just disappeared. *Soon we
will be together,* he promised himself and her. *Soon.*

"Dinner on Friday?" Laura echoed the words in dismay. "That's very kind of you, Squire Everett, but I
thought we agreed my uncertain schedule made it wiser
that I not dine in company." With a nervous glance she
surveyed the group who'd greeted her in the small salon
when she returned from her walk with Lady Catherine.

"But 'tis my farewell party, ma'am," Dr. Mac-

Donovan argued. "Sure, and you'd not be sending me off with a wave of a bandage roll across our sleeping Kit's bed?"

"You're to leave Saturday?"

"Aye. I've just examined the lad's lungs again, and it's clearer still they be. Under your competent care, I've little doubt of his eventual recovery, and it's needed I am back home."

"Yes, you must attend, Laura," Lady Elspeth urged. "I've felt so much better the last two days, I can finally envision dining without revulsion. Since I owe that improvement solely to you, you must help me celebrate."

"At the risk of putting you off entirely, I confess the party is as much in your honor as the good doctor's, ma'am," the squire said. "We owe both of you a great debt, and would like to publicly acknowledge it."

"Publicly?" Laura repeated in automatic anxiety.

"We've had the whole neighborhood asking after young Kit and praying with us for his recovery. 'Tis only fitting that all have the chance to help our distinguished visitors celebrate the good news before their departure."

"If 'tis to be a large party, then you'll surely not need me. It will make the numbers wrong," Laura offered.

"Pish-tosh, Mrs. Martin." The squire waved away the suggestion. "'Tis not some fancy London party, all standing on precedence. And you need not feel shy. Excepting the earl, Lady Elspeth and the good doctor, 'twill be only neighbors you've dined with on several occasions. Oh, and Lady Ardith and Lord Asquith."

Laura looked at the smiling faces—the squire, the doctor, Lady Elspeth. Some inner imperative told her to accept would be dangerous, possibly the most dangerous thing she'd done since coming to the aid of the earl's wounded brother. But as she had no reason to fear any of her neighbors—even the conceited London beauty Lady Ardith, who scarcely acknowledged her existence— Laura could dredge up no excuse to avoid the party that would not either cause offense or give rise to speculation.

Surely the earl would be present, too. The thought shimmered through her, adding to both her longing and dismay. Still, she didn't see how she could avoid this. "You are vastly kind. I shall accept with pleasure."

"Oh—m'sister may call upon you to write out the invitations. Her failing eyesight, you know. If that won't be too much of an imposition?"

Laura had to smile. Lady Winters, an indolent damsel of some seventy summers, had previously called on Laura to assist her after suffering palpitations at the mere prospect of the work entailed by an evening party. "You may assure your sister I shall be happy to assist her."

"Good, good." The squire patted her hand. "Knew we could count on you. Want to send the doctor off with a good proper party, and with you overseeing the arrangements, I know 'twill be top of the trees."

Though Lady Elspeth, bless her, objected it was not quite right that Laura toil on a party given partly in her own honor, she desisted when Laura assured her that she didn't mind in the least. Thanking the group again, Laura returned to her room.

It was only ingrained caution that made her so uneasy. All the guests would be well known to her. Besides, if she handled the arrangements for Lady Winters, she could arrange the dinner partners to suit herself, make a brief appearance in the parlor after the meal, then excuse herself before tea.

Thinking of the guest list again, she had to laugh at her apprehensions. With Lady Ardith promised to appear, no one would give the dowdy Mrs. Martin a second glance.

Late the following afternoon, Laura was returning to her room after going over the party lists with Lady Emily when Lady Elspeth hailed her in the hallway. "Please, could you join me for some tea in my sitting room before you rest for tonight? Being reduced to the company of the squire, Lady Winters and my brother at dinner, I sorely miss the conversation of a rational lady."

Having on occasion been constrained to be the rambling Lady Emily's dinner partner, Laura could sympathize. And after a few day's acquaintance, Laura had largely lost her reserve around Lady Elspeth. Here was a friend in truth, one who, even should she learn of Laura's deception—not that she ever intended to reveal it—would not, Laura felt sure, betray her. And she sincerely enjoyed the company of the earl's charming, cheerful sister.

"I should be delighted."

Laura entered to take the seat indicated on the brocade flowered sofa while Lady Elspeth poured tea. After handing her a cup, her friend gave her a measuring glance.

"I happened to notice that, though you agreed to help Lady Winters, you didn't seem particularly pleased to accept the squire's invitation to dine."

Laura sighed. "I'm afraid I'm painfully shy in company, a fault I've never managed to overcome."

"Please don't be offended, but do you hesitate for fear that, with the very fashionable Lady Ardith attending, you feel you do not possess a suitable gown?"

Laura laughed. "I certainly possess nothing cut up— or should we say 'down'—to Lady Ardith's standards."

"I should hope not," Lady Elspeth agreed with a chuckle. "But I wanted to ask a favor. I brought with me a new dinner gown just received from the mantua-maker that I've never worn, and now I find I cannot. If God wills, and I carry this child, by the time I visit London again fashions will have changed. Though I hope I'm not as vain as Lady Ardith, I doubt I'd wear it then. The color is a lovely green, and would suit you. Would you accept it?

"Please, now—" she held up a hand to forestall Laura's protest "—don't refuse outright. You know I won't insult you by offering payment for the care you gave Kit. Indeed, were I the richest woman in the universe, how could I ever pay you the worth of my baby brother's life? Beside that, a gown is the merest trifle. Still, it is too lovely to waste, and it would please me to have you wear it."

Though she didn't doubt Lady Elspeth's sincerity or kindness, Laura wasn't naive enough to believe this offer a coincidence. With a rueful grimace, she wondered who had whispered in her friend's ear. Lady Catherine, wanting "beautiful dresses" for her friend? Or Lord Beaulieu?

As she hesitated, Lady Elspeth misinterpreted her silence. "What a widget! Of course you can't decide until you see the gown. I'll have Jane bring it immediately!"

Laura tried to protest, but Lady Elspeth had already rung for her maid. Instructions were given, and by the time they finished their tea, the maid reappeared, bearing the dress. The demurral Laura intended to voice died in an inarticulate cry of wonder.

It was simply the most delicate, wondrous, lovely gown she'd ever beheld, a simple sheath of pale green silk whose wispy sleeves and long train were covered with a fairy's cobweb of fine lace. Not even in her debut season had she, limited to the whites and pastels prescribed for unmarried maidens, possessed such a dress.

Before she could muster her scattered thoughts to protest, Lady Elspeth had her on her feet, the maid holding the dress up to her as her friend gave instructions on where to pin, tuck or adjust.

"Ah, Ellie—it's marvelous! But I simply couldn't!"

"Since it's rather obvious you like the gown—" Elspeth paused in her instructions to grin at Laura "—and it becomes you wonderfully, I shall be most hurt if you refuse it."

The sober, responsible, cautious side of her urged that she do just that. But the woman in her slid the sensuous length of silk through her fingers, felt the sigh of lace against her arms, and knew she could never bring herself to turn this down. For one evening, like Cinderella in the fairy tale, plain, dowdy, shy little Laura Martin would be dressed like a princess.

And her Prince Charming, whom she might covertly watch and desire but never possess, would see her in it.

Even in a small gathering, wearing such a beautifully made gown would be sure to draw to her the universal attention of every lady present, and probably that of the gentlemen, as well. Inviting precisely the sort of widespread scrutiny she'd spent nearly three years carefully avoiding. Attending in that gown would be foolish, vain and most unwise.

And she would do it. If her benefactress were present, of course.

"You're sure you will be feeling well enough to attend the party?" Laura asked, grasping at straws.

Lady Elspeth's smile widened. "I wouldn't miss it for the world."

Chapter Nine

"Thank you, Jane. I can manage from here."

"Aye, ma'am. A right treasure you look, and so I'll tell her ladyship!" With a nod of professional approval, Lady Elspeth's maid curtsied and left the chamber.

Lips curving into a smile of pleasure, Laura closed her eyes, enjoying the pure sensual caress of the silk gown against her skin. Not until this moment, the smoky-green fabric swirling about her, did she realize just how much she'd missed what Lady Catherine would call "pretty dresses." After the door shut behind the departing maid, with a giddy laugh, Laura lifted her arms and waltzed around her narrow chamber, dipping and turning in the embrace of her invisible partner.

Cinderella in truth, for the dress was no more substantial than moondust and starlight. After months of wearing the stiff, heavy brown bombazine favored by Aunt Mary, so sheer and weightless did the garment feel Laura could scarcely believe she was clothed at all.

She stopped dancing and cast a worried glance down at her chest. Though fashioned with a décolletage nowhere near as deep as the style favored by Lady Ardith, the dress was still much lower cut than any she'd worn during her brief Season. Perhaps she should have protested more strongly when Lady Elspeth absolutely forbade Jane to sew a lace tucker into the bodice.

Nonsense, she reassured herself. With Lady Ardith present in all her scandalous finery, who would spare a look for little Laura Martin?

Nonetheless, her disquiet increased after she left the secure cocoon of her chamber. Since her near-miraculous recovery from the fever that had almost killed her, she'd worn naught but the mud-brown camouflage of her new identity. Daring to appear in public without it made her feel even more unclothed than the gossamer gown.

Still, if she meant to put off for an evening garments guaranteeing obscurity, nowhere in England could she do so in more safety than in Squire Everett's drawing room. The only guests present would be neighbors who'd long ago accepted Laura Martin, or relatives of the boy whose life she'd help to preserve. None of those, she believed, would consciously seek to do her harm.

Honesty forced her to admit that her unease at descending to the drawing room was directly related to the tall, commanding earl about to gather there with the assembling dinner party. A man who inspired in her this perilous swing of emotion from attraction to avoidance, the man she'd felt impelled to give, for one brief evening, a glimpse of the woman behind the mask.

A man who, should he decide to tempt her out of sanity into temporary dalliance, would tryst with her and forget her the moment his carriage passed beyond the gateposts of Everett Hall. In truth, no matter how glorious such an interlude would prove—and every inexperienced but acutely sensitive nerve shouted that it would be glorious indeed—she could not afford for him to remember her longer.

Laura Martin, you're an idiot, she concluded as she reached the floor on which the main bedchambers were located. As she started past the door to her patient's room, she paused. Perhaps she should check on Kit.

Glad to have a responsible reason to indulge her cowardly desire to dawdle, she knocked on the door. When Kit's valet, Peters, answered it, instead of standing aside to let her enter, he simply stood for a moment, jaw dropped, staring. "Cor, ma'am," he breathed, finally remembering to step back, "but you do look fine."

"T-thank you," she stuttered, not sure whether to be alarmed or flattered.

"Who is it, Peters?"

"Mrs. Martin, master—I think."

Kit Bradsleigh lay propped against his pillows, face pale and drawn. Only in the past two days had her patient been conscious and coherent enough to converse, though his lung ailment perforce limited speech. Still, she'd already come to appreciate the young man's unpretentious charm.

As she approached, his pain-shadowed eyes brightened with interest. "Fine indeed! Excuse my bad manners…not rising…to kiss the hand…of a lovely lady."

She smiled. "After all the hours Dr. MacDonovan and I have expended the last week to bring you to this evening, should you attempt so reckless a feat I'd be more tempted to bash you with the hand than let you kiss it."

"Then I am safe." He gave her a rueful grin. "Already attempted it…when Ellie stopped by. Found movement…most unwise. Must lie here…and admire from afar."

"It is a lovely gown and I do thank her for it. Shall you fare well here? I feel somewhat guilty going down to join the company, leaving you alone but for Peter's care."

He waved a hand. "If anyone deserves…an evening off…'tis you, ma'am! Afraid I've not…been in right frame…to express appreciation…but I want—"

"None of that," she interrupted. "Just praise heaven, as I do, that Dr. MacDonovan's skill and your own strong constitution were sufficient to bring you through."

He nodded, his thin face serious. "No more, then. But an evening…of Peter's company…is small recompense…for my debt…" His words trailed off, lost in a fit of coughing. Concerned, Laura leaned to press firmly against his bandaged shoulder, trying to immobilize the wound until the coughing subsided.

"Hush, now," she said when at last he took a gasping, cough-free breath. "Enough pretty speeches, though I do thank you for them. Peters, make sure he finishes the broth I send up, and no more conversation! You will call me on the instant if you feel I'm needed?"

"Aye, ma'am."

"Good. I'll bring up an herbal tea later." She squeezed Kit's hand. "'Twill ease your breathing and help you sleep." After he nodded acknowledgment, she looked with reluctance to the door. "I suppose I must go down."

She'd moved several steps away when his voice halted her. "Mustn't…be afraid."

Startled, she stopped short and turned back to him.

He managed an encouraging smile. "Beau intimidating…but kind. Never…hurt anyone good." He paused to put a hand to his chest, grimacing through another short cough. "Smile. You have…a lovely smile." He fluttered his fingers at her in a gesture of farewell and then closed his eyes, slumping back against his pillows.

Laura descended the stairs, more pensive still. Was her

agitation when around Lord Beaulieu so obvious? Or had Kit, knowing the reaction normally evoked in underlings by his lofty brother, merely been trying to encourage her?

Too late now to debate the wisdom of coming tonight. Taking a deep breath, she pushed open the parlor door.

A din of massed voices rolled over her. Startled by the noise after years of self-imposed social isolation, Laura halted, alarm skittering across her nerves. Forestalling the butler from announcing her arrival with a short, negative shake of her head, she slipped in, her eyes scanning the room to identify the company.

Lady Winters sat in her customary spot, several neighborhood ladies gathered around her, Lady Elspeth and another guest on the sofa opposite. The squire and his son held forth by the sideboard, glasses of spirits in hand. By the window, surrounded by most of the men of the company, Lady Ardith sparkled in low-cut golden splendor.

A shiver passed through her as she recognized the tall figure toward which Lady Ardith was leaning her impressively bared bosom. The shiver magnified to a tremor as Lord Beaulieu, as if cued by some invisible prompter, turned toward the doorway and saw her.

His look of mild annoyance vanished and his body tensed. While she waited, unable to breathe, his gaze swiftly inspected her—his frankly admiring gaze. And then he smiled, a warm, intimate message of welcome, as if she were the one person for whom all evening he'd been waiting.

He thought she looked pretty. She tried to stifle her guilty pleasure at the realization and swiftly bent her head before he could see the answering smile that automatically sprang to her lips. Both gratified and alarmed, she hurried to Lady Elspeth's comforting presence.

* * *

Beau shifted restlessly, a polite smile in place while he tuned out the drone of Lady Ardith's speech as effectively as he blocked out the quite attractive but entirely untempting display of cleavage she insisted on continually thrusting beneath his nose. Blast, did the woman think him blind?

Had this whole evening been for naught? Despite his sister's assurances and Kit's offer to help if necessary, would Laura Martin fail to appear?

Just as, reining in his raveling temper with an effort, he was about to come to that conclusion, he felt a change in the room, a rush of cool air.

He turned toward the door—and saw her. For a moment he quite literally forgot to breathe.

Her thick auburn hair, twisted at the top of her head into a mass of ringlets, was obscured from his awed glance by only the smallest of lace caps. And to his enthralled eyes, Ellie's luscious green gown revealed with vivid clarity every curve and even more of the glorious ivory skin he recalled from lovingly tended memory of the Vision.

Her restive glance finally collided with his in a connection that was almost palpable. For a timeless moment they simply stared at each other, oblivious to the other occupants of the room.

He wanted her at his side, where she belonged. At the last moment sanity returned and he stopped himself from calling out to her. Instead he smiled, trying to imbue in that silent gesture all his unspoken urgency. *Come to me.*

But though her eyes widened and her lips responded with a smile she quickly bent to hide, she turned to walk not to him, but to his sister.

Beau gritted his teeth to keep from gnashing them in

frustration. *Go easy,* he cautioned himself. He must not crowd her in front of this crowd of people. Not make her nervous by singling her out, or conspicuous by drawing down on her the rancor Lady Ardith would surely display if that calculating lightskirt decided the richest potential lover present was taking undue notice of some other lady.

He must wait, in short. And so he would. But sometime, somehow, he vowed, before this evening ended he would find a way to steal her to himself. After the other guests had departed, for a walk in the garden, perhaps. Just the two of them, alone under an embrace of moonlight.

Mollified by that pleasant thought, he was able to tear his eyes from the fetching silhouette of her slender form before Lady Ardith, presently toying with a portly knight who was Sir Everett's nearest neighbor, noticed his lapse in attention. Fortunately, that lady had so monopolized the other male guests that it seemed none but himself had noticed Mrs. Martin enter.

Just as well. Let them gape at the high flyer—and leave the refined elegance of Mrs. Martin to him.

The dinner gong sounded. Despite her change of attire, Beau noted with an inner smile, Mrs. Martin still managed to remain reclusive, slipping away from his sister as the guests rose from their seats, retreating toward the Squire and Tom before Beau reached her.

As they caught sight of Mrs. Martin, both men uttered exclamations of surprise and delight. Beau gritted his teeth once more as the squire's tone abruptly changed from bluff to coyly gallant. Squire Everett and Tom would not be the only gentlemen captivated tonight by the widow's swanlike transformation, he realized with irritated resignation. However, he promised himself again, regardless of how many gentlemen fell under the spell of her charm throughout dinner, the widow would end her evening in his company alone.

He was less pleased once they arrived in the dining chamber to discover that Mrs. Martin, whom he'd instructed the butler to seat near him at the head of the table, was instead positioned at its foot. He turned to his hostess.

"Lady Winters, this will not do! We're gathered here to honor Dr. MacDonovan and Mrs. Martin, the two individuals responsible for saving my brother's life. We cannot have one of them banished to the end of the table."

His hostess gave him a startled look, but before she could stutter an answer, Mrs. Martin said, "Marsden told me you'd requested that, my lord, but not considering it fitting that I be seated above the more distinguished guests, I had him change the cards, as I knew Lady Winters would wish." She fixed her gaze carefully on the fluttering figure beside him. "Though I am, of course, much flattered by his lordship's kindness."

Her reply attracted to her for the first time the general notice of the entire party. Beau watched with ironic amusement as the faces around the table reflected, first interest in the newcomer in their midst, then puzzlement, then varying decrees of shock, astonishment—and admiration as they finally identified the speaker.

By the time she finished her explanation, all other conversation had ceased and the attention of everyone present was riveted on Mrs. Martin. Finding herself suddenly the focus of every eye, the lady swiftly dropped her gaze to her lap, her cheeks pinking.

A gasp sounded in the silence, followed by a "By Jove!" The vicar, across the table from Mrs. Martin, sat with mouth agape, while the knight seated next to her exclaimed, "Mrs. Martin, what a capital rig. Capital!"

Lady Ardith stared at the widow with a look of shocked indignation, as if one of the stone spaniels that flanked Squire Everett's drive had just turned and bitten her. Nonetheless, she was first of the ladies to recover.

"What an...interesting gown, Mrs. Martin. A hand-me-down from the family of a grateful patient, no doubt. When one is forced to earn one's crust, I suppose one must accept all manner of payments."

Ellie gasped, indignation flashing in her eyes, and though a matching anger flared in Beau, he reached out swiftly to put a warning hand on her elbow.

The high color in Mrs. Martin's face paled. Before Beau could intervene, she raised her gaze to Lady Ardith. Her coolly amused gaze. "Indeed, my lady."

Bravo, Beau thought.

"I hope," Ardith continued, sublimely oblivious, "you've expressed your humble thanks to the squire and his lordship for permitting you to be included in this gathering. I daresay you've never dined in quite this sort of company before."

Did he observe an instant's quiver in her lip? Before he could decide, Mrs. Martin, her expression blandly meek, replied, "You're quite right, my lady." Her eyes dipped briefly to Lady Ardith's jutting bosom before she continued, "I've never dined in such company before."

Beau choked back a laugh, then shot a glance at Ellie. His sister gave him a tiny nod, her eyes full of mirth.

"I do thank his lordship, Squire Everett and Lady Winters for including me tonight," Mrs. Martin concluded.

The vicar gave Lady Ardith a sharp look. "'Tis not so unusual for us to dine with Mrs. Martin. We have on several occasions been blessed with her excellent company."

"Country parties, of course," Lady Ardith replied. "Given the unfortunate lack of numbers often obtaining in country society, 'tis quite amazing the odd parties one is occasionally forced to make up." Noting the vicar still frowning, Lady Ardith leaned toward him, gifting the reverend with a full view of her generous endowments. "Though you, of course, Mr. Blackthorne, would be welcome at any party. And how is your mama, the viscountess?"

Being human, the vicar did gaze for a moment at the display beneath his eyes, but to Beau's grudgingly accorded credit, almost immediately raised his glance back to the lady's face. His closed expression hinted he'd already assessed Lady Ardith's character and found it, unlike her chest, to be somewhat lacking. "Quite well, Lady Ardith," he said shortly, refraining from adding a comment that might prolong the conversation.

Lady Ardith eyed the vicar for a moment, then shrugged at the subtle rebuff. Apparently considering the man not worth the effort—or perhaps writing him off as unattachable—Lady Ardith turned once more to the squire, and conversation became general again.

Beau was too far away to be able to overhear Mrs. Martin's comments to her dinner partners, but as she was seated on the opposite side of the table, at least he could turn occasionally and gaze at her. She sat quietly, speaking little, her head inclined in smiling deference.

Unlike Lady Ardith, who seemed unable to let her neighbors dine in peace. Scarcely had he taken a mouthful before, in a minor breach of etiquette, she waved across the table at him.

"Do you find the fish agreeable, Lord Beaulieu?"

To reply, he was forced to dispense with the bite in one swallow. "Very."

"Alphonse, our London chef, prepares a similar dish—much more elaborate, of course, as one would expect of a French *artiste*. You must stop by and try pot luck with us some evening when you are in town, mustn't he, Asquith?"

Her husband, mouth full and focus fixed on the wine glass the footman was refilling, uttered a grunt that might be taken as assent. Scarcely waiting for her spouse's reply, the lady turned to the squire with a flirtatious sweep of lashes. "How clever of you to procure so excellent a cook here in the country." She leaned forward and stroked one finger slowly down his hand. "I so *enjoy* a clever gentleman."

Having reduced the squire to goggling incoherence, Lady Ardith took another small bite and turned to Dr. MacDonovan. "Ah, delicious!" She slowly ran the tip of her tongue over her lips before saying in a husky voice, "Dr. MacDonovan, do they enjoy such delights in Edinburgh?"

After a sympathetic wink at Beau, Mac grinned at the lady. "To be sure, Lady Ardith. Such treats should be devoured wherever they are offered."

She arched a brow at Mac and gave a soft, throaty laugh. "Naughty man! Though I believe you are correct, Doctor. Lady Elspeth, is he always such a rogue?"

"Always."

"You must excuse me for neglecting you, Lady Elspeth," Ardith continued. "I know the mama of so lovely and clever a daughter as Lady Catherine must want to be speaking of nothing but her offspring and alas, I fear I know little of children, his lordship and I not being so blessed. I try to console myself with the reflection that infants are quite ruinous to the figure. But then I am a silly, frivolous creature, as my lord is ever telling me. Ah, Lord Beaulieu, how do you like the shrimp velouté?''

And so, effectively shutting out the vacant Lady Winters, who seldom exerted herself to converse, and Elspeth, who was too polite to wrench the conversation back in her own direction, Lady Ardith continued to chatter through the meal, punctuating her running commentary with flirtatious glances and suggestive touches to the hands of the gentlemen closest to her, as if to keep them ever mindful of her physical allure.

Beau glanced from Lord Asquith, food-stained cravat askew, to where Lady Ardith was preening coquettishly before Mac, the knight Sir Ramsdale and his bedazzled son. He felt an unexpected flash of sympathy for the lady.

With her glittering blond beauty and siren's body, she'd doubtless been the diamond of her come-out Season, accustomed to being the focus of masculine attention since the day she left the schoolroom. Shackled now to a prominent, wealthy peer who apparently no longer indulged appetites beyond the table, with no children to occupy her time, it was small wonder she felt compelled to practice her wiles on any reasonably attractive male within reach.

Especially since, he had to acknowledge, the majority of his sex would encourage her efforts. Given the lady's alluring assets, few men would deny themselves the pleasure of seizing the several hours of harmless, mindless, full-body amusement her enticing glances promised. Brutal honesty compelled him to admit he might have been tempted to respond himself, had he not first encountered the more intelligent, complex and subtly attractive Mrs. Martin.

Certainly the gentlemen at table with Lady Ardith now were competing to claim that prize. Although her husband persisted in ignoring her, occupying himself solely with the replenishment and emptying of his plate and wineglass, the other men vied for Lady Ardith's attention, responding eagerly to her suggestive banter. The knight's adolescent son, to the neglect of his dinner partners, chewed his meal while staring at Lady Ardith in cow-eyed adoration.

In contrast, Mrs. Martin ate sparingly and spoke but little, though her soft-voiced replies to her neighbors' statements seemed to foster a continuous and lively discussion at her end of the table. Not was she entirely lacking in admirers, Beau noted.

Despite the distracting presence of Lady Ardith at his elbow, the squire nonetheless occasionally sent an appreciative glance toward the lady at the far end of his table. And, Beau realized with an unpleasant shock, the vicar, who sat in privileged proximity just opposite Mrs. Martin, seldom took his eyes off her.

A man of the cloth, Beau thought with an immediate surge of indignation, should not be entertaining thoughts that, to judge by the heated intensity of the vicar's expression, were obviously both covetous and carnal.

Beau turned to find Lady Ardith staring in the direction of his gaze, her eyes frosty as they rested on Mrs. Martin. With a glittering smile, she abruptly angled her head toward the squire's sister, who sat absently picking at her food.

"Lady Winters, you had Mrs. Martin write out your invitation cards, didn't you? Kind of you to offer her employment, which she badly needs, I imagine."

Belatedly realizing she'd been addressed, Lady Winters focused out of her haze. "Employed?" she repeated, looking confused. "No, I don't pay Mrs. Martin."

"Nay, of course not, 'tis as a friend of the family she does it," the squire clarified.

"Well, I knew the moment I received the invitation that someone other than dear Lady Winters had copied out the cards. I vow, one can always distinguish the hand of a true lady. My own *écriture* is so precise, I cannot address more than a handful of cards at a sitting. Before a ball, I must spend the veriest week at it."

That speech evaporated whatever tepid sympathy Beau had previously summoned for the acidic blond beauty. Squelching a strong desire to deal Lady Ardith a sharp set-down, Beau forced himself to remain discreetly silent.

"Quite a pretty hand she has, we think," the squire said with a nod toward Mrs. Martin.

"Indeed?" Lady Ardith raised penciled brows. "Mrs. Martin is fortunate you and Lady Winters are so obliging. I was quite shocked when first I heard that a woman, of supposedly gentle birth, chose to live alone without even the vestige of a chaperone. Did you not, in your good nature, continue to recognize her, I daresay she might not be received by any good family in the neighborhood."

While Beau choked back his outraged response, Lady Ardith leaned confidentially closer to the squire. "Though you might warn her to be more discreet. Appearing in such a—well, coming—gown, and living alone as she does, who knows what sort of thoughts she might inspire in some of the local men? Even the vicar looks quite…taken. Though perhaps that's her intent." Lady Ardith smiled slyly. "Still, she'd best take care. *Exposed* as she is, a very little gossip deeming her 'fast' would be enough to ruin her reputation. Where would she be if the common folk no longer sought her out for their pills and potions?''

Her ''confidential'' advice, uttered in a tone that must have carried halfway down the table, if not all the way to the ears of the lady it derided, was the final straw. Deciding to end the conversation before he lost control and strangled Lady Ardith, Beau abruptly turned to his hostess. ''Lady Winters, is it not time for you to withdraw?''

Again looking startled, Lady Winters goggled at him. After fussing to find her handkerchief and reticule, she rose. ''Brother, gentlemen, if you will excuse us?''

Looking forward to the freedom of the drawing room where at last he could approach his lady, and knowing she would probably seek an excuse to leave the party early, Beau maneuvered the gentlemen out of the dining room after a single glass of brandy. Though Lord Asquith grumbled about being separated from his cigars, the rest of the men, doubtless relishing thoughts of a closer view down the bodice of his wife's dress, greeted Beau's suggestion with approval.

As he followed his host to the drawing room, Beau rapidly developed a plan that, with a little help from Mac, would ensure Mrs. Martin wasn't allowed to flee before the other guests departed. Short of storming her bedchamber—and he wasn't completely sure he'd not resort to that extremity if pressed—he was prepared to do whatever it took to get her alone.

Chapter Ten

It was, Laura decided, the nicest dinner party she'd ever attended. Despite the sparkling gown that had initially drawn her to the attention of the company, the far-more-glittering presence of Lady Ardith guaranteed that she was soon able to return to her preferred role as a quiet observer. And so, wearing a dress that made her feel like a princess, being treated with kindness and even a touch of deference by her neighbors, she could relax and with perfect propriety let her gaze stray down the table to Lord Beaulieu.

Who was without question the most impressive gentleman in the room. The midnight-black of evening dress suited his raven hair and dark eyes, and the stark simplicity of the color and cut of his garments merely emphasized his breadth of shoulder, litheness of body and aura of power. Though she could not make out his words, even at a distance she could tell how, despite the impediment of Lady Ardith, whose rapid, laughter-punctuated banter scarcely paused long enough to allow her to draw breath or consume a morsel, he skillfully handled his end of the table, managing to coax even the normally silent Lady Winters into the conversation.

Occasionally he glanced in her direction. When he caught her eye, his mouth would curve in that compelling, intimate smile, and she would again be seized with the absurd notion that despite being surrounded by a tableful of people, one of whom was an accredited beauty, he was interested in her alone.

Absurd, but on this magical night when like Cinderella she'd appeared in borrowed finery and caught the eye of a prince, she'd ignore the prosaic voice of common sense.

Giddy delight, like champagne bubbles rising, swelled in her breast, and she could not help smiling. How different this evening was from the mostly wretched dinner parties she'd attended as a shy and nervous debutante, then as an inexperienced young bride.

The smile faded. She'd come to hate social functions, knowing her hawk-eyed husband would observe her every gesture and remark, and after the guests departed subject her to a scathing critique. She was too forward or too timid; she spoke too little or too much, played cards badly, danced too frequently or too seldom.

Even after she'd stopped caring about his good opinion, realizing it impossible to obtain, she so dreaded those post-party diatribes she could scarcely eat during dinner. Especially since as Charleton seemed to sense her will to please him diminishing, over the passing months he became increasingly angry, demeaning—and violent.

An involuntary shudder passed through her. With an effort, she shook her thoughts free. She mustn't spoil a moment of this perfectly lovely gathering—the only occasion she would ever appear outside her dull brown persona—fretting over demons who were, she reassured herself again, safely consigned to the past.

"Is something the matter? You look...disturbed."

The vicar's question startled her. "N-nothing!" she

replied, damping down an automatic alarm. "I was wool-gathering, which was terribly rude. Please excuse me."

"No forgiveness necessary. I must simply redouble my efforts to entertain you. 'Twould be a crushing blow to my self-esteem to know the loveliest lady in the room found my dinner conversation dull."

She dutifully smiled at the compliment, though in truth the only mild distress she'd experienced since coming to the table was generated by rather too solicitous attention of Reverend Mr. Blackthorne. It seemed, as the courses were brought and removed in turn, that every time she glanced in his direction, she found his admiring and uncomfortably intense gaze resting on her.

"It is the excellence of your address, I fear, that condemned you to this end of the table, so far away from the belle of the evening," she replied, gesturing toward Lady Ardith. "For that I must truly apologize. Knowing how skillfully you converse with every member of society—" with a nod she indicated the querulous dowager to one side of him and the shy spinster on the other "— I'm afraid 'tis I who placed you here."

Mr. Blackthorne glanced at Lady Ardith, currently laughing as she plied her lashes at Dr. MacDonovan. "It cannot be lost on any gentleman present—" he leaned forward to murmur in a voice pitched for her ears alone "—who the true belle of the evening is. A lady whose beauty of countenance is matched by gentility of manner."

Unsure how to politely discourage his ardency, Laura blessed Lady Winters, who rose at that moment, signaling the ladies to withdraw. "You will excuse me, sir?"

"If I must," he said. "Until later, then."

I certainly hope not, Laura thought as she followed her hostess from the room.

'Twas time for Cinderella to depart, and not just to evade the attentions of the unexpectedly solicitous Mr. Blackthorne. Protected by the length of a dinner table, she'd been able to indulge her frivolous fantasies about Lord Beaulieu. But once the gentleman returned, there would be no barrier to his approaching her. Better to leave now, before Lord Beaulieu brushed away the fragile cobweb of her silly dream by ignoring her completely.

Or worse, made it all too real by approaching her.

In the parlor, the ladies took seats by age and inclination, save for Lady Ardith who, denied any other masculine attention, stood by the door dazzling a young footman. After the lad sprang away to fetch the wine she commanded, the lady drifted over to the window and stared out over the moonlit garden, one slippered foot tapping rhythmically against the floor.

Laura approached Lady Winters, intending to present her compliments and withdraw. But before she could utter a word, Lady Elspeth called to her.

"Please, Mrs. Martin, come sit by me." Lord Beaulieu's sister indicated the place beside her. "I've not had a chance to speak with you all evening."

Much as Laura would prefer to leave forthwith, she could not do so without being rude to the lady who'd befriended her. Forcing a smile, she walked to the sofa.

"How fortunate you are, Lady Winters, to have such a charming, intelligent neighbor as Mrs. Martin. No, my dear, you must not blush!" Lady Elspeth patted Laura's hand. "Dr. MacDonovan has sung your praises since the moment I arrived, and he is not a man to offer idle compliments. Indeed, have I not witnessed your skill for myself? I'm breeding, you see," she informed the others, "and have been most horridly ill. Mrs. Martin prescribed a tea that has eased the discomfort."

The neighborhood ladies all nodded. "'Tis a rare blessing she is to the whole county, just like her dear aunt, Mrs. Hastings," the knight's wife said. "Especially since one never knows whether or not Dr. Winthrop will be…available."

"All the more rare to find such skill in a lady of gentle birth," Lady Elspeth continued. "How comforting it is to be able to discuss intimate matters with an *equal*." She cast a glance toward Lady Ardith as she emphasized the word.

As if pricked by the remark, that lady looked back toward the company, her disdainful gaze coming to rest on Laura. It seemed she would speak, but apparently deciding that without a masculine audience to exploit she'd not bother, she turned back once again to the window.

"With me feeling so peevish, Mrs. Martin has kindly stepped in to take my daughter for her walks," Lady Elspeth continued. "What a champion you have there, Mrs. Martin! Catherine can scarcely be contained until it is time for her outing, and comes back chattering of the clever things you've shown or said or read to her."

"Ah, children," said Lady Ardith from her window. "Charming creatures! So inexperienced, they possess no discrimination whatsoever."

"The intelligent ones do, from quite an early age," Lady Elspeth replied. "A shame you've apparently never encountered the like among your own family and friends."

Lady Ardith pivoted to face Lord Beaulieu's sister, a martial light sparking in her cold blue eyes. Fortunately for Laura's peace of mind, at that moment the parlor door opened. In a rush of conversation flavored with the lingering odor of cigar, the gentlemen entered.

With a smile as glittering as her gown, Lady Ardith at

once made for Lord Beaulieu. "Ah, my lord, thank you for joining us so speedily!" she cried, latching onto his arm. "Deprived of your company, we women are such dull creatures. Babies and potions...I declare—" she swept a dagger glance at Lady Elspeth "—Squire Everett's winter garden is more interesting than the conversation we summon up."

Dr. MacDonovan halted beside them. Was it Laura's imagination, or did a subtle glance pass between the two men? "Ah, lass, I canna believe the lips of such an exquisite creature could pass on anything less than... delicious. Come," he urged, taking the hand the lady had pressed on Lord Beaulieu's arm, "let us find some wine. Then ye must speak to me and prove the yea or nay of it."

It appeared that the lady might refuse, until the doctor leaned closer and murmured something that brought a satisfied smile to her face even as she laughed and batted his arm. "La, but you're wicked," she reproved, allowing Dr. MacDonovan to lead her to the sideboard.

Before Laura could look away, Lord Beaulieu's gaze met hers. He rolled his eyes briefly, a gesture so indicative of relief she almost laughed out loud. Then he smiled again, a slight curve of lip and fire of glance that once again ignited every nerve and set the champagne bubbles dancing through her veins. His eyes holding hers, she sensed more than saw him approach.

"Thank you, brother, for the rescue," Lady Elspeth murmured. "I was in dire danger of becoming... unladylike."

Lord Beaulieu bent to kiss his sister's cheek. "That, I could never believe," he said with a grin.

With Lord Beaulieu a mere forearm's length away, Laura could feel the heat emanating from his body, catch the faint scent of shaving soap and brandy. Almost, she could feel his hand once more resting on *her* shoulder, those lips dipping to brush *her* cheek. A shiver swept over her skin.

He turned to her, his grin fading as his imperious eyes found and commanded hers. Scraps of conversation, the popping of the fire, the clink of glasses faded, until she heard only the rapid beat of her pulse. While they both remained motionless, staring, she forgot even to breathe.

"Mrs. Martin," he said at last. "How very beautiful you look tonight."

"Th-thank you, my lord."

"I had hoped we might—"

"Excuse me, my lord," Squire Everett's hearty voice startled her. "The card tables are set, and Lady Ardith is demanding we choose partners now and begin play."

"Play," the earl repeated, and shook his head as if to clear his thoughts. "Yes, of course. If you'll excuse me, ladies." He made them a quick bow.

Almost dizzy with happiness, Laura watched him walk away. *He thought her beautiful.* As she'd dreamed all evening, he'd come to her, stood by her, gifted her with that special smile that transported her to a magical realm where nothing existed but the two of them alone.

Better to leave now, before anything occurred to mar the perfection of an evening she would recall with wonder the rest of her days. Cinderella, mirrored in the eyes of her prince as "beautiful."

In a daze, she murmured thanks to Lady Winters and Lady Elspeth and floated toward the door.

Before she reached it, Lord Beaulieu called out, "No, Mrs. Martin, we cannot have you departing so early! Squire Everett needs a fourth at his table."

"Aye, madam, ye've had evenings enough of sick lads

and laudanum,'' Dr. MacDonovan said. ''Having kept vigil late these past days, ye canna be weary yet.''

''You must stay, Mrs. Martin,'' Squire Everett said. ''My sister declares she will not play unless you join us.''

Desperately as she wished to break free, to tuck away this fragile gem of an evening in a protective tissue wrap of memory so she might preserve it forever, once again civility dictated she remain.

And so she let the squire lead her to the table, knowing in truth that the reticent Lady Winters, an indifferent card player, would be wretchedly uncomfortable unless matched with a forgiving partner.

And besides, depending on where Lady Ardith maneuvered Lord Beaulieu, she might be able to observe the earl a bit longer, add a few more gilded treasures to the trove that must warm her through the long lonely days after he departed. As soon he must.

A surprisingly bitter regret spiraled through her. Damping it down, she took her place.

Laura gamely played through several rubbers, though her modest skill was not sufficient to outweigh some of Lady Winters's disastrous discards. Their team ended by being solidly trounced, much to the delight of the squire and his partner Sir Ramsdale.

Naturally, Lady Ardith had snared the earl and Dr. MacDonovan for her table, with Lady Elspeth making up the fourth. The beauty seated the gentlemen—deliberately?—so that Laura could view only the back of his lordship's head, but from the frequency of Dr. MacDonovan's hearty laugh and the coos and squeals emanating from Lady Ardith, Laura surmised their table was enjoying a rousing good game.

The other tables were finishing up. Repressing the desire to linger, Laura turned to the squire.

"Thank you and Lady Winters both for such a delightful evening. I must go check on our patient now."

"Nonsense," Lord Beaulieu said, surprising her by appearing behind her chair. "Kit's valet will summon help if the need arises. Lady Winters, shall we not have some dancing? This handsome chamber seems designed for it."

"D-dancing?" Lady Winters repeated faintly.

"Capital idea!" Squire Everett said. "We've numbers enough for a respectable set. You can play for us, Emily."

Lady Ardith walked over then to put an entreating hand on the earl's arm. "Oh, yes, you must dance with me! Do say you will play for us, dear Lady Winters."

"Nay," Lord Beaulieu said, slipping his arm from under Lady Ardith's grasping fingers in one smooth movement. "I insist on leading my charming hostess into the first set. I've heard, Lady Winters, you were such a belle at your debut Season the gentlemen called each other out over the privilege of escorting you."

"Aye, a regular diamond our Emily was," the squire confirmed proudly. "Winters was smitten the moment he saw her. Weren't the only one, neither—even the old Duke of Clarendon came calling on her."

"I'll wager she can outdance us all still," Lord Beaulieu said. "If you would do me the honor, my lady?" He made her the exaggerated leg of a Georgian courtier.

"Oh, la," Lady Winters said, her face pinking with a mingling of pleasure and alarm. "I—I…"

"Excellent," the earl said. "Squire, Dr. MacDonovan approaches, so you'd best be quick if you wish to capture Lady Ardith for the first set." Ignoring the dagger glance that lady shot him, he turned to the rest of the company. "Ladies, gentlemen, choose your partners."

He turned back to Laura. "You will play for us, Mrs. Martin? I understand you are quite skilled." Without awaiting a reply, he offered his arm to the blushing Lady Winters and led her to where the couples were assembling.

Laura made her way to the piano, trying not to feel so...deflated. What had she expected—that the earl would ask lowly Mrs. Martin to dance? A woman who, whatever her origins, now occupied a position less elevated than a governess. A woman who, as Lady Ardith had cogently reminded the company earlier, had to earn her own bread.

She should focus on that fact and forget the seductive magic so briefly evoked by a borrowed gown.

"Let me help you find some music."

Mr. Blackthorne stood beside the piano, distracting her out of her dispiriting reflections.

"A country dance, perhaps?" he suggested.

She nodded, as perversely comforted now by his attention as she had been unsettled by it earlier. After selecting a piece, she began to play.

Within a few moments, joy at the mellow chords produced by the squire's fine instrument succeeded in dissipating her melancholy. She glanced up to the dancers—and found the reverend's eyes focused on her with alarming warmth. A smile leaped to his face as their eyes met and he winked. Then, as he bent to turn the page of music, he placed a hand on her bared shoulder.

She jumped, missing the next chord. The earl whipped a glance over to them and frowned. Removing his hand, Mr. Blackthorne stepped back, but she had to struggle to recapture the beat, her quiet enjoyment shattered. Though he did not touch her again for the remainder of the piece,

Laura remained uncomfortably conscious of his presence beside her.

After the music ended, Laura looked up to find the earl regarding them frostily. "Mr. Blackthorne, we have ladies in need of partners. I'm sure Mrs. Martin can keep her place in the music without assistance. Lady Ramsdale, did you not request the reverend's escort?"

"If you please, sir," the knight's wife said. "You're ever so fine a dancer."

Laura thought for a moment Reverend Blackthorne would refuse. Then with a sigh, he murmured, "You will excuse me?" and walked to the dancers.

Waiting for a cue to begin the next piece, Laura watched the earl bow over the hand of Lady Winters who, flushed and laughing, shook her head in demurral. Whatever he said in those deep, even tones must have been persuasive, for after a moment, still shaking her head, she let him lead her once again into place beside him.

To her horror, Laura felt a shaft of bitter envy pierce her.

If she were reduced to resenting the gentle, silly Lady Winters, it was long past time to depart. The minute the dancers tired of their sport, she would take her leave.

Laura tried, but was unable to recapture her previous delight in the music itself. After the current dance ended and the earl, insisting Lady Winters dance now with Dr. MacDonovan, turned to claim a waiting Lady Ardith, what tepid enthusiasm she had mustered dissipated completely.

She tried to ignore the girlish giggles and arch tones that disrupted her concentration whenever the movements of the dance brought the earl and Lady Ardith nearby. When, after the last chord faded, the beauty immediately implored Lord Beaulieu to partner her again, Laura had to fight to keep from grinding her teeth.

She should have escaped earlier. Now her lovely memories of the party would be soured by the sound of Lady Ardith's breathy voice and high-pitched titters.

Which is exactly what she ought to recall, argued the wiser, more cautious part of her. She'd been given a lovely gown and treated with deference by the company, which was everything and more than a woman in her position could expect or desire. She should banish once and for all every other moonstruck fancy.

"Yes, my lord, one more dance," Lady Ardith cooed. "And we simply must make it a waltz!" She looked over at Laura, her expression a mixture of triumph and disdain. *How dare you try to garner any attention at my party,* it said. "You do know how to play a waltz, Mrs. Martin?"

Ignoble but instinctive fury shook Laura. But before she could mendaciously deny she knew anything about the waltz, Lord Beaulieu intervened. "A treat we shall have to postpone, my lady. Our hostess is looking fatigued."

Lady Ardith's smile faded to a moue of annoyance, but the earl had already relinquished her hand to stride toward the small group gathered around Lady Winters. Their hostess did in fact look ill, swaying on her feet as her brother supported her and Lady Ramsdale fanned her rapidly.

"Lady Winters, are you all right?" the earl demanded.

"A bit overcome by the heat," the squire replied. "I think I'd best take her up to bed. I've instructed the staff to bring in the tea tray. Mrs. Martin, would you kindly pour for us?"

With a flare of irritation, Laura nearly refused performing this additional service. If she did so, however, she knew the hostess's task would fall to Lady Elspeth, who ought to be delivered a cup and allowed to rest. "Of course, Squire Everett."

"She'll be as right as a trivet once her woman gets her tucked up in bed," the squire assured the rest of the company. "Come, my dear, and wave your goodbyes to our guests. I'll have you upstairs in a hound pup's lick."

"Please allow me to assist," the earl said, "and selfishly steal a few minutes longer with the most graceful dancer of the evening." Having received a weak smile from Lady Winters, he motioned in the servants who stood at the doorway, heavily loaded trays in hand. "Mrs. Martin will serve." Taking Lady Winter's other arm, he helped the squire lead her from the room.

My lord of Beaulieu was certainly good at ordering people about, Laura thought resentfully as she took her place behind the tea tray. But the small civilities of serving tea and the friendliness of Lady Elspeth, who insisted on installing herself at Laura's elbow, gradually soothed her irritation. By the time the squire and the earl returned to the parlor, Laura was able to prepare their cups with a fair measure of her usual calm.

Don't meet his eye. Don't listen for his voice. Pour the tea, smile politely, leave. Now that, at long last, she was finally about to depart, she felt an irrational sadness that the evening was truly going to end. Cinderella, returning to sackcloth and ashes.

"Another round of cards?" Reverend Blackthorne suggested. "I've not yet had the pleasure of partnering Mrs. Martin."

"Not for me, I'm afraid," Lady Elspeth said, smothering a yawn. "My daughter has me up betimes. My warmest regards to all, but I shall have to retire."

"I expect we should leave, as well," Sir Ramsdale said. "A capital party, though, squire! Be sure to convey our warmest thanks to Lady Winters."

Amid murmurs of agreement among the other guests, the squire motioned the butler to summon the carriages.

"I'm past needing to check on our patient. Please excuse me," Laura said with a curtsey to the company.

"I should like to look on him, as well," the earl said. "Squire, my lords and ladies, a delightful evening. If I might escort you, Mrs. Martin?"

Beau climbed the stairs beside Mrs. Martin in a silence that was both edgy with awareness and paradoxically, companionable. After Peters answered their soft knock, Mrs. Martin walked to the side of his sleeping brother's bed. "Has he been resting comfortably?" she asked the valet.

"Aye, ma'am. He argufied some, but I got 'em to drink all his broth."

"Good." She reached out to touch Kit's forehead, ran her fingers down to his temple, then moved them to the pulse at the base of his jaw and let them rest there. Beau felt a sharp, involuntary pang of envy.

"Fever is not much elevated, and his pulse is quiet," she observed. "Has he been coughing?"

"A bit. But not what's you might call excessive."

She nodded, then carefully laid her head against his brother's chest. Beau sucked in a breath, thinking it might be worth getting shot to be in Kit's place. Especially with a tad fewer witnesses and a lot fewer garments.

"Just a bit of a whistle in his lungs, and his breathing is easier," she said. "I expect he should do fine tonight, although perhaps it would be best if I—"

"There's no need, Mrs. Martin," Beau interrupted

hastily. "Dr. MacDonovan would not have turned Kit over to Peters if he had any doubts about his well-being."

"You get some rest, ma'am," Peters said. "Young master will be fine."

Kit murmured and stirred. Beau took that opportunity to place a hand under Mrs. Martin's elbow. "Come, we don't wish to disturb his slumber."

She hesitated a moment before nodding. "Very well. Good night, Peters."

"Good night, ma'am, your lordship."

His hand still at her elbow, Beau urged her toward the door. He paused at the threshold to glance back—and caught Kit watching them. His brother flashed him a wink before snapping his eyes shut. Suppressing a chuckle, Beau led Mrs. Martin from the room.

At last he would have her to himself. Anticipation surged through his veins.

"You missed your walk with Lady Catherine this afternoon," he said, willing his voice to calm. "Or so she informed me during our ride, with no little indignation. You mustn't neglect your exercise, though, and so unless you are fatigued, I suggest you take that walk now. The evening is clear with no trace of wind, the garden near bright as day under a full moon, and with a wool wrap you should be perfectly warm."

"What an appealing thought! I believe I will." She smiled. "I've always wondered if roses smell as sweetly at night."

"Shall we find out?"

Her smile dissolved, her eyes widening. "W-we?"

"I can hardly allow you to walk about the grounds after dark without an escort. And since 'tis I who urged you to it, 'tis only fitting that I do the honors."

"Oh, but my lord, you said you had work...I could not—"

"My papers will wait. Lady Winters's white garden was designed to be seen in moonlight, she told me. I should like very much to inspect it with you." His touch feather-light, he put a finger to her chin, tilting it up so her eyes were forced to meet his. *Come with me,* his gaze implored. "Please, Mrs. Martin."

He held his breath, frantic with impatience as he awaited her response. She had no guile; he could read on her face the distress, uncertainty—and longing his invitation evoked. All his energy concentrated in wordless imperative, he willed her to yield to the desire that warred with caution in her eyes.

Each moment she did not flee brought her closer to consent. Acquiescence trembled on her lips, and he sought to help it find voice. "Does a white rose truly smell as sweet at midnight? I, too, should like to know." His eyes never leaving hers, he offered his arm. "Let us see."

Say yes, say yes, say yes. The refrain beat so loudly in his head he might have spoken it aloud. If she demurred now he wasn't at all sure he could make himself leave her.

The briefest flicker of a smile creased her lips. "It would be much wiser if we did not. But..." She uttered a small sigh, as if having won—or lost—some great struggle. "Let me fetch my shawl."

Relief, excitement and gladness shot through him like an exploding Congreve rocket. Knowing he was grinning like an infatuated schoolboy but unable to help himself, he said, "My cloak is in the library. 'Twill be warmer."

Before she could change her mind and bolt, he clasped her arm and led her downstairs, across the deserted entryway where the case clock ticked loudly in the stillness, and into the library. Snatching up the cloak he'd left there after his late ride, he fastened it beneath her chin with care, the deliberate avoidance of contact with the soft skin so tantalizingly near his fingers a delicious game of heightening awareness.

"Come," he whispered. Taking the gloved hand she offered, he led them out the French doors onto the terrace. As they descended to the garden, Mrs. Martin gave a gasp.

"It is a fairyland!"

Illumined by moonlight, each urn, bench and planting stood in its usual place, yet the silvered light and the odd, amorphous shadows it cast gave everything a strange, otherworldly aspect.

His senses seemed uncommonly acute, as well. He heard the plaintive call of an owl, the scurrying of some small animal in the bushes, the crunch of the gravel under their feet, the silken rustle of her skirts. Her subtle scent carried on the chill night air, teasing his nose with the warmth and fragrance of her. Moonlight painted her dark hair, silhouetted her small straight nose and delicate lips with a crystalline line. Each time she took a step the opaque darkness of his cloak parted to reveal a sparkling flash of gown, as magically luminescent as phosphorus in the wake of a ship.

In awed silence they walked down the center allée, then turned toward the west wing into the white garden.

Ghostly roses glowed against a shadowed trellis on the stone wall opposite them. The silver leaves of artemesia and curry drifted onto the pathway, a splash of stardust at their feet, while tiny white brushheads of asters stood out like dots of exclamation against a dark mass of greenery.

"It's beautiful," Mrs. Martin whispered.

He lifted her hands to his lips, exulting when she did not pull them away. "You are beautiful," he said as he kissed them, his voice husky. "Not a lady in the room tonight could compare."

She laughed, her voice unsteady. "With your sister and Lady Ardith present? Mendacious flattery, my lord."

"Absolute truth."

She made a scornful noise. "I am to Lady Ardith as a candle flame to a Yule log's blaze."

"You are to her as fine gold to dross. And so I would have told you earlier, but your having endured enough of her spiteful tongue at dinner, I did not wish to single you out and attract more sweetly acid commentary."

She tilted her head and gazed up at him with that inquisitive look he found so endearing. "It would not have been fitting in any event."

"Is propriety so important, Sparrow?"

"You must not call me that." The quiver of a chuckle belied the stern tone of her reproof. "Nor am I sure I like being called a plain brown sparrow, even were it proper."

"But you *are* a sparrow—quiet, observant, intelligent. Endlessly fascinating and entirely overlooked. Although tonight you were transformed into a swan, glittering and graceful." He held up a hand to forestall her protest. "And now I'll revert to observing the proprieties. I shall call you 'Sparrow' only when we are alone."

He heard her choke of stifled laughter and grinned. She'd caught his little joke, clever Sparrow that she was.

"As if our being alone together were not much more improper," she replied. "I should not have allowed you to accompany me."

It was too soon to ask, but the urgent need to know overrode caution. "But you wanted my company?"

For a long, anxiety-ridden moment she remained silent. "Yes," she said finally, her voice a low whisper. "Having admitted that, now *I* shall observe the proprieties, and leave you."

"Wait!" He caught her shoulder as she turned. "I've a question I've not yet asked you."

She lifted one hand, and for an instant he thought she meant to place it over his, strengthening his hold on her. Instead, she let it flutter back to her side. "One question, then."

"Will you dance with me?"

Her eyes registered surprise. "Dance?"

"Here, now." He gestured to the sky above them. "Accompanied by a symphony of stars, to the music of the wind's rustle."

"You want to dance with me here?" She repeated, her tone still incredulous.

"I didn't dare ask you in the drawing room, fearing my proper Sparrow would probably refuse. But there are no prying eyes now to criticize or condemn. So, my lady beautiful, dance with me." Beau held out a hand.

For a moment she simply stared at him. "This is madness," she murmured at last. And slipped her fingers in his.

He eased her into waltz position, shocks jolting through him as they touched at shoulder, waist, hip. How well she fit against him, he thought; how absolutely right and natural it seemed to have her in his arms. Tucking the silk of her hair under his chin, he moved her into rhythm.

Under the spangle of stars they dipped and twirled while Beau hummed a tune in her ear. The racing of his heart owed little to the exertion of the dance, everything to the feel of Laura Martin's hands clutching his shoulders as he swung her in ever-faster spirals, the press of her torso against his through the maddening thickness of his cloak, the warmth of her rapid breaths floating up to caress his face. Not until she gasped an inarticulate appeal did he slow, then halt, though he could not bring himself to let her go.

He didn't want her to leave the dance or his side, he realized suddenly. No, he wanted her solemn eyes and incisive mind and wood sprite's charm beside him for the rest of this night. Perhaps for always.

Still clasping her waist, he raised his other hand to trace her trembling lips. "I've been waiting all night to have you in my arms," he murmured.

But he lied. He wanted much more than that. He hungered to arouse the vision he'd glimpsed in her cottage garden, the siren with tumbled hair and passion-languid eyes and soft mouth tilted temptingly to his own.

Beyond strategy and caution, he bent his head toward her lips. To his joy, with a murmur she clutched his shoulder and strained up to meet his kiss.

He retained enough sanity not to plunder her mouth with the urgent need that pulsed in him, luring her instead with quick, glancing touches meant to tantalize, entrance. Not until she twined fingers in his hair, tugged his head closer did he deepen the kiss, licking and sucking at the fullness of her lips until on a moan they parted.

A tremor shook her, shook him when their tongues met, before she darted hers away. An unexpected tenderness welled up—amazingly, his Sparrow did not even know how to kiss. Holding in ruthless check the desire to swiftly conquer and possess, he made himself slow, his tongue once more teasing within the softness of her mouth, letting her accustom herself to the feel of him. After a moment, she rewarded his patience as, tentative, uncertain, her tongue sought his.

He returned that guarded tap, the oblique contact like the sparing blades of cautious fencers. And when she met him again, lingering this time, he boldly stroked her tongue's full length in a hot velvet slide that struck sparks to every atom of his body.

A strangled moan escaped her throat and he felt the bite of her fingers at his shoulder, her other hand delving into his coat, nails scratching at the buttons of his shirt-front as if seeking entry.

In some dim corner of his mind he knew control was eroding, that he was rapidly approaching the point where not even the October chill of the moonlit garden could rein in his desire. But before sense was lost in a mindless search for a bench, a terrace, even a softly yielding patch of grass, she abruptly wrenched her mouth from his.

In automatic response he tried to pull her back. She fended him off with one hand, her eyes focused on something behind him.

And then he heard it. A woman's high-pitched, provocative laughter, emanating from the chamber just beyond the garden.

He turned. Through the mullioned window, he saw Lady Ardith standing with her bodice undone, candlelight and moonlight illuminating the bareness of her breasts. Mac leaned toward her, sliding up her skirts as he bent to capture one shadowed nipple in his teeth, while Lady Ardith fumbled with the straining buttons of his trouser flap.

The consternation he felt was reflected in Laura Martin's horrified stare. Before he could utter a word, she shoved him away and fled down the path toward the library.

Chapter Eleven

Heart drumming against her ribs, gasping from her headlong flight across the garden and up the stairs, Laura closed the door to her room and sagged against it.

Moonsick madness. That's all it had been, enchantment spun from her silly dreams and a touch of moonlight.

Sensible Laura Martin would never behave so again.

But even as she tried to excuse the episode, shame flooded her chest, thick and stifling.

She could not blame the magic of the garden, her foolish fancies or even Lord Beaulieu's overpowering presence.

'Twas her own folly alone that had brought her to this near catastrophe. Her weakness in accepting an escort she should have refused at the outset, her fault in underestimating the strength of her own greedy desire that had almost led her to commit the same wantonness she'd witnessed through the west wing windows.

How could she be disgusted by Lady Ardith's lechery when she'd felt the same imperative pulsing in her blood?

Lord Beaulieu had enticed her, certainly, but 'twas she who'd eagerly responded. Heat burned her face as she remembered the shivering shock of his lips against hers, the rasp of his tongue releasing a scalding flood of sensation that seemed to melt her bones, turning her fluid in his arms, starving for something she could not name but frantically sought. Craving the touch of his hands, his mouth, closer, deeper, as man desperate with thirst craves water.

And she craved it still. What she'd felt for her young suitor in her mother's garden years ago was but a feeble precursor to the raging desire she'd discovered within herself tonight, like the tepid sunlight of an early spring morning that precedes a blazing July noon.

What she might have done, have allowed Lord Beaulieu to do, had that graphic vision of lust not shocked her into recognizing her own, she could only imagine.

And what must Lord Beaulieu think of her now? A woman who'd mouthed propriety, then shown herself as ready for a mindless tumble as the most amoral society matron. Regardless of the tangle of her own wildly contradictory feelings toward his lordship, in light of her behavior tonight his opinion of her must be humiliatingly clear.

A lonely woman, ready for the price of a few compliments to become his convenient during the short time he remained in the country.

Tears burned her eyes as she stumbled to the bed and struggled to strip off the beautiful, never-to-be-worn-again gown.

Cinderella, home at last among the shattered fragments of her dream.

Frustrated and furious, Beau paced the moonlit paths. Damn Mac and the randy Lady Ardith for choosing that particular chamber for their blatant display. He wanted to pursue his Sparrow, comfort her, recapture the magic shattered by that unintentional glimpse of mindless coupling, but some inner sense warned him she was too upset now for him to attempt it.

Tenderness softened the edge of anger. For all her mature calm, she was such an innocent, 'twas little wonder she'd been shocked. He'd been dismayed, as well, and he had far more experience than she.

Though brutal honesty compelled him to admit, had that unfortunate episode not occurred, he'd have been driven as urgently as Mac to unbind the spangled cloth veiling the lady he wanted so badly, to gently tutor her through every nuance of pleasuring and being pleasured. Even now, the desire to do so still thrummed in his veins.

But only when she was ready, only as far, as fast as she would willingly follow. Unlike the meaningless tryst they'd stumbled into viewing, their eventual joining would contain a joy and tenderness that fired lust into something purer and more lasting. A single night would not be nearly sufficient to satisfy his craving. No, he wanted all of her—heart, mind, as well as body—for the indefinite future.

She knew that—didn't she? A niggle of doubt troubled him. Surely she didn't think he'd lured her to the garden only to use her body with the sort of casual carnality they'd inadvertently observed?

The doubt occurred only to be dismissed. They had shared the burden and worry of Kit's illness, chatted of books and herbs and philosophy, touched each other's thoughts and emotions in countless small, significant ways before ever their bodies touched. She couldn't possibly think he viewed her as an object of temporary dalliance.

No, she'd been startled, repulsed, a reaction he treasured for the modesty and discretion it displayed. Nonetheless, just to be sure, he'd proceed carefully tomorrow, treat her with a special gentleness that, combined with a night's sleep and the prosaic perspective of daylight, would erase from her mind the event that had caused so abrupt and dissatisfying an ending to their walk.

She would leave today, Laura decided as she looked out through the raindrops slipping down her windowpane. Clouds enveloped the garden in a mist-shrouded drizzle, changing the silver walkways, urns and plantings of last night into soggy brick and sodden earth utterly devoid of magic.

As her life must be. She walked to the wardrobe and pulled out the plain brown bombazine. The gown seemed heavier than she remembered, its muddy hue uglier compared to the frosted emerald of the dinner dress. A little brown sparrow, Lord Beaulieu had called her, unnoticed and insignificant.

So she was. So she must be. And if desire could so blind her to that fact, if her protective instincts had eroded so badly that she could stray as far from that role as she had last night, then she must depart at once.

For the truth was, scold herself ever so severely in the fastness of her chamber, she knew if the earl were to walk in the room this minute, her hands would still itch to resume tracing the contours of his body, her mouth yearn to meld with his and see what new delights he could teach her. It shamed and horrified her to discover within herself such a deep vein of carnality, but in the stark light of morning, she was too honest to deny its presence or power.

Intensified by admiration and affection, such a force would be nearly impossible to resist. And if fully satisfied in a connection both physical and emotional, it would create a bond that would shatter her soul to sever.

She'd likely given him her heart already, a gift he'd never sought and surely wouldn't appreciate. At least if she prudently fled now, she might avoid completing the disaster by bonding with him in body, as well.

A leaden despair settled in her gut. Even if they both wished it, there could never be anything legal or permanent between them, nothing beyond a fleeting, temporary liaison. Besides, she had only her girlish fancies to suggest that the earl even desired her for more than assuaging the same need for which Lady Ardith had met Dr. MacDonovan.

She had more self-respect than to stoop to that.

Kit Bradsleigh no longer required her round-the-clock presence. Her garden needed tending, her dog craved companionship, and she ought to seek the solitude necessary to reconstruct the boundaries that protected her.

That isolated her.

She reached out to stroke the silky lightness of the dinner gown, still draped on a chair where she'd abandoned it last night. She closed her eyes, allowing herself for a moment to relive the feel of Lord Beaulieu's arms around her, the taste and touch of his tongue. A ragged sigh born of pain and loss slipped from her throat.

Then with quick, efficient moves she donned the brown gown, hung the spangled emerald dress back in the wardrobe, and left the room.

After handing Peters the chessboard, Laura turned back to Kit Bradsleigh. "I'll be coming by daily to check on you and follow any orders Dr. MacDonovan leaves for your care." Written ones, she hoped. After last night, she'd rather not meet the doctor again in person.

Kit eased himself painfully back against the pillows. "Both of you…deserting me at once."

"Dr. MacDonovan has sicker patients to tend. And I'm close by. Soon you'll be able to get downstairs to dine and receive callers, so I daresay you'll not be so bored." She smiled. "Most of them probably won't beat you at chess."

He grinned back. "Like a challenge. Besides, I'm not…quite myself yet. I demand a rematch."

"Soon," she promised.

As she rose to depart, though, he caught her hand. "Can't begin to thank you—"

"Nonsense!" she interrupted. "I thought we'd settled this long since."

He shook his head. "With you so stubborn and me so incapable, we just…stopped discussing it. But you must know…our family considers your service an unredeemable debt. Beau especially." He paused, stifling a cough. "No, let me finish. We're a small family…just Beau, Ellie and me. Parents killed in a carriage accident…I was too young to remember. But Beau was there…in the carriage. He seems to think it his duty now…to protect us from all harm. And after this, you, too. Should you ever need us, need anything, you have only to ask." He paused, unsuccessfully trying to keep the gasp from turning to a cough.

Laura took his hand. "There is no obligation."

Gripping his shoulder to damp down the cough's vibration, Kit once more shook his head. "Lifelong vow," he said when he could breathe again. "Word of a Bradsleigh." He squeezed the hand she held.

Protect her from all harm. Oh, that the Bradsleighs or anyone else could do that! But despite his influence, even the mighty Earl of Beaulieu was not above the law.

Whatever safety she found must come, as it had since she'd chosen this course, solely from her own efforts.

"Rest now," she urged, gently withdrawing her hand. "I'll stop to bid you goodbye before I leave."

He squeezed her hand again and closed his eyes. With a nod to Peters, she left the room.

She'd snatched a hasty breakfast this morning, not wishing to encounter the earl, and now hoped he'd be occupied with his London satchels long enough for her to slip in a visit to Lady Elspeth and explain that she was returning home. After that, 'twould take little time to pack her few possessions. While the family was at luncheon she could pay her last call on Kit and depart.

Back to the safety of her cottage. Her books, her garden, her life of loneliness.

Before she indulged in greensick moping, she'd best remember on just how thin a thread that life still hung.

At her knock, Lady Elspeth bid her enter. To her delight, Lady Catherine was there, too.

"Miss Laura, come see! John Stableman gave me kittens!"

"Your mama lets you keep them here? I should think they'd rather be living in the stables."

"Oh, no," the child assured her. "They want to be here with me and Mama."

Over the girl's curly head, Laura looked up to see Lady Elspeth roll her eyes.

"You must thank your mama and the squire for letting them remain in your rooms, then. And be gentle with them," she cautioned as the girl reached to pluck one small furry body from the basket she'd fetched.

"Uncle Beau showed me how to hold them. He said they can break, just like my doll." She offered Laura a squirming, hairy handful. "Isn't he beautiful?"

Laura accepted the small creature, which mewed reproachfully at being removed from its cozy basket and regarded her with indignant blue eyes. "Handsome indeed. I'm glad you have some new friends to play with. Soon, your uncle Kit will be well enough to play with you, too. In fact, he's so much better I'm returning to my own home today. I'll stop by daily to check him, of course, but—"

"No!" Lady Catherine wailed. "You cannot leave!"

Laura deposited the kitten back in its basket and took the little girl's hands. "I shall not forget my friends."

"Catherine," her mother remonstrated, "Mrs. Martin has a house of her own which she must be missing. She's been kind enough to stay here to help Uncle Kit, but of course now that he is better she wants to return home."

The child patted Laura's dress and frowned. "If we gave you more dresses, would you stay? Uncle Beau will buy them! He told me he loves buying ladies pretty things."

While the girl's mother tried to explain to her why that would not be proper, Laura briefly wondered how many "pretty ladies" the earl had bought gowns for. A fair number, she imagined. Never her, she vowed.

Catherine's blue eyes filled with tears. Clearly unable to comprehend why anyone she'd befriended would wish to leave her, she turned from her mother back to Laura. "But who will take me for my walk? Silly Mary doesn't know anything. And you tell the bestest stories!"

Laura bit her lip. For as long as the earl remained in residence, she wished to keep her visits to Everett Hall as brief as possible. But knowing how little there was to occupy a lively child—and recognizing poor Mary really was dull-witted—she couldn't withstand the appeal on Lady Catherine's face.

"I will walk with you every day, after I've checked your uncle," Laura conceded.

"But you will not stay?" the girl said, her lip still quivering.

"I'm sorry, poppet. I really cannot."

"Catherine, you must not tease." Lady Elspeth tried to soothe her unhappy daughter. "Miss Laura has already done so much for us. She's promised to visit you—and me, too. After all—" she smiled at Laura "—we have plans to make."

Before Laura could inquire what sort of plans Lady Elspeth had in mind, a quick knock at the door was followed by the entry of the one person Laura had most hoped to avoid—Lord Beaulieu.

While Lady Catherine threw herself at her uncle, chattering about kittens, Laura retreated to the window seat, disgusted to note her heartbeat accelerating merely because the earl had entered the room. She'd take no part in the conversation, avoid his eye, and make her escape at the earliest possible moment.

But she'd reckoned without her champion. Laura edged to the door while the earl duly inspected the kittens, but before she could slip out, Lady Catherine pointed at her.

"Uncle Beau, Miss Laura says she must go home today, and I don't want her to. Please make her stay!" The little girl gazed up to give her uncle a melting smile. "She'll stay if you ask her. Everyone does what you wish."

The earl's smiling face sobered abruptly. He looked over at Laura, brows creasing in a frown. "Going home today? You made no mention of it to me."

His eyes impaled her, almost—accusing. Laura forced herself to look away, shaking her head to clear a sudden light-headedness. "Mr. Bradsleigh is recovering nicely, so there's no need for me to remain in residence."

"But with Dr. MacDonovan departing, it would be wise to have someone of skill standing by, at least for the first several days. Surely you'll not abandon your charge now, Mrs. Martin."

She couldn't let him make her weaken. Moistening her lips, she replied, "I'm not abandoning him Dr. Mac-Donovan assures me Kit no longer needs care through the night. I shall check him every day and faithfully administer any treatments the doctor believes necessary. But I do have a household of my own that needs tending."

"A household which could manage without your presence for a bit longer, I should think."

"Perhaps. But I should be more *comfortable* returning there," she said pointedly. Damn him! He would have her close to bewitch at his leisure. Well, she'd not allow it.

His belligerent manner softened suddenly. "I had hoped to offer you every comfort here," he said quietly.

She felt the insidious longing invade her again. What could a few more days hurt? She could be strong.

Liar.

She shook her head. "I—I appreciate all you have done. But I really must go."

"Even should I beg you to stay?"

She forced herself to resist the intensity of his gaze. "Even then."

After a long moment he gave her a stiff nod. "Very well. Go, then."

Lady Catherine had been watching the exchange with a smile, evidently entirely certain of her uncle's powers of persuasion. At that, however, she jumped up. "No, Uncle Beau! You cannot let her go!"

Lady Catherine ran to Laura and seized her hands. "Please, can you not stay? The kittens will miss you too."

Laura knelt down and gave the girl a quick hug. "Friends can still be friends even when they're not living in the same house. I shall walk with you every day, I promise. And if your mama permits, you can visit me. I have a dog who would love to have you throw sticks for him, and there's a walk by the river we could explore."

The girl looked up at Laura. "A friendly dog?"

"Very friendly. I've also got a big tabby cat and a pond full of frogs."

After a moment, Lady Catherine nodded. "I suppose you have to go home. Your dog and cat and frogs must be lonely."

Laura rose. Lord Beaulieu stood watching her, arms crossed over his chest, looking angry and—surely it wasn't hurt she read on his face. She jerked her glance away and walked toward the door.

"Return to your little household, Mrs. Martin," the earl said, a bitter edge to his voice. "Your very small household. Given how clever you are with children, 'tis a great shame your late husband didn't bless you with any."

The pain was instantaneous, automatic, and even after more than two years, devastating. Without thinking she whirled to face him. "How true, my lord," she snapped. "Especially considering that I buried one." Dipping a curtsey, she fled the room.

Chapter Twelve

The slam of the door echoed in the sudden silence.

After giving him a speculative look, Ellie walked over to her daughter. "Let me ring for Mary, sweeting. She can help you take your kittens out for some air. Beau, if you would please wait, I'd like to speak with you."

While his sister took her daughter away, Beau tried to master his anger and make sense of his disordered thoughts.

How could Mrs. Martin leave now, when he had so little time left? He understood why the events of last evening might have upset her, but why flee from him, as if he were the perpetrator of that scene? It shocked—and he had to admit, hurt—him that she apparently had so little trust in his honor. When had he ever attempted to push or coerce her into doing something she didn't desire?

It hurt, too, that she seemed so willing to give up the little bit of time they had left together—time that had become increasingly precious to him.

But if Mrs. Martin wanted to ignore the connection between them and return home, so be it. Given a few moments to accustom himself to this unexpected development, he'd be able to deal with it. 'Twas only natural, having had his self-esteem unexpectedly bashed, that he'd succumbed to that rare fit of temper.

An uncomfortable tweak of conscience jabbed him. He'd have to pen her an apology after that gibe about her being childless. The idea of reaching out to her, even via the impersonal medium of a letter, suddenly lightened the sense of...dismay he'd experienced when she'd refused to be dissuaded from leaving.

Perhaps he'd call on her and deliver the apology in person. As that thought warmed him even further, the fact finally registered, too glaring and inescapable for him to evade the truth any longer.

He couldn't lose Laura Martin. The idea of going through a day without experiencing her smile, her wide-eyed sparrow look of inquiry, the jolt of pleasure that excited his nerves just to be near her, was simply un-thinkable. Beyond the ever-present physical pull, she had become that rare friend who challenged his opinions and resisted his commands even as her wit invited his laughter and her quick intelligence piqued his mind.

He'd been looking forward with impatient anticipation to becoming more than friends. Exactly what form their long-term relationship should take, he hadn't yet figured out, but there would be time enough later for them to determine that together. First he had to ascertain what had so upset her, and coax her back.

Beau paced the room, trying to make sense of her be-havior. Given the strength of the connection between them, despite her innocence he simply couldn't believe a mere display of lust would have horrified her into retreat. He'd given her no reason to suddenly fear he'd try to coerce her into similar behavior.

A radical thought popped into mind, a theory that

would settle all the jumbled pieces into place so neatly, he halted in midstride.

What if Laura Martin wasn't what she claimed? What if she was not Lieutenant Martin's *wife*—but rather his cast-off mistress? A gently born girl who'd been seduced, disgraced and abandoned to bear alone a bastard child who later died?

Having forfeited through indiscretion the life of comfort and the respect that had been her birthright, estranged from everyone in her family save a kindly aunt, naturally she would wish to live quietly, zealously guarding the tiny niche she'd carved out in this rural society. Betrayed by a man she loved, with neither family nor dowry to protect her, she might well distrust the motives of men, and deliberately seek to discourage their interest.

And certainly she would flee if tempted to commit once again the folly that had led to her ruin. Seeing the writhing couple last night might have shocked her into remembering all she risked by allowing Beau too close.

There'd been too much raw pain in her tone for him to doubt that she'd lost a child. But what of the rest of what she'd revealed about herself in Merriville?

His analytical mind already speeding, Beau determined to send word by return pouch today to have his secretary launch an immediate inquiry into the family background of Lieutenant Winnfield Martin of the Thirty-third Innisford Greys, the man the squire told him had been her late husband.

Whether or not Laura Martin had suffered such a disgrace mattered not a groat to him. The woman who enthralled him had honor, intelligence and character written into her bones. Nothing that had occurred in her past could dissuade him from wanting her by his side.

Whatever the truth of her story—and well-honed instinct told him there was much more than she'd yet re-vealed—he must somehow persuade her she had nothing to fear and everything to gain by confiding in him, a man who regarded his family and close friends as both gift and sacred trust. He must seize another chance to con-vince her he would never betray her, that he wished in-stead to hold, protect and care for her the rest of her days.

He was still trying to decide the best way to approach Mrs. Martin when Ellie reentered the room. With his re-turn to London imminent, he couldn't afford to wait for answers to an inquiry.

"An illuminating conversation, brother dear," Ellie said as she walked to his side. "And don't pretend you don't understand. You were very severe with Mrs. Mar-tin."

He gave her a rueful grin. "You are right. I was…surprised. I shall have to apologize."

"I should think so." She pointed a reproving finger at him. "You do so hate it when someone within your pur-view makes a move without your consent."

"A despot, am I?"

"Absolutely." She kissed his cheek. "A benign one, but a despot nonetheless. Still, in this instance I think Mrs. Martin is being wise."

"And why is that?" he demanded, surprised and more than a little affronted.

"I've seen the…attraction between you. Not knowing you well, she might be fearful of what you mean to do about it. After all, Laura Martin is a woman living all alone, without family or defenders. Unlike that demi-rep of a sharp-spoken bitch, Lady Ardith, she's not the sort to indulge in idle bedsport. If you've dalliance in mind, brother dear, I recommend you confine your attentions to that one. She's eager enough."

"Such language, sister mine," Beau replied with a quiver of amusement. "And thank you for kindly advising me to take myself off to someone you've just pronounced to be an acid-tongued witch."

"She's beautiful enough, I'll grant. And quite suited for the casual interludes you men seem to enjoy."

"Is that what you think I seek?" Beau clapped a hand to his heart. "How wounding that my own sister holds my sex in such low esteem. I assure you, idle dalliance is of little interest to me."

"Then your intentions toward Mrs. Martin are more…serious?"

Careful, Beau cautioned himself. Being not quite sure yet just what form his long-term intentions for Mrs. Martin might take, he had no intention of revealing anything to his deceptively disinterested sister. "Minx!" he said, tapping her on the nose. "Suffice it to say that I would never allow the lady to come to harm."

Ellie's air of detachment dissolved. "You value her that much? Oh, splendid, Beau!" She took her brother's hand and kissed it. "I cannot tell you how relieved that makes me. Serene and competent as Mrs. Martin appears, there's about her an air of such…fragility. I worry about her future, alone in that little cottage with no kin to assist her. But if you, dear brother, have decided to watch over her, I can rest easy. Who knows better than Kit and I how safe and comfortable you make those lucky few you commit to your protection!"

"You like her very much, don't you?"

"Yes. And Catherine adores her." At his grin, she added severely, "You'll say a mama would dote on the devil, were he sufficiently attentive to her child, but I assure you, children are fine judges of character. Laura is so good with Catherine. How tragic that she lost a babe!''

Ellie paused, sighing. ''What a sad life she's had. No surviving family, apparently, and widowed so young.'' She shook her head. ''From time to time I've made reference to Arthur, how I miss him when we're parted. Not once has she ever volunteered a word about her late husband.''

''Prying, dear sister?''

''Certainly not,'' she retorted with some heat. ''You men are close as monks about your feelings, but women often speak to each other of such things. That Mrs. Martin does not, leads me to believe her union cannot have been a happy one. As far as it lies within my power, I intend to see that her future holds the promise of better. You'll assist me in convincing her to come to London next Season?''

Beau laughed. ''If you can persuade the very independent Mrs. Martin to accompany you to London,'' he offered, sure her future would have been decided in much different fashion by then, ''you may tell your husband I'll frank the expense.''

''We shall see her settled for certain.'' Ellie gave him an impish grin. ''But given the interest hereabouts, if you refrain from appearing to dally with her, I may well not need a London Season to achieve that goal.''

Did his sister mean the vicar? Instantaneous irritation ignited at the thought. Having Laura Martin wed the well-connected reverend was certainly not in his plans. Suppressing the sharp remark that vision engendered, he replied instead, ''No matchmaking schemes, Ellie. Let the lady choose her own way.'' *Our way,* he added mentally.

''Yes, brother,'' she replied with deceptive meekness.

Best to depart before Ellie tried to tease any more reactions from him. "Tell Catherine I'll ride with her before dinner." After kissing her cheek, he escaped to his room.

It being absolutely unavoidable, he'd work through the day on his papers, he decided, pulling out the first of several document satchels. Though he had a strong desire to confront Mrs. Martin again before she left, prudence said it might be better to let her depart unopposed. Allow her to regain the tranquillity of her safe haven—and carefully prepare his approach before seeing her again.

Despite that resolve he paused, paper in hand, a bleakness invading him as he envisioned the long expanse of afternoon and evening which, for the first time in more than two weeks, would not be brightened by the sight and voice of Laura Martin.

As soon as he'd processed this stack of documents, he'd set about figuring out how to change that. *If you think me easily discouraged, you are mistaken, Sparrow.*

Figure it out and act upon it. Tomorrow, he promised himself as he sorted the papers on his desk, as early as he could reasonably expect her to be up and about, he'd pay a call on the newly resettled Mrs. Martin.

Wiping her muddy hands on a rag, Laura sat back on her heels and surveyed the weed-free herb bed. Misfit dozed in an early morning sunbeam nearby, a hot pot of tea and a fresh loaf of bread waited her in the kitchen, and she ought to be quite pleased with the results of her first morning home in over a se'ennight.

But she'd found upon arriving yesterday that the snug cottage she'd regarded for two years as a welcoming haven had somehow lost its power to comfort. Though she could still sense the presence of her beloved Aunt Mary, the small rooms echoed with emptiness. The conviction that her guardian angel watched over her yet had as little effect in raising her sagging spirits as the sputtering fire had in driving two weeks of chill from the room.

Another voice whispered through her dreams now, bringing her to wakefulness time and again awash in poignant longing. Another face appeared before her eyes as, weary of attempting sleep, she rose early to busy herself with weeding, gathering and replenishing her supply of herbs.

She missed the earl, missed even more sharply the energizing possibility that she might at any moment encounter him—at breakfast or tea or out walking with Catherine. 'Twas the height of foolishness to mourn the loss of a friendship which had never really been hers, yet she could not seem to banish the deep sadness that dogged her. Nor could she, to her mingled chagrin and shame, deny that the one spark of pleasure in this gloomy day was the knowledge that she would return to Everett Hall this afternoon to check Kit Bradsleigh, walk with Lady Catherine—and perhaps catch a glimpse of the child's uncle.

Soon Lord Beaulieu must return to London, beyond the possibility of a chance encounter. Her foolish partiality, she assured herself, would then wither and die, as it must. She should be proud she'd had the sense to tear herself away before she committed some irretrievable folly.

She wasn't.

A lick on her hand startled her back to the present.

Tail wagging hopefully, Misfit nudged her. With a short bark, he bent to pick up the stick he'd dropped at her feet.

Laura sighed. "Since you were the only one to enthusiastically welcome me home last night—even the cat having deserted me—I suppose I owe you a game.''

Prancing in agreement, Misfit released the branch, then stood eyeing it avidly. He tensed as Laura held it aloft and swung it behind her back.

The instant she released it the dog tore off. She laughed, thinking ruefully how simple a dog's needs were: food, affection, an occasional game of fetch. Why could human vessels not be equally reasonable?

When after several moments Misfit did not return, she frowned, certain he could not yet have tired of the game. Then she heard his bark—the short, sharp one that meant he'd discovered something. Fervently hopeful that it wasn't another from a litter of skunk babies he'd tracked several weeks previous, she set off in pursuit.

She rounded the corner of the cottage—and stopped short. Smiling down at the prancing dog, who offered him up a stick, stood Lord Beaulieu.

Beau looked up to find Laura Martin staring at him from behind the gate that separated her herb garden from the country lane. Though she wore another worn gown faded to nondescript gray, the strengthening sunlight transformed that prosaic garment, outlining her slender figure in a halo of light and turning the stray curls that escaped the confines of her shapeless mobcap to copper fire.

Even with a smudge on her nose and mud on her apron, she looked beautiful, he thought, his heart swelling with gladness at the sight of her.

Were those shadows under her solemn eyes? Had she slept as little as he, tossing with impatience for the day that would bring him back to her?

He realized suddenly they'd both been standing, silently gazing at each other for some moments. Evidently she did, too, for she jerked her glance from his.

But not before he'd seen the surge of gladness in her face turn to wariness.

"Don't!" he cried, brushing past the dog to approach her. "Don't be afraid of me."

For a moment he thought she'd retreat back into the garden without even permitting him to speak, but at the last moment she stood her ground. She even managed a tremulous smile.

"Good morning, my lord. And—I'm not afraid of you."

He offered his hand. After a small delay, she extended hers. He savored the small courtesy of bringing it to his lips. "Are you sure? I've been much dismayed, worrying that somehow I drove you away."

"Not you. Prudence. Did...did you need something?" Sudden alarm crossed her face. "Kit has not suffered—"

"No, Kit is fine. Awaiting a rematch at chess this afternoon, he bade me tell you."

Her face relaxed. "Good. Did Dr. MacDonovan send you for supplies?" She tilted her head up, giving him that inquiring Sparrow look he'd come to treasure.

How fiercely he'd missed her after just one day. "No. I came to apologize."

A blush stained her cheeks. "There is no need—"

"There is. But I should do a better job of it seated. If we might?" He gestured toward the cottage.

He held his breath as alarm, indecision—and longing played across her expressive face.

Yes, she still cared for him. Exultation mingled with restraint and a fierce desire to embrace her, kiss away the caution in her eyes, seize the opportunity here, far from prying eyes, where they might recapture and deepen the wordless intimacy they'd found in the moonlit garden.

Too soon yet, he told himself, stilling fingers already curled with anxiety to hold her again. "You are too kind to deny me that opportunity, aren't you?"

Before she could reply, the sound of galloping hooves approached. Beau looked up to see Lady Ardith, resplendid in a fur-trimmed riding habit, bearing down upon them, and cursed under his breath.

The lady drew rein and smiled down at him. "Lord Beaulieu, good day to you! Is it not a brilliant morning for a ride?"

Did a grin flit briefly across Mrs. Martin's lips? Before he could be sure, she curtsied. "Lady Ardith."

The blonde regally inclined her head. "Mrs. Martin." Her horse danced sideways and she tightened the reins, her trim posterior bouncing against the sidesaddle.

A deliberate move? Beau wondered cynically. With Mac departing this morning, was the wench already trolling for a replacement?

It won't be me. "Fine indeed, Lady Ardith. Do not let us keep you from your ride. Mrs. Martin, shall we?" Beau gestured to the cottage.

"If you should wish me to delay a few moments until you finish your business with Mrs. Martin—" Lady Ardith plied her long lashes and gave him a smoky glance "—I could be persuaded. 'Tis so enjoyable to ride with a partner."

Mrs. Martin made a choking sound, which she turned into a cough. "I can bring any necessary supplies with me when I call on your brother," she volunteered.

"No need for you to tarry then, my lord," Lady Ardith said. "Have you ridden the trail by the river? 'Tis wonderous scenic once you reach our land. My husband had several little grottos constructed that are charming and quite…private. Shall we race?'' She inclined her head to the stallion he'd secured to the fence. ''Your beast looks quite fresh, and my mare—'' she sidled him a glance ''—is nearly the best mount in the county.''

''Do go, my lord,'' Mrs. Martin said, her innocent tone at odds with her suspiciously twitching lips. ''I shouldn't wish to you to miss Lady Ardith's kind offer.''

He shot her a sardonic glance. The grin she returned looked entirely unrepentant.

''Another day, perhaps,'' he told the horsewoman.

''Come now, I dare swear you've time for a little sport,'' Lady Ardith persisted. ''I promise you'll not regret it.''

Beau had no desire to conduct his business with Laura Martin while this lightskirt lay in wait for him outside the cottage. Giving Mrs. Martin an indignant glance that caused her to choke down another gurgle of laughter, he turned his attention to the necessity of getting rid of the annoying Lady Ardith.

''A short ride,'' he said.

''Excellent.''

Ignoring the lady on the sidesaddle, he turned back to Laura Martin. ''I shall see you later, ma'am.''

A devilish twinkle lighting her eyes, she dipped a demure curtsey. ''My lord, Lady Ardith.''

Not bothering to acknowledge Mrs. Martin, Lady Ardith brought her horse closer. ''Can that stallion of yours perform as well as my mare? Let's see!'' With that, she spurred her mount.

''Soon,'' he warned Mrs. Martin, and set off.

Half an hour later Beau brought his stallion to a halt at the shed behind Laura Martin's cottage. He was not, he thought smugly as he dismounted and tied the horse to a post, the only person who could fob off an unwanted escort.

Leaving his mount hidden back here, where no passer-by could see it and decide to interrupt his visit, Beau stealthily traversed the garden, intending to enter by the back porch door.

Memories of the vision he'd stumbled upon the last time he'd silently approached down these herb-lined pathways kindled a flicker of heat in his stomach. Unbidden, the feel of her waltzing in his arms under the spangled stars, the taste of her lips meeting his eagerly, welled up in him, fanning the flicker.

Not yet, he told himself, curbing the memories. He'd not have the wit to calm her fears and win her trust if he walked in with his body aflame.

He paused by the door and raised his hand to knock.

And heard something—Mrs. Martin's high clear voice interspersed with deeper tones.

Not again. Frustration humming through his veins, he paused on the threshold, debating whether to wait out the annoyance of a second visitor or to slip away and return later.

He'd first determine who her caller was, he decided. Silently he eased the back door open and crept down the hallway until he could see into the front parlor.

The scene he spied there paralyzed both thought and movement. In front of Mrs. Martin, who sat on the sofa by the window, he saw Reverend Blackthorne down on one knee.

Chapter Thirteen

Disengaging her hand, Mrs. Martin backed away from the vicar—straight toward Beau. Recovering his frozen wits in an instant, he leaped aside to flatten himself against the staircase wall, knowing it imperative he remain hidden until he'd sorted out what to do about this extremely disagreeable development.

His first furious reaction—to stalk into the parlor, seize Reverend Blackthorne by his shirt collar and haul him bodily out of the cottage—he quickly discarded as impolitic, if eminently satisfying. His second thought was a throat-drying fear that in his self-absorbed concentration on maneuvering Mrs. Martin into the sort of relationship that would best satisfy *his* desires, he'd let this underestimated rival steal a perhaps insurmountable advantage over him.

If Blackthorne did in fact assuage Mrs. Martin's distrust of men by offering marriage, and she accepted him, how was Beau to counter that? He might lose her before he'd barely had a chance to press his own claims.

Cold purpose focused him, let him shake his mind free of angry dismay. *There had to be some way to stop this.*

Without a particle of remorse, he focused on overhearing as much as possible of the conversation.

"Please, Mr. Blackthorne, I beg you proceed no further," said Mrs. Martin, distress in her cool voice.

That reassuring request was followed by the soft pad of Mrs. Martin's footsteps, but in his current position Beau could not see where the occupants of the parlor now stood. *Move away from him,* he silently urged.

"Surely my feelings cannot come as a surprise," Blackthorne said, a bit of reproach in his tone. "I've long held you in esteem, as our dealings with each other must have shown."

"I felt you esteemed me as a member of the community who attempted to assist those in need, as I esteem you," she replied. "Nothing more."

"Perhaps I was not as…forthcoming as I should have been," he conceded. "A man of my position must naturally be circumspect to avoid becoming fodder for the local gossips. But I regret that restraint, if it left you in ignorance of the steadily increasing warmth of my regard. So much that I must beg you let me continue!"

Beau heard heavier footfalls, and grimly concluded the reverend must have pursued Mrs. Martin. "Please, sir—"

"No, dear lady, you must allow me voice! Granted, had certain…events not transpired I should not have chosen to approach you in so precipitous a manner, but at this critical moment both personal desire and my duty as your spiritual advisor demand that I address you now."

Beau heard Mrs. Martin's ragged sigh. "Continue then, if you must."

"I beg you will acquit me of conceit if I state what I see are the advantages to you of this match. At this moment I occupy a position which might appear to offer little worldly gain, but I have an income independent of this living and the ear of my father, who is, I assure you, a most influential man. My wife and children will want for nothing. For months I've been increasingly drawn by your modesty, excellence and nobility of character, a beauty of soul surely the equal of your lovely countenance. I think we could pursue a common purpose. While I cannot claim to be without flaws, I hope I bear no more than my human share. Should you do me the honor of becoming my wife, I should earnestly strive to make you happy.''

Though Beau could hardly have hoped the vicar would offer a lady of his parish carte blanche, still the formal proposal shook him to his boots. A widow in Mrs. Martin's tenuous position, unless she held her suitor in absolute abhorrence, would be a fool to refuse such an offer.

Torn between dismay and hopeless anger, Beau waited in wretched silence for the inevitable acceptance.

''Mr. Blackthorne, please understand I am fully cognizant of the brilliance of your offer. A woman who occupies as humble a position as I could not help but be honored that a man of your birth and position would consider her for his wife, but—''

''You are a lady born, as any *gentleman* could see, quite worthy to be offered a man's hand and name,'' Blackthorne said with some heat.

''Thank you, sir. But flattering as it is, I—I must decline your proposal.''

Beau sagged back against the wall, shock and gladness weakening his knees. He could not imagine why she would reject so clearly advantageous an offer, but at this moment, having little doubt that Reverend Blackthorne would probably attempt to persuade her otherwise, he focused all his thoughts on willing her to persist in refusing it.

"You…find me disagreeable?" Despite himself, Beau felt a grudging sympathy at the mingled pain and humility in the reverend's voice.

"No, of course not. It's just…" Beau heard her soft, quick step, as if she were pacing the room. "I…can only tell you that my…experiences with the wedded state were such that I cannot envision ever entering it again. Pray, do not press me further."

So Ellie was right—her marriage had not been happy. Apparently the vicar had not been aware of it, for several moments of silence followed her declaration.

"My dear lady, I deeply regret any unhappiness you may have suffered," he began again, apparently taken aback but undaunted. "Still, I vow that if you will but entrust your future to me, I will do all in my power—"

"Sir, I beg you say no more! My resolve on this matter is unshakable."

"If you forbid me speak, I must honor that request, but you cannot silence me on a matter of even graver import. No, madam—" Beau heard the soft tones of her protesting voice under the vicar's more strident ones "—this must be said. It has not escaped me that recently you have become the object of interest to…a man of great position. Indeed, he has singled you out to a degree that has already begun to cause speculation in the neighborhood. I must warn you that I seriously question this nobleman's intentions toward you."

"Indeed, sir, I am sure you are mistaken!" Mrs. Martin's gratifying prompt response mitigated Beau's immediate desire to spring from his hiding place and plant the disparaging reverend a facer. "I am much too far beneath that person's notice," she continued, "for him to have any designs upon my person whatever. I agree that both he and his sister have singled me out to an extraordinary degree, but that is only because of the service I've rendered their kinsman.''

"Dear Mrs. Martin, it does honor to the purity of your character that you view Lord Beaulieu's actions in that light, but in this you must bow to my superior knowledge of the world. I have closely observed the manner in which his lordship looks at and treats you. I wasn't called to the church until after I'd been some years on the town, and speaking as a fellow aristocrat who knows how such men's minds work, I assure you in the strongest possible terms that you do indeed stand in danger.''

Another fraught silence followed that impassioned speech. Hands itching for the feel of the vicar's throat under his thumbs, once again Beau had to exercise supreme discipline to keep from bursting into the room. Damn the man's effrontery in so viciously maligning Beau's interest in Mrs. Martin! As if he desired only some hasty, meaningless backstairs coupling. Surely Mrs. Martin knew better than that. He might truly murder the vicar if the man weakened the fragile trust Beau had been working so hard to build.

"Y-you cannot believe that *I* encouraged—"

"Of course not! I'm sure I know your character better than that. But others will be less discerning and more judgmental. Believe me, Lord Beaulieu's very particular attentions, if they continue much longer unchecked, will create enough speculation that your character *will* be impugned and your standing in this community *will* suffer, be you innocent or not.''

"I would stand condemned even if innocent?'' A note of outrage colored the distress in her voice.

"Such is the world. Which is why I felt strongly that

I must make now an offer that, I assure you, I have been contemplating for some time. Your becoming a married lady would put a halt to any untoward advances as well as preserve the purity of your reputation.''

''I am to marry you solely to preserve my reputation?''

''For much more than that, I trust! I hope I do not err in believing that you cherish for me at least a modicum of affection—affection that two like-minded individuals committed to a life together could enrich and deepen. As my own emotions are already considerably engaged, I cannot stand by and see you harmed by one grown so accustomed to having his every wish and whim deferred to by others that he neither sees nor cares what harm he may do!''

''Mr. Blackthorne, having, as you've noted, spent much time with Lord Beaulieu, I must protest that harsh assessment. Whatever his intentions—and I still take leave to doubt he has any toward me at all—I cannot believe he would knowingly harm me.''

Bless you, sweet lady, Beau thought, both gratified and humbled by her avowal.

''Given my own aspirations, perhaps I am too harsh,'' the vicar allowed. ''But the danger to your reputation, even should his lordship's interest be as fraternal as you assert, is nonetheless grave, and grows daily more acute. Please, my lady, I beg you to let me take your hand, offer you the protection of my name and my heart.''

''Sir, you will please release my hand.''

''Not until you've given me the assurance that you will carefully consider what I've said. I cannot leave until you guarantee me at least that.''

''M-Mr. B-blackthorne, you are d-distressing me. P-please let go my hand now!''

"You will consider my words? You'll promise me that?"

"Y-yes—no, oh, I don't know! J-just go, I b-beg you!"

That ragged speech, followed by a choked sound suspiciously like a sob, had Beau poised on the balls of his feet in murderous rage, ready once more to burst into the room and drag the persistent clergyman away.

Before he could proceed, Mr. Blackthorne said, "I'll withdraw now, ma'am, as you request. I am heartily sorry to have distressed you by speaking so forcefully, but I reiterate, the matter is grave. Rest assured I shall keep an eye on the cottage. We will speak further when you are calmer. Your servant, Mrs. Martin."

Much as he'd like to go a few rounds with the vicar, Beau had no desire to have the man catch him hiding in the shadows like a petty thief. Quickly he slipped back down the hall and out the porch door.

Where he stood, irresolute. Standing out most clearly in the confused swirl of violent emotions racking him were a total incomprehension of why Mrs. Martin would refuse Blackthorne's proposal and an immense relief that she had. Fear of the vicar's repetition of his offer warred with a buoyant hope that it was not too late for Beau after all, humility at her trust in his honor, and the fervent need to prove himself worthy of it. A renewed imperative to claim her for his own fired up, fueled in part by anguish at the thought of her trapped in a distasteful marriage. How could any man not have cherished so gentle a heart, so sterling a character?

It seemed his careful theory lay in tatters. Apparently she *had* been wife rather than mistress to her lieutenant. Not only had her flat statement about marriage been utterly convincing, but a woman anxious to redeem her character should have leaped at, rather than refused, an honorable offer.

Unless her emotions were already elsewhere engaged. A rush of elation followed the thought. Dare he hope she might have refused the vicar at least in part because of the connection calling them together?

He'd find out—right now. Be she widow or wayward miss mattered naught—only their future together was important. He turned back toward the door, took two strides, and halted once more.

The vicar had been right in at least one assertion— Mrs. Martin was too distraught to receive anyone. Strongly as instinct called him to her side, prudence counseled him to give her time to recover from the turmoil created by the vicar's visit. He should call again later.

But as he reluctantly turned toward the garden, the sound of a shuddering sob stopped him.

The first was followed by another, then another. He stood paralyzed as a series of deep, gasping sobs flayed his already raw emotions, wrenching from him both the desire to flee the premises immediately and the need to return and comfort her.

Mama, Mama, don't cry! I'll help you.

Can't help...darling. Too...late.

Sweat broke out all over his body as he jerked his mind from the echo of his nightmare of that long-ago accident. He hadn't been able to help then, his mama and the unborn child she carried dying even as the frantic six-year-old jerked and tugged at the skyward-staring door of their shattered carriage. But much as the sound of Mrs. Martin's sobs ignited a revulsion that shuddered through him, he knew he couldn't walk away and leave her alone in her anguish.

He forced himself back down the hallway into the parlor. She still stood in the center of the room, face buried in her hands while sobs convulsed her frame. Neglected wife? Abandoned mistress? Whatever had befallen her, the agony shaking that slender body said the experience had been unendurably painful.

The remaining shreds of nightmare dissolved beneath an overwhelming need to help her. "Mrs. Martin," he called softly, not wishing to startle her.

In a gasp of breath, the sobs halted. Before he could take a step, she jerked upright, eyes wide, face contorted.

With fear, he realized. "Don't be alarmed—it's Beau Bradsleigh."

It took a long moment for the words to penetrate, before the alarm faded from her eyes. "M-my lord?"

"I—I was passing by and…and chanced to hear you. What has happened to so overset you? Please, let me help."

At first she stared at him as if his words had no meaning. An expression of infinite weariness gradually overtook the misery in her eyes. "T-thank you, my lord. But 'tis nothing that can be helped."

"Everything can be helped."

Her tear-stained eyes examined his face. *Tell me,* he silently willed her. She opened her lips, hesitated. Closed them again with a sigh.

And then, almost as visibly as if a curtain had descended, her face changed to a mask of distant politeness. "D-did you require something, my lord?"

He could not let it go, not now when he knew—*he knew*—she had come so close to telling him the truth. "I rather thought you might."

Alertness leaped back to her face. "My lord?"

"I could be of greater assistance if you would but answer me one thing. Who are you, Laura Martin?"

Chapter Fourteen

It was her worst nightmare come to life. Discovery.

Sheer panic blinded her. As the first shockwave receded, leaving behind a fear that seeped into every pore, her vision cleared and she saw Lord Beaulieu standing before her. Staring, his face intent and questioning.

In that moment she realized with bitter certainty that her overlong hesitation had just given her away. 'Twas too late now to summon up some glib remark, to feign bafflement. Even had she the inner resources left after her interview with the vicar to find the appropriate words.

Wearily she closed her eyes and stumbled to the window, leaning her forehead against the cool glass. She sensed Lord Beaulieu follow her. Like the vicar, who would not take her polite refusal and go away, who had pursued her, cornered her, seized her hand in a move so reminiscent of Charleton she'd almost become physically ill.

A faint spark of anger flickered and caught. No, she had not endured all she had suffered to live to this moment, managed day by painstaking day the recreation of her whole being, to let it end now.

Before she could decide how best to counter him, she

heard Lord Beaulieu's soft voice behind her. "Whatever troubles you, know I only want to assist. Please, let me help you."

She felt a touch to her shoulder and whirled to face him, the reaction too ingrained to suppress. "Help? And just how do you intend to do that? By hinting to the community that I am not what I seem? Destroying my name, my reputation? Seeing me cast from the meager niche I've carved out for myself here, as a king would crush a bothersome insect?"

"Of course not! How could you think that of me? Who you were—who you are, does not matter to me as much as solving what causes you such distress. Will you let me?"

She stared at him with ferocious intensity, evaluating the angle of his body, the set of his expression, every remembered nuance of his voice. Her heart, her mind, her instincts all told her he was telling the truth.

He would not betray her.

Relief washed through her in a dizzying wave. "Y-you will say nothing?"

She must have swayed, for he reached out a hand as if to steady her. Drew it back as instinctively she stiffened. "I will say nothing without your leave." In his eyes she could read only a warm concern. "But that does not touch the heart of the matter. Tell me, sweet lady, how can I help you?"

The dregs of panic drained away in an upwash of emotion. How she loved him, this principled man devoted to his family who wanted only to ease her suffering, as she had eased his brother's. Who had power that nearly rivaled the king's, yet would not hold her against her will. Who coupled strength with gentleness, as her father had.

Not until the vicar's warning had she fully realized the

depth of her desire to be with the earl, talk with him, touch him, become his lover for however short or long a time he would grant her. Not until then had she fully realized how impossible of fulfillment that desire truly was.

The vicar spoke the truth, however unpalatable. Now that Kit Bradsleigh was healing, to remain on any terms of intimacy with a man so superior to her in rank and fortune would be interpreted by the world in only one fashion. To be thought the earl's *chère amie* in the so-phisticated, amoral world of the London ton would be unremarkable—probably even elevate her status. In the more rigid, moralistic society of rural England, such a perception would ruin her reputation, make her an outcast from local society and very likely destroy her livelihood.

Being with the earl was but a foolish, impossible dream, and had been so from the very beginning. Strange that having to destroy it hurt so much.

She turned her face from the earl's too penetrating gaze. "If you truly desire to help, stop calling upon me. Do not speak with me except in greeting. Do not be seen with me outside in your brother's sickroom."

"That is what you want?"

She hesitated. "That is what must be."

"It need *not* be. Not if you want, as I do, so much more for us both. Would you throw away all that we could mean to each other without even trying to find another way? You know I would never allow anything to harm you! Please, can you not trust me?"

Oh, how she wanted to trust him. But with her liveli-hood, perhaps her very life, hanging in the balance, she dare not.

Unsure she could resist if the plea in his eyes matched the urgency of his voice, she walked away to once more gaze out the windows. "You will soon leave here. I must stay, live among my neighbors. If you agree to say nothing about me, I will be secure. That is the best thing you can do for me, the only thing I desire."

"I don't believe that. Look at me, Laura! Look me in the eye and swear you want me to walk away."

Back in a past she tried to forget, she'd managed to face up to Charleton and lie, even knowing her life might be forfeit if he caught her out. She could lie now if she must.

Laura took a trembling breath and, blanking her face of all expression, slowly raised her gaze to meet the earl's. "Please go, my lord, and do not come back." She paused, forcing herself to add with a touch of scorn, "I hope you will not insist on haranguing me to tears before you're convinced to comply?"

Something sparked in his eyes—anger, perhaps hurt. Ruthlessly she suppressed the pang of guilt, the need to explain. After a silent moment during which her cold mask did not melt under his fevered stare, he made her a curt bow.

"As you wish then, madam. I bid you goodbye."

Laura held herself unmoving while his footsteps retreated down the hallway, through the porch door's slam. Not until the jingle of harness and clip-clop of iron-shod hooves on the lane outside faded, signaling Lord Beaulieu's final departure, did she stagger from the center of the room to the sofa.

She collapsed upon the soft padded surface, unable to move or think, conscious only of a bone-deep weariness made weightier by piercing sadness.

It was over. Over, really, before it ever began. Lord Beaulieu, accustomed to giving orders rather than taking them, summoning ladies of his choice rather than being dismissed by them, would not be back.

She was still safe, though. Surely some days or weeks or months later, when she could bring herself to truly acknowledge that fact, her heart would agree his loss was worth that gain.

Spurred on by fury and frustration, Beau drove his mount at a flat gallop through the woods back to Everett Hall. Damn and blast, the woman was stubborn! He could almost feel a kindred sympathy with the rejected reverend.

But perhaps, his normal clear thinking obscured by the unaccustomed depth of the emotions Mrs. Martin roused in him, he'd misconstrued Mrs. Martin's reactions over the past few weeks. Perhaps she had not responded to him to the degree he'd thought. In any event, her icy dismissal clearly indicated that she did not harbor the same intensity of feeling for him that he did for her.

Perhaps she had no wish to wed the vicar and disdained the whole institution of marriage because she abhorred men in general. Such women existed, he knew.

Whatever her reasons for refusing the vicar, the fact that she had also rejected both Beau and his offer of help was gallingly unambiguous. *Scornfully* rejected, he recalled with a renewal of ire, as if he were an impotent, bumbling schoolboy.

Well, he certainly had enough other problems to solve. Now that Kit was on the mend, easing his anxiety about his immediate family, he should apply himself to the weighty matters demanding his attention. He'd pack up and return to London tomorrow at first light.

Righteous indignation carried him through the swift disposition of the papers brought him by today's courier,

a short afternoon interview with Ellie and Catherine and
dinner with the assorted company. During that interminable affair, Lady Winters seemed more than usually vac-
uous, Ellie tried his patience by several oblique refer-
ences to Mrs. Martin and the squire chatted on about
trivialities with thick-headed obliviousness. With a little
difficulty, he managed to squelch the nasty but entirely
understandable desire, when Ellie brought Mrs. Martin's
name into the conversation for the fourth time, to drop a
tiny hint that the lady might not be who she seemed.

Regardless of how little others might esteem it, his
sense of honor was unbreachable, he told himself when,
after the brandy, he was at last able to escape back to his
room. He *was* a man worthy of the highest trust—had
not even kings and cabinet ministers deferred to his in-
genuity and discretion? And he certainly was *not* suffering pique at having his desires thwarted, overlayed by
more than a little hurt that his regard had been so igno-
miniously spurned. He was merely…disappointed.

By the time he'd finished packing his bags, however,
the smoldering fury that had carried him through the day
had burned itself out. In the cold void left after the heat
of anger evaporated, the dispassionate logic upon which
he prided himself belatedly resurfaced.

Mrs. Martin's wholly unexpected rejection of his over-
tures had shaken his certitude, but now that he calmly
reconsidered the evidence, he was once again convinced
he had not misinterpreted her reaction to him. The desire,
both physical and emotional, that bound them together
was strong and mutual. Why would she then send him
away with such cold finality?

The subtle signals she'd sent during that interview,
nagging all day at the edges of consciousness, suddenly
combined with everything else he'd observed these past

few weeks to coalesce in a conclusion. One in which the apparently disjointed pieces of the puzzle that was Laura Martin fell perfectly into place. The utter certainty of it swept through him with the force of a gale wind.

Of course she had refused the vicar. Of course she lived quietly, deliberately discouraging the notice of society in general and men in particular. Of course she begged him to leave her in obscurity, proclaiming there was no remedy for the malady that distressed her.

Laura Martin was neither an abandoned mistress nor a widow. She was a wife. Some powerful man's runaway wife.

His heartbeat sped as he tried to grasp all the implications. Laura "Martin" had lived in this small community for nearly two years. If she feared her husband enough to remain in hiding that long—a fear, he realized now, he'd often been puzzled to see lurking in her eyes—the villain must be both a man of far-reaching influence—and dangerous.

"'Tis nothing that can be helped," she'd said. Under ordinary circumstances, she'd be right. The law gave a husband absolute ownership of his wife's property and person, a power neither her family nor any legal authority could contravene, regardless of circumstance. A husband could not be legally convicted of rape or assault if the victim of those crimes was his wife.

That the sole legal redress would not be easy and would probably damage his own prestige irreparably, Beau dismissed without a qualm. He had considerable influence in the House of Lords and he would use it. Difficult though it be, he would force the loathsome coward who'd called himself Laura's husband to petition parliament for a bill of divorcement.

Perhaps deep within he'd known the truth of it even

before the vicar's unexpected proposal shocked him to awareness, but regardless of when the realization struck, he knew it now. Laura Martin was the companion for whom he'd been waiting all his adult life. In order to keep her by his side, however, he must first free her from the man who had dishonored his husband's vows and abused her trust. Once she was free, Beau could then beg for her hand and the right to guard and protect her forever.

His most immediate task, however, would be to move her out of that vulnerable cottage, where there was naught but one disreputable mutt to safeguard her. He'd transport her to some location where he could watch over her while the legal proceedings moved forward. He blessed the fact that in his job he'd accumulated contacts who could help with that, as well.

The disappointment, anguish, hurt of the previous hours dissolved in an upsurge of joyous excitement. Over the past several years he'd perfected his calling, pursuing the enemies of the state with methodical precision, quietly content to have rendered valuable, if unheralded, service to his nation. Now he would use the skills honed in that service to rescue the woman he loved and fashion a place for them to be together for a lifetime.

He remembered then her stark avowal—that she would never again consider entering the state of wedlock—and some of his ardor dimmed. Would he be able to persuade her to once again trust in a man's vows to love, cherish and protect?

He refused to consider now the bleakness his life would become if he could not. But regardless of whether he was eventually successful in winning her hand, he pledged on his sacred honor that he would see her freed of her sham of a marriage, freed of fear, free to live once again in the open.

When he left for London at dawn tomorrow, Laura Martin must go with him. Now all he needed to do was to convince her.

The midnight air was cold and clear, the moon full enough that its light cast shadows across the cottage porch as thirty minutes later, Misfit gamboling joyfully at his heels, Beau stood at Laura Martin's door.

He fisted his hand to knock and then hesitated. Would an unexpected pounding on her door at midnight terrify her with fears of her husband's pursuit? Or had she been a healer long enough that she would merely think some individual sought emergency aid?

He decided on a single sharp rap. "Mrs. Martin, it's Beau Bradsleigh!" he called through the night stillness. "Please, I must see you at once!" Apparently deciding to add voice to the summons, Misfit began to bark.

By the time he'd quelled the dog's enthusiasm, he saw a light approaching. Her body obscured by a voluminous dark wrapper, the ubiquitous cap on her head, Mrs. Martin cautiously moved to the door.

Her eyes glanced off him into the empty darkness beyond. "My lord? Pray, what is wrong? Your brother—"

"No, Kit is well. Please, may I come in?"

She stood a moment, eyes examining his face, as if struggling between acceptance and refusal. Then, with a slight smile, she nodded. "This is certainly not wise, so it had best be brief." She gestured him inside.

He followed her into the parlor, dark and chill with no fire in the grate. After setting her candle upon the table, she sat and invited him to do the same.

He hesitated, searching for the most convincing words.

"Forgive me for intruding upon you so late, but I leave for London in the morning and there is something we must settle before I go."

"Excuse me, but I thought we had already said everything that was needful." Sudden alarm flashed across her features. "Unless you've changed your mind—"

"I mean you no harm, as I assured you this morning. Quite the opposite, Mrs.—it isn't 'Martin,' is it?"

Her eyes fell. "No," she said softly.

"Nor is it the 'widowed' Mrs. Martin?"

She jerked her head upright, dismay in her eyes. She opened her lips. Closed them again.

"You're still married, aren't you? That's what—who you're hiding from. That's the matter that 'cannot be fixed.' Isn't it?"

She sighed. "Why could you not accept the surface appearance of things, as everyone else does?" She smiled, her expression half rueful, half self-mocking. "All of England, and I must take refuge in the one small community whose squire's son is friend to the Puzzle-breaker's brother. So now you've guessed the whole of my secret. But as long as you honor your pledge not to betray me—and I think you will—what is there to discuss?"

"You believe yourself in danger, do you not?"

Her smile faded. "Yes."

"Then you must come with me."

That startled an incredulous laugh from her. "Go with you! To London where the chance of Ch—of discovery would be so much greater? You must be mad! Why do you think I chose so obscure a location?"

"Obscure or not, you just admitted that, should your husband discover your whereabouts, you would not be safe here. I can keep you safe."

"I beg to differ, but you cannot! Clever though you be, you are not above the law. Should my husband find me, no one has the right to keep me from him."

"You think I would let him find you? A man who has used you so badly you felt it necessary to go into hiding to escape him? Think, Laura! I've many more contacts than you. I can see you settled secretly, somewhere safe. Where you can stay while I persuade him to pursue a bill of divorcement."

"Divorce?" She uttered a short, scornful noise. "Now I know you're mad! He's…an important man, fiercely proud of his family and his lineage. He'd never tarnish it with the stain of divorce. He'd see me dead first."

Beau shrugged. "If he is proud of his family, he'll want sons to carry on his name—which I trust you've not yet provided?" When she said nothing, he continued, "He'll not get heirs without a willing wife. 'Tis in his own interest to divorce you and find another. And should he refuse to proceed, he'll be made to do so. A man who causes his wife to flee cannot be a saint. There must be some stain on his honor he would not want revealed, something that would be more damaging to his name than divorce. If necessary, I'll guarantee him it *will* be revealed." Beau smiled slightly. "As you know, I'm rather good at ferreting out secrets."

Laura shook her head. "He will not be coerced. Only remember—society, law, custom are all on his side! Alerting him to my presence would only encourage him to arrange the one thing that truly would make him free…" Her fervent voice faded to a whisper. "My death."

"Do you think me so poor a champion?" Beau asked, appalled, frustrated and more than a little stung by her lack of faith.

She looked up, her eyes lit with tenderness. "You are a wonderful caretaker to those who depend on you—your sister and brother and niece. But you cannot protect me. Even if I had some valid claim to your protection."

"Do you not, Laura, my sweet?" He reached for her hand, and she let him take it, bring it to his lips. "Your fierce spirit laid claim to my heart that first long night we toiled together at Kit's side. Every day that passes, each moment we share deepens that claim. A bond and obligation quite apart from what my family owes you, a link between you and I alone. Surely you feel it, too."

A statement, not a question. Her lips trembling, she squeezed his hand. "Y-yes. But it cannot—"

"It *can!* We *can* be together, if you will only believe in me, trust me. I want you with me, Laura. I want to protect you and care for you and love you. I'll pledge my life to prevent any harm coming to you. And I will do whatever is necessary to set you free."

Tears welled in her eyes, the candlelight reflected in their watery sheen. "I believe you. But you do not know him. You don't know what he's...capable of. I promise you, he would never consent to a divorce. Soon I'll be...safer, as safe as I shall ever be in this life. But only if I stay here, if you promise to take no action that might bring to his notice some hint of my whereabouts."

"Laura, that's nonsense! Only a divorce will truly make you safe. Won't you tell me the whole, help me set the process in motion?"

"I cannot!"

Damn, but the woman was stubborn. Fighting exasperation and fatigue, Beau tried again. "Laura, I must leave tomorrow. How can I go, knowing you are alone and unprotected? I realize you've built a life here, and it's only natural that you are reluctant to abandon it. But if I managed to piece together the truth, someone else might as well. Or what if, one day as you passed the village posting inn on your way to tend a patient, the door of a private carriage opened and your husband stepped out? What then?''

If Beau had harbored any vestige of doubt about the depth of Laura's fear, the stark look of panic that widened her eyes and paled her skin at that possibility would have erased them.

The urgency of persuading her goading him ever more acutely, Beau pressed his argument. ''It could happen, Laura. Please, come with me! I swear on my family's honor to keep you safe and to see you freed.''

Pressing her lips together as if to still them, she pulled her hand free and backed away from him, stumbling as she encountered the wall behind her. Swaying with the force of her agitation, she remained there, eyes riveted on his face, while doubt, confusion and dismay played across her expressive face.

He let her retreat. ''Trust your heart, Laura,'' he urged her softly. ''Trust me.''

Knowing there was nothing more he could say or do, Beau simply stood, willing her with all his strength to agree.

Finally, as he watched in consternation, a distant, shuttered look descended on her features, as it had this morning. She gave her head a small, negative shake. ''I'm sorry, but I must stay. Please, do not urge me further.''

Beau grit his teeth and resisted the urge to shake her like a disobedient child. How could she not admit the superior logic of his plan? He took a deep, calming breath. ''Laura, I know you are afraid, but—''

''Lord Beaulieu, must we part in anger? I will not go, and nothing you can say will change my mind. If you intend to depart at dawn, I suggest you return to the squire's and get some rest before your journey.''

As if they'd just finished some innocuous social chat over tea, she turned away, apparently intending to lead him to the door.

Irritation and the daunting knowledge that he hadn't succeeded in convincing her roughened his voice. ''Damn it, Laura, I can't just abandon you here!'' As she tried to bypass him, he seized her by the shoulder.

With an inarticulate cry she wrenched out of his grasp, scuttled sideways and whirled to face him, arms raised protectively over her head.

As if to ward off a blow. The realization exploded in his brain and radiated in shock waves through his body. He'd known, intellectually, that her husband must have abused her. But not until this moment, as she half crouched before him, her breath coming in gasps, her eyes dilated and feral as a cornered animal's, had the reality of what she must have lived with, fled from, truly registered.

While he stood there staring at her, incredulous and horrified, she slowly straightened, lowered her arms back to her sides. Her wide, watchful eyes never left him.

Blind rage filled him, a sick revulsion at the indignity she must have suffered. Though given the evidence he'd just witnessed there was little need to ask, he couldn't seem to stop himself from voicing the awful truth.

''He hurt you.''

She nodded, a quick jerk of the chin.

''Often. Badly.''

She pressed her trembling lips together and squeezed her eyes shut, displacing a single tear that tracked down her cheek, a glaze of liquid diamond in the moonlight.

''Ah, Sparrow,'' he whispered against the ache in his

throat. "I'm so sorry." And walked over to gather her against his chest.

She trembled within the circle of his arms, trying not to weep. He'd guessed her most shameful secret, and yet he'd not turned from her in disgust after she cowered before him like some sort of brute beast. Instead, he sheltered her in his embrace, offering her refuge while she regathered the few tattered shreds of dignity Charleton had left her. For that mercy alone, did she not already love him, she would surely have given him her heart.

Not for more than a year, since Aunt Mary had entered her final illness, had Laura been embraced by another human soul. How she had missed the sweet peace conveyed by simple physical closeness. For long moments after she'd recovered her composure, she could not make herself move away. But when finally she did force herself to push against his chest, he released her instantly.

"How long?" he asked quietly.

Even now, 'twas best not to be too specific. "A number of years."

"And he…misused you from the first?"

She sighed. "Nearly."

"Did your family not suspect?"

"I ran back to them the first time. But he came after me, so charming and regretful, that he convinced them—and me—'twas all a silly misunderstanding, that I was young and overreacted. I believed him—until the next time. And then it was too late. I was watched too closely."

"Until one day you felt you could stand it no more?"

He cannot be a saint…there must be some stain on his honor he would not want revealed… But no, Charleton was too clever. Even if she told Beau what had happened, it would end up her word against her husband's—and which was the court likely to believe? Better, still better to say nothing. "Until I could stand no more," she agreed.

He took her hand and kissed it. "Were these medieval days, I would find him and kill him, but we are supposed to be more civilized now. Won't you leave with me, let us fight this together?"

So he might protect her from Charleton. Her champion. Another tear escaped her. "N-no. I'm sorry, but I cannot. I've suffered much to construct a haven here. Please, please do nothing to jeopardize it."

"Only legal action can prevent that," he repeated, and then smiled, his voice softening. "Though I truly believe it best, I'd never force you. You know that, don't you?"

Gentleness with strength. Not sure she could reply without her voice breaking, she merely nodded.

"I'll be back for you, Laura. Soon. With plans to win your freedom so foolproof and irrefutable you shall have to agree to them."

He wouldn't be back, of course. There was no safe haven for her beyond this place—and in any event, once Lord Beaulieu returned to London and the press of his business there, he would soon forget the dowdy, troublesome little nurse who'd dared oppose his authority. During his rare moments of leisure, he'd doubtless have any number of lovely ladies eager to distract him from remembering.

An upsurge of longing swelled in her, and a bitter regret for the closeness they'd almost attained. Swallowing hard, she nodded.

"You are right, my sparrow, I must get some sleep, else I'm likely to fall asleep in the saddle tomorrow. But before I go, would you grant me one favor?"

"If I can."

Slowly, as if to ensure he did not alarm her, the earl reached over to caress her cheek with one knuckle. "Would you take down your hair for me?" he asked. "Let me see the moonlight cast shadows on that lovely auburn hair, as the sun did that first morning in your garden?"

His reverent touch, as if she were a precious object to be handled with awe and respect, melted any remaining caution. When he started to move his hand back, Laura caught it, held his palm against her temple. With her other hand, she stripped off the nightcap, splayed her fingers to comb out the braiding, then shook the tumbling plaits free to cascade over her shoulders, down the back and sides of her worn woolen wrapper.

"Like this?"

Moonlight silvered his sliver of smile. "Like that."

Emboldened, she sought his other hand, brought it up to twine in her rippled locks, arched her neck and bent her head back, thrilling to the feel of his fingers against her scalp, the delicious shivery pull of his hand through her hair.

He caught her chin, steadying her. And bent his head toward hers.

He was going to kiss her, as he had the garden. A rush of memory awakened every sense, and a greedy exultation filled her.

She'd never be the mistress he'd hinted she become, never have days or weeks or months to delight in his company. But perhaps, if she could entice him to it, she might have tonight, just one night in which the coming together of man and woman held all the joy and tenderness that most intimate coupling should contain. A joy she had never yet experienced, and once he left her, likely never would.

Please, her mind whispered like a prayer as she raised her mouth to his. *Give me one perfect night.*

Chapter Fifteen

She opened her mouth to allow him entry. Encouraged by his moan of response, the sudden tightening of the fingers cupping her face, she tentatively moved her tongue to stroke his. She felt his body shudder, and in one swift move he slid his hand from her face to wrap his arm about her shoulders, binding her closer.

Yes, she wanted closer, wanted the plush of his tongue probing, exploring, igniting shivers of sensation that tingled all the way to her toes. She reached up to tangle her fingers in his dark hair, pull him nearer so she might launch her own exploration into the delicious peaks and valleys of his mouth.

The warmth of him heated her despite the barriers of greatcoat and wrapper, but she craved more contact, yearned to feel the bone and muscle of his body against hers. Impatient, she pulled loose her robe, tugged at the buttons of his coat.

With a shuddering gasp he broke away, pushed her back. "Ah, Sparrow, I want you too much. I must leave now, while I still can."

"No!" she cried, catching his hand. "Please...don't go. Not yet."

He went entirely still, turning the full force of his gaze upon her. She stared back, desperate with hope and yearning.

"Are you sure?" he asked. "If I stay, I cannot promise to stop."

"I know," she said. "Please, stay."

For another long moment he studied her. "So be it," he said hoarsely, and kissed her hand.

Trembling at her unaccustomed boldness, she tugged him into motion and led him down the shadowy hall to her small bedchamber.

Through years of marriage she'd endured the invasion of her body, from the painful initiation on her wedding night until the last time Charleton had taken her, barely recovered from childbed. Each time, she'd accepted but never welcomed the forcible joining of a man's flesh to her own. But now she wanted it, wanted the heavy weight of the earl's flanks across her thighs, tautness of his belly against the roundness of her own, her breasts crushed under the muscle of his chest. Something feverish and urgent pulsed within her at the thought of that vital, thrusting part of him buried deep within her. She wanted the sound of his breathing gone crazed and ragged as he approached the peak, his cry of fulfillment as he surmounted it. And she wanted the sweet peace of his head pressed to her bosom as, sated and spent, he collapsed against her.

If she were fortunate, perhaps instead of springing up immediately afterward, he would be content to lie beside her, gifting her with the music of his breathing as it slowed. And if she were exceptionally lucky, perhaps he might doze while she held him close, daring to lightly trace the lines of his body, storing in her memory the contours of the strength and vitality she'd once been privileged to briefly hold to her breast.

While the earl closed the door behind her and deposited the candle on the bedside table, Laura stood, suddenly uncertain. Was the earl ready? Sometimes before the act, Charleton had required her to…stimulate him.

She turned to see the earl regarding her gravely. "Second thoughts?"

"Never."

His eyes lit. Smiling widely, he shed his greatcoat and pulled loose his cravat. "Then come to me, Sparrow."

Pulling off her wrapper as she went, she ran to his arms. He caught her, lifted her, laughing softly. Set her back on her feet and bent his head.

He kissed her gently this time, light, teasing, touches like the brush of rose petals against her lips, her chin, her cheeks. She murmured a protest, wanting more, and he obliged, tracing the outline of her mouth, sucking softly. The blade of his tongue found hers, the clash setting off shudders deep in her belly.

She swayed on her feet and he caught her against him. She shuddered again at the evidence of his readiness, surprisingly large and hard against her belly. Fire sparking at the center of her, instinctively she rubbed herself against it.

He moaned and took the kiss deeper. Panting now, she urged him to the bed, trying with one hand to pull up her night rail while she settled back against the pillows. She parted her legs and drew him toward her, her trembling fingers fumbling with the buttons of his breeches.

He caught her hand and stilled it, then moved her cupped palm slowly over his rigid length. "S-sweet," he gasped, the sound nearly a groan. Then, to her surprise, he pulled her fingers away and kissed them. "But not yet."

"Not yet?" she echoed, bewildered. "But...are you not—ready?"

"You are not," he said.

"But...I am!" she wailed, fretful with need and mystified at the delay. "D-do you want me to do...something else?"

He chuckled. "Nothing, my sweet sparrow. Just let me look at you."

She stared at him, wondering if they were speaking the same language. "You...are looking at me," she pointed out.

"True," he returned gravely, though his lips twitched as if at some private joke. "But I can't see nearly enough."

"Then light another candle," she said crossly and bit her lip, tears threatening. Was she doing something wrong? Suddenly she felt awkward and unsure. Had her boldness revolted him? Surely he wouldn't— "You're not going to leave?" she blurted.

His smile changed, from amusement to tenderness, and the warmth of his gaze held her motionless. "Never, my sparrow. I'll never leave you."

The words caught her like a blow to the chest. Scarcely able to breathe through the tightness, she'd not have managed a reply even had her brain been functioning well enough to formulate one. All she knew was she wanted to be joined with him, her body a gift offered joyfully, gratefully for his pleasure.

Leaning on one elbow, she reached back for him. But before she could seize his breeches flap, he reached over to grasp her ankle. Puzzled once more, she stilled, watching as he bent low over her leg. And kissed the soft skin at the instep of her foot.

She gasped, the sensation both ticklish and powerfully pleasurable. The vibrations he set off there seemed somehow to directly intensify the prickly, achy tenderness of her breasts, the pulsing fullness between her thighs. Then he lifted her foot and stroked the hot wetness of his tongue across her toes, took the littlest into his mouth and sucked it.

An immediate response rocketed through her. She seemed to lose control of her limbs, felt herself sag back against the pillows, her heartbeat loud and rapid in her ears, as if she'd been chasing Misfit while playing fetch. Seeming oblivious to her disintegrating faculties, the earl made a leisurely progress across her toes, stimulating each in turn, then inching her night rail higher to kiss her ankle, tantalize her shins with his tongue.

By now well beyond the ability of speech, but for her rasping breaths she lay silent, in thrall to his touch. With excruciating, intoxicating slowness he explored the curve of her calves, the dimple beside her kneecap. She rejoiced with incoherent gasps as he moved over her knees to the trembling smoothness of her inner thighs, his caress of that exquisitely sensitive flesh so intense it neared pain.

He halted when she flinched away, chuckled deep in his throat when she seized his neck to urge his mouth back down to her. He slowed his pace still further, letting her accustom herself to the shocking newness of his intimate touch. Some remote part of her mind watched in horrified titillation as the wanton creature who now resided in her body begged with whimpered moans and a clenching of hands for him to continue his deliciously slow progression toward a goal she could hardly yet believe.

When at last he reached there, gently urging her thighs wider so he could caress the outer petals and seek the hidden bud within, she could wait no longer. With an inarticulate cry she pushed him back, jerked free the buttons of his straining breeches. "Now," she begged, desperation giving her voice. "Please."

"Sparrow," he said on a gasp as at last she felt the weight of his bare chest against her. She clutched his sweat-slick shoulders as he fitted himself to her aching passage, and unable to wait a second longer, thrust her hips to carry him within.

So incredibly sweet was the joining, tears sprang to her eyes. But as he began to move in the ancient rhythm she thought she knew so well, the subtle friction immediately and dramatically magnified the throbbing sensations within her. Her skin grew feverish, her fingernails biting into his back as she writhed under him, trying to remain properly passive while her body demanded movement.

"Ah, yes, sweeting," he murmured against her mouth as, helpless to prevent herself, she rocked her hips to mimic his motion. The tautness within her spiraled tighter, tighter, a nearly unbearable torment, tearing a deep moan from her throat. Then suddenly, tension exploded in a brilliant shower of sensation that cascaded through her, a flashflood boiling through every nerve.

For a few moments afterward she lay stunned, barely conscious, barely breathing. Dimly she was aware of Beau rolling her with him to her side, and then she surrendered to the heavy lassitude stealing over her.

Sometime later she struggled back to consciousness, to find she was still wrapped in the earl's warm embrace. His steady heartbeat vibrated against her chest; his breath warmed her hair. Utter contentment filled her, and once again her eyes stung with tears.

No matter how long or short the life she was destined to live, she would thank heaven for this precious night.

She looked up into his faintly smiling face and the love she'd tried to avoid and ignore caught her full in the throat, strangling her voice. How could she bear to let him walk away?

She cursed the tears that welled up, brushing them away with an impatient hand. She would not spoil the wonder of this night by regretting what could not be.

She wanted to pour out her love, tell him she'd never known such closeness nor tasted such pleasure, that she would treasure these moments the rest of her life. But nothing beyond tonight was possible, and so she swallowed the ardent vows she must not make and searched for something permissible. "How can I thank you?" she whispered at last.

With the gentleness that so captured her heart he rubbed his knuckle against her cheek. "How can I thank you?"

She struggled to lift herself on one elbow. He would leave now, as he must, but resigned though she was to the inevitability of it, still she sought some way to delay.

"Can I get you something? Do anything before you…go?"

"Some wine, if you have it. But, Sparrow—" his voice deepened "—I'm nowhere close to being ready to leave."

The teasing promise in his tone stopped her breath. Surely he couldn't mean…what she thought? Her experience argued against the possibility of any further coupling—but then, everything else tonight had been far beyond any previous experience. At the mere hint of it, nerves she'd thought too exhausted to function were beginning to stir and spark. "I'll g-get you wine," she said hurriedly.

"Wait a moment," he said, catching her hand as she reached for her wrapper. "Let me look at you."

She'd never been naked in front of a man before. But as he held her at arm's length, his ardent plea echoing in her ears, her self-consciousness faded. She nodded, dropped the wrapper, and stood fully unveiled before him.

Slowly he examined her, from her bare toes up her calves, her thighs, across her belly to taut, tight peaks of her breasts, her shoulders, her neck, her chin, cheeks, hair. "You are so lovely, Sparrow," he murmured. "Now, wine please, and hurry before you catch a chill."

Any tendency to chill evaporated as, before he released her hand, he leaned forward to capture one erect nipple and tease it with his teeth. She gasped, delight at this new sensation coursing through her, and grabbed his shoulder to steady herself.

With leisurely slowness he moved his mouth to tantalize the aching peak of her other breast. She was melting, nearly boneless when he at last stopped.

"Wine," he said, skimming his hand over her belly to touch the tight curls beneath. "We've not much time, and there's so much more—" he moved his finger to stroke within the warm folds "—to experience."

Somehow she managed to totter to the kitchen and bring back wine without spilling it all over. He greeted her with a kiss, pulled her close under the bedclothes to warm her, and fed her wine. And then, after they'd sipped, and talked, the earl proceeded to demonstrate just how ignorant this long-married wife had been.

He taught her, a voraciously greedy and willing pupil,

how he could set off the same incredible explosion with his fingers, his tongue. How she could ready him again for joining with the urging of her hips, the goad of her mouth. Through the swift and shimmering hours of that short, matchless night he showed her how pleasure could be stimulated and conveyed, rapture a current flowing from him to her, from her to him, until it swept them together over the precipice in a timeless, sense-stunning cascade to completion.

Sometime in the quiet dimness near dawn Laura woke to find him still beside her. Joy that he had not crept away while she slept swelled in her, and she leaned up to kiss his cheek.

"Sparrow," he murmured, angling his head to take her kiss on his lips as he pulled her into a rib-bruising embrace.

She clung to him, knowing the time to delay had passed. "You must go now," she said when at last he released her.

"Yes. I'd best get back to Everett Hall before first light, lest I encounter some farm boy on the way to market who might carry tales. I'll be off for London an hour or so after." He paused, looking down at her. "Let me stop here for you on my way."

Quit Merriville. Part of her yearned to silence her mind's automatic clamor about the danger, respond only to the leap of gladness that urged her to go with him. But once again, fear and caution won out.

"I cannot. Please, I'm sorry, but—"

He stopped her apology with another kiss. "I know, Sparrow. Though I leave you here alone under protest, I'll not take you with me by force. But when I return—and I will return, soon—you *will* agree to depart with me."

She said nothing, the bittersweet agony of his impending loss thickening her throat and preventing reply. While he dressed she threw on her wrapper and poured him more wine, then walked with him to the porch door.

He bent to kiss her, then lifted her into his arms and hugged her close. "Keep yourself safe, Sparrow. And dream of me until I return."

"I will," she said as he set her back on her feet. *The whole of my life,* she added silently.

Heart already aching, she watched him mount his horse, and with a final wave, ride off into the waning night.

After an exhausting journey that finally saw him installed back in London several days later, Beau sat at the desk in his study, reviewing the latest evidence in the embezzlement investigation. All the reports confirmed his suspicions. Now he must anticipate the perpetrator's mood and movements in order to construct the most foolproof trap to bring him down.

Sighing, he put the dossiers aside. Having done all he could at the moment to move the case forward, he might now turn his attention to the personal concern that had haunted him all through his long voyage south.

Though Laura seemed to feel she was safe in Merriville, every instinct had rebelled at leaving her there alone and unprotected. And he'd been bitterly disappointed that he'd not succeeded in winning her confidence. Though she'd confirmed the basic facts after he guessed them, she'd not let slip the smallest detail that would make the search for her real name—and thus the path to protecting her—easier or swifter.

That placed him at a disadvantage, but not an insurmountable one. After all, there were but a limited number of men wealthy and influential enough to necessitate a fugitive wife's going into hiding. Amassing a list of potential names and checking them would be a tedious process, but he would have it done. Armed with all the possibilities, he had every confidence he would eventually deduce the identity of the man he sought.

But how much time would that require?

He begrudged every day he would have to wait while the necessary information was assembled. Each one he spent apart from her heightened the urgency of his desire to claim her, tightened the spiral of anxiety about her safety. Grimly he vowed that he'd give the search no more than a month. Regardless of whether the investigation was complete by then or not, he would return for her.

Now to set the search in motion. He rang a bell to summon his secretary.

The slender, sandy-haired man entered, smiling in welcome. "My lord, good to see you back! I trust this means Kit is recovering?"

"Good to be back, James, and yes, Kit is doing much better. Thank you for doing your usual excellent job to keep the dispatches coming. I believe I've perused all the latest. I see our sailor songbird is still chirping."

The young man smiled grimly. "It appears he participated in bringing in several more cargoes on which the duty charged on the manifests exceeded the legal amounts owed, the excess being siphoned off into coffers other than those of the government. As you will have read, by covertly following the boasting sailor we've been able to definitely establish three other links in the chain. I assume, as usual, you intend to leave apprehension of the lower-level miscreants to other authorities?"

Beau nodded. He seldom concerned himself with apprehending petty criminals like the corrupt sailor. Instead, he felt it his special calling to track and eventually bring down their leaders. That men of birth and privilege who should consider it their duty to serve the nation should betray that trust inspired in him a loathing as deep as it was visceral.

"The evidence thus far does seem to point to Lord Wolverton as head of the operation," his secretary continued. "Did your observations of him in the north support that conclusion?"

"Yes—the bastard." Beau sighed. "Another page in the all-too-familiar story of a younger son outspending his means by indulging a weakness for gaming, women or vice. Though in my noble Lord Wolverton's case, it seems to be a combination of all three." With a grimace, he shook a finger at the secretary. "Promise me, James, if you ever develop such proclivities, you'll come to me before doing something stupid."

"So you can straighten out my warped thinking with a well-placed left hook?" His secretary gave a slight smile. "Surely you know, after what happened to my father, I'd be the last man on earth to—"

"I know, James," Beau interrupted. "An attempt at levity to relieve my disgust at the pathetic circumstances."

"I'm afraid I can't find any humor in it," the young man replied, bitterness in his tone. "Not when my father's reputation was nearly destroyed by the false accusations of such a man. If not for you, he would have been disgraced—"

"None of that now." Beau waved his secretary to silence. "I suppose I'm indebted to the villain. Had your father's predicament not outraged me into vowing to uncover the identity of the real traitor, I might still be naught but an idle dandy playing at puzzles.''

"As if you were ever such!'' his secretary scoffed. "I'm just glad your intervention in my father's case brought you to Lord Riverton's notice, and that his lordship succeeded in persuading you to continue the work. And as always, I'm honored that you trust me to contribute my small part. Speaking of which, what would you have me do now?''

Beau hesitated. "I need to investigate another matter. A personal and highly delicate one involving a lady, which must of course be conducted in strictest secrecy.''

"I hope you know you can rely on my discretion.''

"That I do not doubt. However, since I'm determined to tap my usual network in pursuit of wholly private concern, a somewhat…irregular practice, I admit, you may not feel comfortable being part of it. If you choose not to become involved, I will not hold it against you.''

"My lord,'' the secretary replied, "since it is you who fund that network, I cannot see that there would be any impropriety in your using it however you see fit. And even if there were, after all you have done for my family, I'm hardly likely to question any contrivance of yours. Now, what should you like me to do?''

Beau smiled, gratified by the young man's loyalty. "I need you to compile me a list of gentlemen who have, ah, 'lost' a wife sometime in the past two years. The woman will probably have been reported dead, although it might be claimed she is tending distant relatives or off on a lengthy journey of some sort. She might even have been declared insane. The lady would be of good family and should have been about three-and-twenty at the time of her…departure.''

Beau had the dubious pleasure of knowing he'd confounded his normally unflappable secretary. After staring a moment, with commendable discretion, James managed to swallow the curiosity he obviously felt. "Very well, my lord. How soon do you require the completed list?"

"As soon as possible. It's a matter of considerable urgency." Beau gazed out the window, seeing again Laura Martin's small form hunched before him, fragile arms and puny fists braced against a blow. Anxiety twisted in his chest. He must persuade her out of Merriville, and soon.

He turned back to his secretary. "As you may have surmised, the husband in this case has violent proclivities. Try to determine if any of the prospects are rumored to be abusive. And, James… "

"My lord?"

"Your help in uncovering this shall more than repay any service I may ever have done your family."

His secretary hesitated. "The…lady is that important to you."

"Yes."

James Maxwell bowed. "Then I shall begin the search immediately."

A month later Laura Martin deposited her newly harvested herbs on the garden bench and wearily sat beside them, shivering in the tepid warmth of the fading late-afternoon sun.

Full winter would be upon them soon, with its inevitable complement of snow, sleet and drenching rain that would render the roads snow-drifted, iced over or deep in mire for indefinite periods until next spring's thaw.

That irrefutable fact made her shiver with a chill that had nothing to do with the wind blowing over her chafed hands. For with her woman's courses two weeks overdue, she had to face the frightening possibility that she might be with child.

Unfortunately, there was no way to know for certain—not until the child quickened, by which time the evidence of her indiscretion would be only too apparent to the entire county. But she'd never missed her time before, unless she was increasing. As she'd learned during her years of marriage, her cycles were most regular. Indeed, as a new bride, she'd counted the days, wanting to please her husband by offering him the possibility of the son he so desperately craved. But all too soon, she'd come to regard the advancing end of each cycle with dread, knowing the evidence that she'd not conceived would send Charlton into a fit of violent temper. At first, he'd been only verbally abusive, vilifying her as graceless failure of a woman, a disgrace to her normally prolific family he would never had deigned to marry had he known she was barren. Later her mouth would dry with fear, knowing the best she could hope for would be a slap across the face. Twice he'd beaten her so severely that she'd required the whole of the next month to recover.

Twice she'd conceived, a short-term protection from his aggression. She closed her eyes on a shudder. Even now, she could not bear to remember the terrible outcome of those pregnancies.

Once she'd watched the stable boys with a mouse they'd found in a grain bin. They'd teased it with a stick, pushing it this way and that, while the small creature, hemmed in between the probing stick and the tall straight walls of the bin, ran frantically this way and that.

She knew now what that mouse must have felt.

"Your character will be impugned and your standing in the neighborhood will suffer," she recalled the vicar warning. Simple speculation could cause that much harm.

But to bear a fatherless child nine months after the earl's departure? She'd have no reputation left—and no livelihood, either.

How to preserve both? Swiftly she ruled out both accepting the vicar's offer and remaining in Merriville. She wouldn't serve Reverend Blackthorne such a turn, even if such a marriage would be legal, and to face down her neighbor's scorn would simply condemn herself and the child to slow starvation. No, if time confirmed that she was with child, she mustn't remain here.

Instinctively her hands slipped down to cradle her still-flat belly. Despite the risk, despite the fear that uncoiled thick in her veins at the mere thought of relocating, she couldn't regret that night. Nor could she regret the child who might have been conceived from it. A child to cherish and protect, tangible reminder that a love encompassing heart and body was not a fanciful imagining, but for one wondrous night, had truly been hers.

A child to protect as she'd failed to protect Jennie. That stark thought instantly refocused her thoughts.

For time was critical. If she wished to preserve her reputation—and the possibility of returning to her livelihood in Merriville—she'd have to leave before her condition became apparent. And if she wished to be assured of getting away, she'd best depart before full winter and the possibility of ice or blizzards that might strand her here for weeks.

Too agitated now to sit, she jumped up to pace the length of the porch. Inventing a plausible pretext to depart was no problem; as a healer, she could always say she'd been called away to assist some distant relative. But where to go?

A flurry of pacing merely confirmed the stark truth. When she'd made the decision to come here, she'd deliberately broken all ties to her former life, to family, friends and any acquaintances who might have come to her aid. Only one individual remained who knew her true identity, and she was the one link by which Charleton might yet trace Laura.

Her former governess, Miss Hollins, whose sister ''Aunt Mary'' had secretly conveyed back to Merriville a battered, dying runaway wife. Having initially come to Miss Hollins's home to tend a young governess, incapacitated by influenza at the local inn while journeying to her new post, Aunt Mary arrived to find at her sister's cottage both that unfortunate—and Laura. After the poor woman died, the two sisters had buried her in a grave bearing Laura's name. If Charleton retained any suspicions about the identity of the remains beneath the simple granite marker he'd been shown when he finally tracked Laura to Miss Hollins's cottage three months later, he'd still be watching that house—and Miss Hollins.

Another five minutes of pacing left her with the same worrying conclusion. She simply didn't have funds enough to support herself unassisted in some faraway community for nearly a year. If she were going to relocate for a time, she must have some assistance. Miss Hollins was the only person she could both trust with the truth and ask for help. She would have to risk contacting her again.

She hugged herself, fighting the bitterly familiar spiral of fear that clogged her veins and tightened her stomach. *I will protect us, Jennie,* she vowed.

There is one other option, a small voice argued. *You could seek out the earl.*

The thought brought back the image of his face, the echo of his voice, the dearly remembered touch of his gentle fingers. Longing rippled through her. Ah, how good it would be to make her way to London, to relax her constant vigil in the comforting warmth of his powerful presence, to cast this dilemma into his capable hands!

She smiled wryly. Given the circumstances, at least he'd know she wasn't trying to trick him into marriage.

The smile faded. But as she'd told him that night, powerful as he was, he was not above the law. If she risked going to London and Charleton discovered her, Lord Beaulieu could not prevent her husband from seizing her.

An even bleaker realization dawned, so awful the lingering desire to run to his lordship evaporated on the instant. As she was still legally Charlton's wife, any child she bore was also his. Were Charleton to find her, he could claim the child. Their child. Beau's son.

And he would do it, finding the act a fitting revenge. No, she resolved, let her flee to the ends of England, but should she be discovered, let Charleton believe the child she carried the by-blow of some farmer or curate, not worthy of being claimed as his own. Let him never discover the babe's true father.

Her resolve established, the fear retreated to a grim, ever-present shadow. She'd spread word of her intended departure to the squire and several of the neighborhood ladies. Briefly she considered sending a note to Lady Elspeth, who'd borne her much-recovered brother back home with her the previous week, and swiftly decided against it. The fewer who had definite knowledge of her plans, the better. She'd not even send a note ahead to warn Miss Hollins.

Misfit rubbed against her hand, whining for attention. Absently she leaned down to scratch his head, already aching with regret to leave behind the peace of her cottage, her garden, the kind solicitude of the squire and the families of their small neighborhood. Resolutely she put aside the grief, focusing her mind on beginning the necessary planning. She would leave within the week.

She couldn't risk even the smallest possibility that Charleton might get his hands on Beau's child.

Chapter Sixteen

A few days later Beau sat at the desk in his study, reviewing the nearly completed dossier on Lord Wolverton. Over the past three weeks the investigation had picked up speed, all the meticulous details painstakingly gathered by his operatives finally coming together to create a clear picture of the embezzler's web. Once Beau received the last overseas reports for which he still waited, he'd have sufficient evidence to present the dossier to Lord Riverton.

Normally by this point he'd be experiencing the deep satisfaction of another puzzle solved, tempered by the sadness of confirming once again human nature's frailty. But he'd had to exert all his self-control to keep his mind focused on business. For his private investigation of Laura Martin had not proceeded nearly as well.

Initially he'd expected to uncover her identity so he might return to Merriville before Ellie transported the recovering Kit from Everett Hall. But once his lungs cleared, Kit had improved more quickly than anticipated, a fact of which Beau could only be glad, and Ellie decided to move her brother the shorter distance to her country estate rather than trespass upon Squire Everett's hospitality until Kit was fit enough for the longer journey to London.

Beau could not now cloak a visit to Mrs. Martin under the guise of checking on his brother. To journey to Merriville and call on her without such a socially acceptable excuse would be so glaringly remarkable as to immediately give rise to precisely the sort of speculation and possible censure the vicar had warned about. Beau dared not approach her now until he had all the facts necessary to persuade her immediate removal. And those facts had not yet fallen into place.

Was she still safe? She'd been so ten days ago, for the message Ellie had written him when she'd arrived home at Wentworth Hall pointedly mentioned they'd left Mrs. Martin with their warmest thanks and a promise to meet again *soon*—his sister had underlined the word.

With more fervency than his manipulating sister could have dreamed, Beau wished to meet Laura Martin again *soon*. The month since he'd last seen her seemed an eternity. He would never have imagined that in the brief few weeks they'd spent together she would have so infiltrated his heart and mind that being away from her would create this raw sense of loss.

He missed the subtle loveliness of her presence, even garbed in hideous brown gowns, her low-pitched voice expressing some pithy comment or shimmering with humor as she joked with Kit. He missed the soft rose scent of her perfume, the polished mahogany sheen of the curls that escaped those ridiculous dowager caps. He craved the sight of her inquisitive eyes and angled chin as she gazed up at him with that endearing sparrow look.

Knowing he'd otherwise go mad with frustration and fury, he cut himself off from remembering any detail of their last night together, when she'd given herself to him with such innocent eagerness, proving to his amazement that a woman who'd borne a child could still be so heart-breakingly ignorant in the ways of pleasure. And yet he'd been fiercely glad that he was undoubtedly the first to unlock its secrets for her, exulting to know that special bond was theirs, theirs alone.

Though he might by supreme act of will block out the memories, he could not filter from his blood the sharp edge of need she'd created in him. In a curious way, the sense of her with him, in him was nearly as acute now, when hundreds of miles separated them, as it had been across the narrow space of her bed.

Each day that passed without bringing him the information he needed to claim her intensified both his impatience and his urgency, destroying his sleep, shortening his temper such that increasingly he found himself biting back the first, acid comment that came to his lips.

In fact, he realized with mild chagrin, given the lowered voices and apprehensive looks his household staff had treated him to for the past week, he must have been less successful in stifling such comments than he'd thought. A knock at the study door interrupted his resolve to do better.

His secretary entered, a sheaf of papers in his outstretched hands. "The reports from the West Indies and Bombay for which you'd been waiting, my lord."

"Thank you, James, and be seated, if you please." Indicating the armchair in front of his desk, Beau quickly perused the documents.

"We have in our possession the ledgers listing bills of lading as they were filed upon the ships' landing in London?" Beau asked after a moment.

"Yes, my lord, and as you expected, the cargo amounts on the bills of lading from the ships' port of origin are less than those in the landing ledger by several hundred pounds per commodity. They do match exactly the amounts in the ledgers actually forwarded to the customs office. But do we have any positive proof Lord Wolverton was involved?''

''Nothing that would stand in a court of law. Fortunately we don't need to prove a case, and in any event, the government prefers not to have such messy affairs dragged into the public forum.''

''But if the payoffs were made in cash, such that his involvement cannot be proven, how can you force his resignation?''

''By applying the weight of some telling, if circumstantial, evidence. We know he's been sustaining heavy gambling losses for years, got himself entangled with the cent-per-centers. Suddenly he paid off the loans, even though we've ascertained that his estates generated no more income. Threatened with transportation or the noose, I don't doubt the couriers who carried him the purloined funds will be only too happy to confirm whatever details we wish. Once Lord Riverton acquaints Wolverton with the evidence, I expect he will see the wisdom of resigning quietly.''

James frowned. ''It seems somehow unfair that the others will go to the dock while Lord Wolverton escapes prosecution.''

Beau shrugged. ''The ton knows how these things work. To be stripped of his office and his income will ruin him as effectively as imprisonment. And the corruption will stop, which is perhaps the most important point.''

''When will you present the information to Lord Riverton?''

''He's out of London at present. When he returns.''

"Will you continue to observe Lord Wolverton?"

Beau smiled grimly. "I've half a mind to invite him to the Puzzlebreaker's Club, then propose to the membership that we unravel an embezzlement scheme such as he's been running, just for the pleasure of watching him squirm. But Lord Riverton prefers I keep my involvement in these investigations covert." He sighed. "Usually the personal satisfaction of decoding the mystery is more than enough compensation. Now, have you any more information on the...other matter?"

Without doubt James knew full well why the solution of this present case had engendered in Beau so little enthusiasm. With commendable tact, he'd refrained from commenting on the shadowed eyes and grim weariness his employer had worn this past week like a cloak.

"As you requested, I've gone back and rechecked the records of all the nobility and gentry." His secretary gave him a wry smile. "Who could have guessed there would be so many dead or absent wives among them the past two years? I'm still awaiting confirmation that Lady Worth did indeed depart with her father on a trip to collect data on indigenous peoples of the East Indies, and that Mrs. Dominick is truly visiting her cousin in Italy, but those two are the last. The other missing wives have turned up and the deaths of all the dearly departed have been confirmed by family members not directly related to the husband." He eyes Beau with concern. "I'm sorry, my lord. Shall I begin to check among the wealthy merchant class?"

It couldn't be. He must have missed some clue, somewhere. Beau clenched his hands, tightened his jaw to prevent the raging frustration from escaping in some violent profanity. James was doing everything he could; Beau would not vent his anger on his hapless secretary.

"Oh, I did collect one memento," James said into the tense silence. "That epidemic of influenza two winters ago claimed the lives of several wives on my list. Thought I'd get out and do a bit of sleuthing on my own—"

"I've been that difficult to work with?" Beau interrupted with an attempt at a smile.

After raising a suggestive eyebrow, James continued, "Since several of the families are in London for the Season, I decided to call on them." He held up a hand to forestall Beau's protest. "In quite an unexceptional manner. Told them the government was collecting information on the influenza outbreak for a report."

"A sort of updated Doomsday Book?"

James grinned. "Something like."

Beau sighed, amused despite himself. "James, I begin to worry about you."

"At any rate, the deaths were confirmed unconditionally. Including that of the lady whose husband was previously my prime suspect—a thoroughly nasty individual whom reports suggest may have been capable of violence. However, in the interests of furthering research, the lady's father, a rather scholarly gentleman, lent me a miniature of his daughter. I thought perhaps you'd like to see it."

You're quite a scholar. No, but my father was. As the words echoed out of memory, Beau's heart skipped a beat and his mouth went dry. With a hand that suddenly trembled he reached for the small oval portrait his secretary was extracting from his waistcoat pocket.

"Apparently Lady Charleton contracted the influenza before she'd fully recovered from losing a babe in childbirth..."

The rest of his secretary's sentence faded out as Beau

brought the figured gold case close enough to distinguish the features of the shyly smiling lady portrayed within. A young lady with Laura Martin's glossy auburn locks, Laura Martin's piercingly blue eyes.

For an instant he couldn't draw breath. He shut his eyes tightly, clutching the portrait in his fist, nearly dizzy as relief, euphoria and aching need rocked him in successive waves.

He opened his eyes to find James staring at him. "That…is the lady?"

"Yes. Find me everything you turn up on Lady Charleton's death, everything you can uncover about her husband. Send operatives to both families, if they're now in London—use as many men as you need. And report back to me at three o'clock with whatever you've found."

"Yes, my lord."

"And, James—"

His secretary, already at the door, halted to look back at him. "My lord?"

"Thank you."

Later that afternoon Beau returned to his study. In the intervening hours he'd conducted some research of his own. He knew little of Lord Charleton personally, the viscount being more than a decade his senior, but casual inquiries at his club elicited several intriguing tidbits.

Lord Charleton was regarded with respect but not warmth by his contemporaries. Accounted a good shot, a fair sportsman, a punctilious landlord ruthlessly precise in his duties, he drove a hard bargain in any transaction. A cold, proud man obsessed with his lineage, after being twice widowed he still had no heir, his first wife having produced only daughters and his second, the youngest child of Lord Arthur Farrington, having died two years ago of influenza after complications from a stillbirth.

In three days' time Charleton was to marry again, a Miss Cynthia Powell, daughter of ancient Devon gentry.

Soon I'll be safe, Laura had told him. And so, in a certain sense, her husband's remarriage would make her.

That his Laura Martin was the supposedly dead Lady Charleton he had no doubt—the evidence of the miniature was too compelling. And the few details he'd yet gleaned of Lady Charleton fit what he knew of Laura Martin's arrival in Merriville.

She had been gravely ill. She'd lost a babe. Whether Charleton had invented the notion of her death to derail speculation about her disappearance or whether Laura herself had somehow engineered it, Beau would soon uncover. Now that he had her name, the rest would be easy.

A thoroughly nasty individual, James had described Laura's husband. Did Charleton in fact believe her dead? Or was he still watching, waiting, as Laura believed?

Regardless of what further information would reveal, one indisputable fact had seized Beau the moment he learned her husband was about to remarry. If Charleton did not discover Laura's whereabouts until after his remarriage, he could then neither claim her nor reveal her true identity, lest he leave himself open to charges of bigamy. Though to Beau's thinking, Laura would still not be absolutely safe—Charleton would be secure from scandal only if his inconvenient former wife were truly dead.

But more than her lack of security bothered him. If Charleton's remarriage prevented the viscount from revealing the past, it also prevented Laura's escaping it. She might come to Beau as they both desired, but she'd have to remain in the shadows, unable to use her real name or assume her rightful place in society. Have to remain permanently hidden, too, from the still-grieving family that believed her dead. And most important from Beau's point of view, she'd never be able to become what he most wanted her to be—his lawful wife.

One way or another, he had to stop Lord Charleton's remarriage. One way or another, he had to convince the man to seek a divorce before remarrying.

And he had three days in which to do it.

A burning desire consumed him to order his horse this moment, to ride to Merriville with all speed. Beyond the ever-present compulsion to be with Laura again, it would be wisest to have benefit of all she knew of this tangled affair before Beau confronted her husband. But given the distance, it was impossible for him to ride there and back in only three days.

He paced the room, too restless to sit, impatient to hear whatever news James had garnered. And then, information complete or not, within the next day he must proceed. Without whatever assistance Laura Martin might have been able to offer.

Beau thought again of Laura's slight form cowering before him, her eyes distended with fear, her fisted arms raised, and the smoldering rage within fired hotter. He already knew enough of Charleton to know the man must be legally and permanently removed from Laura's life. His fists itched to deal out to the viscount a liberal measure of the sort of domestic bliss he'd offered Laura.

While he stood at the window, envisioning with grim pleasure that satisfying prospect, a knock sounded, followed by the immediate entry of James Maxwell.

The mantel clock chimed three. "Bless you, James," Beau offering a wry smile as he moved to the sideboard. "Let me pour some wine, then tell me the whole."

***

At just before three the following afternoon, Beau stood in the parlor of Viscount Charleton's imposing Georgian town house. As he paced the gray marble floor, awaiting his host, he surveyed the tasteful arrangement of green brocade Hepplewhite chairs and sofas, the immaculate white plaster detailing of the ceilings and overmantel that proclaimed the room the workmanship of the Adams brothers, and tried to imagine Laura here, greeting her guests in this cold, impersonal mausoleum of a room.

A few moments later Lord Charleton entered. Every nerve stiffening in automatic dislike, Beau made him the bow decorum demanded.

Charleton, a portly gentleman of middle age, barely inclined his head. Without any of the usual civilities, he demanded, "You insisted on seeing me, Lord Beaulieu? I trust the matter is of sufficient gravity. I am expected momentarily to drive my betrothed to tea."

Already simmering from the deliberate insult of not being offered so much as a chair, Beau remained silent, allowing himself a long moment to inspect the viscount, from his silvered hair to his immaculately polished topboots. The man's face was a pasty hue that contrasted unpleasantly with the dark shadows beneath his glaring eyes. One vein pulsed at his temple, and he tapped his fingers against the smooth seam of his breeches.

As Beau allowed the silence to continue, a flush of irritation reddened the unhealthy pallor of the viscount's cheeks. *So you are easily angered,* Beau thought. *Good. Anger often makes men careless.*

"You mock me, sirrah? I shall have my servant throw you out." He turned as if to go to the bellpull.

"Not quite yet," Beau interposed, holding out a hand

to block the viscount's path. Charleton stared down at it, his red color deepening.

Slowly, Beau pulled back his hand. "I understand I should congratulate you on your imminent nuptials. A happy event which will soon blot out the tragedy of your late wife's premature demise."

"You delayed my departure to tell me that? I thank you for your good wishes, but you might just as easily have sent a note. And now I bid you good day."

"I was also somewhat curious, I admit, about the circumstances of your late wife's death. Influenza following hard upon childbed, wasn't it?"

"Yes. Tragic. She was a dear young thing, my poor Emily. Now, if you will excuse me—"

"Emily Marie Laura Trent, she was, yes? Curious though, that although the child's birth took place at your country estate at Charleton's Grove, your wife was buried nearly a hundred miles away, in Mernton Manner."

The viscount waved an impatient hand. "Still distraught over the child's death, she begged to visit her old governess and I hadn't the heart to deny her. She took sick there, and by the time I arrived—" he uttered a deep sigh "—it was too late. My poor dear Emily was already two weeks buried."

The speech sounded so carefully practiced, Beau had trouble hanging on to his own temper. "Two weeks to journey a mere hundred miles to the side of your beloved and desperately ill wife? That seems a trifle…tardy."

The viscount gave him a frosty glance. "As it was—"

"As it was, you weren't in Charleton's Grove when your wife left your house—but in London. And once your staff notified you of her disappearance, it took you another ten days to track your 'poor dear Emily' to Mernton Manner, which is why you arrived after her tragic demise.''

The vein at Charleton's temple pulsed faster. ''I hardly see how my personal affairs are any concern of yours, Lord Beaulieu. So if you would leave my house—''

''Just one more thing, my lord, and I'll go.'' Beau braced himself to pose the crucial query. ''Lord Charleton, are you sure the woman buried at Mernton Manner is in fact your wife Emily?''

Surprise that could not be feigned swept over the viscount's features. ''What are you suggesting?''

Beau held up the miniature James had obtained. ''Is this a portrait of your late wife?''

Charleton glanced at it quickly. ''And if it is?''

''Then I must inform you, Lord Charleton, that your wife is very much alive.''

Chapter Seventeen

Charleton stared at him. "You must be out of your mind. My wife died two years ago at Mernton. Her governess, Miss Hollins, swore to me it was so."

Beau smiled thinly. So Laura had devised the ruse, with the help of her friends. "I'm sure she did. To protect the woman she knew you'd abused throughout the whole of your marriage. A woman who still lives, Charleton."

"How do you know this?"

"Because I've seen and talked with the woman in this portrait, barely a month ago. A very retiring, very private woman who lives alone and carefully avoids public notice. A woman hiding from a past—and a man."

The viscount stood absolutely still, his eyes locked on Beau's unflinching gaze, as if trying to read there the veracity of his claim. It seemed after a moment Beau convinced him, for the pale skin mottled with rage.

"So she lives, that pathetic excuse for a wife? And has hidden herself from her obligations to her lawful lord for two whole years? I'd not have thought the quivering coward capable of so successful a deceit."

Gritting his teeth, Beau held himself rigid, resisting the demand steaming through his blood to mill Charleton down here and now. While he struggled to keep himself under control, the viscount took a few agitated steps, then whirled to face Beau.

"And your interest in this matter? Ah, of course, now I see it! You must be the little slut's lover! I should have taken a thicker strap to her years—"

Unable to stomach more, Beau grabbed the viscount by the neckcloth, effectively choking off any further speech. "Say one more disparaging word about your *'dear* departed wife' and I swear it's your funeral, not your wedding, the journals will announce." He released the neckcloth and pushed the man back. "Since your previous comments have rendered unnecessary any further testaments of inconsolable grief, let us dispense with pretense. You care nothing for the former Lady Charleton, and indeed are on the point of replacing her. You could, of course, choose not to believe me and proceed. However, should events prove me to be correct, taking a new bride whilst still in possession of another legal wife might later prove rather…embarrassing."

Only then did the implications of Laura's existence seem to penetrate. The viscount turned white, then redder than before, a froth of foam developing at his mouth as his eyes bugged out and his hands and body shook with rage. For a moment Beau feared the man might succumb to an apoplexy right before him.

"A…disconcerting turn of events, I will agree," Beau interposed before the livid viscount could spew more venom. "Which is why I recommend that you take the prudent course of divorcing your current wife before claiming another."

Again, Beau seemed to have surprised Charleton. He inhaled sharply, pulling himself up to full height. "Divorce? Impossible! There's never been such a stain on my family honor!''

''A tad less of a stain than bigamy,'' Beau pointed out. ''And I'll be happy to provide the grounds. You may accuse me of criminal consort. I shall take full responsibility before the lords, so there will be no trouble getting a bill passed. Indeed, my friends in the upper chamber will insure the process is as speedy and private as possible. Perhaps your current intended could be induced to wait until the bill is finalized, though I fear the natural speculation surrounding so unusual a case may cause an abrupt cooling in that lady's sentiments. In that instance, you have my profoundest regrets.''

He made the viscount a mocking bow. ''I realize this comes as a shock. I shall invite myself to a chair while you think it over, after which I am sure you will realize there is but one viable course. Once you've given me your word as a *gentleman*—'' Beau nearly choked over the word ''—that you will meet with your lawyers to begin drawing up a bill of divorcement, I will bid you good day.''

The viscount's eyes narrowed to slits. Clenching his hands into fists, he took a step toward Beau.

Come on, Beau urged silently, nearly bursting with eagerness to get his fists around the older man's throat. But then, conscience forced him to warn off an opponent whose age and condition made him no match for Beau. ''Don't tempt me, Charleton,'' he breathed.

Doubtless the villain preferred victims who couldn't fight back, Beau thought, disgusted, as with a flash of fear in his eyes, the viscount backed away. Charleton staggered to a sofa and dropped onto the seat, panting, then extracted a handkerchief from his waistcoat pocket and mopped his brow with trembling hands.

The actions looked somehow calculated, Beau thought. Playing for time? After giving the man a few more minutes to compose himself, Beau repeated his demand.

"A quiet divorce, my lord. You'll give me your word."

Charleton mopped his brow again. "I—I cannot reply now. Be reasonable, Beaulieu! I've just sustained a shock, a terrible shock! I cannot be so sure what the best course of action might be."

"Surely the best course cannot be to either blunder into bigamy or to watch yourself made a laughingstock when your supposedly dead wife turns up. Proceed immediately, and I will endeavor that the entire matter be kept out of the journals and conducted with as much discretion as the subject will allow. Fight me on this…and I might be forced to make public matters even more damaging to your esteem."

The mopping handkerchief stilled. His nervous prostration vanishing, Charleton whipped a hard gaze to Beau. "What are you insinuating, Beaulieu?"

"Tragic to have lost both wife and child. But the babe wasn't stillborn, as the papers reported, was she?"

"N-no, not precisely. She was young enough, poor tot. A fever, such as infants are so prone to contract. Given the…distress I was suffering at the time, you can hardly fault me for not troubling to correct the journal accounts."

"Your memory of the events does appear a trifle hazy, Charleton. Let me refresh it. The child didn't die of a fever, either—the nurse tending her reported the child was well and thriving. Until the morning two weeks after her birth when you entered your wife's chamber, shouting that you would take the worthless daughter she'd produced and have the brat fostered out. While you beat the nurse away from the cradle and dragged her out of the room, Lady Charleton struggled from bed to try to protect her child. When the maid crept back after your departure, she found the babe dead in her bed and your wife unconscious on the floor.''

For a telling instant, the viscount stared at him in silence. "I'll listen to no more scurrilous innuendo. You will leave my house this instant, or I shall have you forcibly ejected."

Beau nodded. "I shall leave readily enough, as soon as you give me your promise to start divorce proceedings. Quick and private, or long and...untidy. But either way, a divorce. Which course do you choose?"

"I cannot answer that now, today! I—I must consult my lawyers, decide what is best. And the shock to the delicate nerves of my dear betrothed! As a *gentleman*—" Charleton sneered "—though I have a difficult time applying that description to a man who has assisted in hiding a wife from her lawful husband—you must allow me more time."

"As a husband who repeatedly violated his vow to cherish and protect, you've even less right to it," Beau snapped back. "I'll have your word."

"I cannot and will not give it! You may sit in my parlor until midnight, but I'll tell you nothing today."

Beau studied the viscount's face, beating back anger, impatience and disgust to make a dispassionate assessment. His observation forced him to reluctantly conclude that he would not be able to wrest an agreement out of the man today.

So be it then.

He gave Charleton the briefest of bows. "I'll return tomorrow. I'm sure by then your counselors will have convinced you a swift and private divorce is preferable.

For make no mistake, if you still refuse to cooperate, I will initiate legal proceedings against you in the matter of your daughter's death. I expect the notoriety of a trial for infanticide would be even more damaging to your betrothed's delicate nerves.''

Charleton made no reply. Beau turned and walked out, his satisfaction soured by an edgy unease.

He'd gotten part of what he needed—a confirmation of Laura's identity and the initiation of the demand for a divorce. If by tomorrow the viscount still refused to take the necessary action, Beau would set his lawyers in motion.

As Beau had assured Charleton, having long ago accepted that a divorce, with all its potentially scandalous repercussions, was the only way to make Laura legally his, he truly did not care whether doing whatever it took to free her was discreet or the subject of ribald conjecture in every scandal sheet in the metropolis. His elder sister was well established, protected from harm by the influence of her husband's family even should the proceedings render Beau himself a social outcast, as well it might. Kit was young enough that the worst of the scandal would have died away before he was ready to marry. In any event, Beau thought cynically, the possession of a handsome fortune tended to erase any lingering blots on a prospective suitor's escutcheon.

It might—or might not—render him worthless for Lord Riverton's purposes—that would be for his lordship to decide. But even if taking this step ended his clandestine public service, freeing the woman he loved mattered more.

And as for Laura—how would she react to being dragged into prominence in so controversial a case? Having been dead to the world for two years, he hoped with all his heart she would conclude that the boon of being freed from Charleton's menace was worth possibly being ostracized by society afterward.

If she did not, he realized that chances were good that she might never forgive him for making this move without consulting her. But with so little time left to buy them a future, risking that was a chance he simply had to take.

His sleep troubled by images of a howling Charleton hovering over a cowering Laura, Beau awoke early and unrefreshed. Waiting only for a shave and a tankard of home-brewed, he called for James.

The first item in his secretary's morning report rocked him to his toes. Charleton, the agents Beau had detailed to watch his movements reported, had departed London at first light.

An unease speeding uncomfortably close to panic coursed through him and he set his mug down untasted. Though he'd been careful to not divulge either the name under which Laura was hiding nor her current location, he couldn't shake a deep, instinctive fear that somehow her brute of a husband might manage to trace her. His mind working frantically, he heard not another word of James's comprehensive review.

The conviction bubbled up, too strong to be ignored. Full information available or not, he was going back for Laura Martin today. And agree to it or not, she was coming away with him.

Several days later Laura sat in her small parlor finishing up tea with Squire Everett. "So you see, I shall be departing as soon as possible. The note from my husband's cousin was most urgent. His family was always kind to me, and I cannot let them down now."

"Aye, one cannot ignore the demands of family. We shall miss you exceedingly here in Merriville, though! How long do you expect to be away from us?"

Laura laid a hand on her belly. "I'm afraid I cannot say. I shall send word later."

"You needn't worry about the cottage or the hound—I'll see they are both looked after. You're sure you'll not accept the loan of my carriage for the journey? It fair distresses me to think of a gently-born lady like yourself traveling on a common mail coach."

"It's terribly kind of you to offer, but—"

"Ah, well—" he waved a hand to forestall Laura's protest "—you'll not take it, so there's an end to it. Just send word when you're ready to depart. I'll drive you to the coaching inn myself—and on that I'll not budge, so resign yourself to it! We'll at least see you safely on your way. There's my Tom, waving at me through the windows, so I'll be off."

Laura felt a wave of affection and regret for the kindly squire whose hopes she would never be able to reward. "Thank you again, Squire Everett."

She walked her guest to the door and waved goodbye. She ought, she thought with a flicker of shame, to have invited Reverend Blackthorne to this farewell tea, as well, but she hadn't been sure she could have faced either the silent appeal she knew his eyes would contain—or his questions about her plans, which were likely to be much more probing that the genial squire's.

By late afternoon she'd dispensed the last of the treatments to the patients she'd been tending and headed toward home. Tonight she'd finish packing her small trunk of books and clothing, to be ready for departure in the morning.

The early dusk of a crisp winter day silhouetted her

cottage against a sky painted in streaks of violet and crimson as she rounded the corner of the country lane. After pausing a moment to appreciate the delicate beauty, she trudged wearily up the front steps.

Not until she'd entered the front door and walked to the parlor did it strike her as odd that Misfit, who usually heard her approaching footsteps well before she reached the house, had not scampered to greet her with his usual joyous chorus of barks.

She'd proceeded one step into the room before her eyes adjusted to the dimness and she stopped abruptly, shock and panic icing her in place. Standing before the empty grate, cloaked in a many-caped driving coat that magnified the malevolent darkness of his bulk, stood the man she'd hoped never again to see in this life. Her desperately unmissed husband, Lord Exeter Charleton.

"My, Emily dear, how down in the world you've come. Not even a fire in the grate or a servant girl to tend you. I can't believe you left me for this—'' He waved an arm to indicate the tiny, modest room.

When she remained mute, her mind still unable to grasp the enormity of the catastrophe playing itself out in her parlor, he advanced on her. "After all this time, have you no word of welcome for your lord and master? Didn't I teach you better manners than that?" As she belatedly scooted backward, he leaned over to grab her by one arm.

She dug in her heels, resisting with all her strength, but as always, she was no match for him. He dragged her to the small window, brought one beefy hand up to seize her chin and force her face to the fading light, his fingers biting into the skin.

"Humph," he snorted. "Still no beauty. Can't see

what a fancy Corinthian like Beaulieu sees in you. Though we both know what he's planted in you, don't we? Say something, wench!'' He dropped her chin to seize her shoulders and gave her a shake that snapped her head back.

''I—I don't know what you're talking about,'' she replied, forcing the words out evenly. She'd not give him the satisfaction of hearing her stutter with the terror he knew she must feel. The terror he'd thrived on inspiring in her even as he despised her for succumbing to it.

His lip curled. ''Liar,'' he said, and backhanded her across the mouth.

The blow sent her reeling into the side chair. She lost her balance and fell heavily, putting both hands around her stomach to protect it as she went down.

He walked over to glare at her in triumph. ''Don't know what I'm talking about, eh? Don't have anything in that barren belly to protect? Shall we test that little theory?'' He moved a booted foot back and poised it to strike.

''Don't!'' she cried, rolling herself into a ball, more desperate to prevent whatever harm he might try to inflict on Beau's child than to protect herself from any outrage he could deal her. *Never again,* she'd promised Jennie. Never again while she still breathed would she let him harm a child of her flesh.

Laughing softly, he placed his boot back on the floor. ''Sniveling coward. So you're carrying his lordship's brat. Better than you managed for me, you worthless excuse for a wife. What a sorry bargain you turned out to be!''

Before she could think to react, he suddenly kicked out. Pain exploded at her elbow. Tears squeezed under her eyes and dripped onto her cheeks as she gritted her teeth to muffle her cry. He'd proved his point—should he wish to harm any part of her, she was helpless to stop him.

He regarded her thoughtfully. "I married a tongue-tied homely bluestocking for the bountiful crop of progeny every other female of her line had always produced—and got not a single surviving son. But cheer up, my darling, we're not done with each other yet. If you provide the heir I need, I might even be induced to keep you, despite all the trouble you've caused me. The indignity of having to contrive an excuse to delay my nuptials…at least until I could determine whether or not you are in fact going to do your duty by me at last."

He laughed again. "Yes, I should enjoy flaunting the brat in Lord Beaulieu's handsome young face, with him knowing it impossible to wrest the child from me. I hope the bastard looks just like him."

Laura lay motionless, not wanting to give Charleton any excuse to kick out again. Somehow she had to get away.

He gave Laura a vicious nudge with his boot. "So up with you, my cherished wife! I shall have to keep you safe and closely guarded—until you're delivered. If it's a boy…we shall see. If you miscarry or produce another worthless female…" He shrugged. "This time I shall have to ensure your childbed fever is truly fatal."

He jerked her off the floor and set her on her feet, maintaining an iron grip on her arm. Laura flicked her eyes around frantically, searching for anything she might use as a weapon. If she could just stun Charleton long enough to break away, she could flee by a backwoods path the viscount wouldn't know, to the squire's or the vicarage—

Charleton hauled her closer, put his lips to her ear.

"Don't bother plotting to slip away again, my pearl," he murmured. "I know your little tricks, and stripped this miserable excuse of a dwelling of anything you might use before you returned. If you took a poker to me, I might grow so angry I wouldn't be responsible for my actions—we both know how you love to anger me, disrespectful, disobedient wife that you've always been."

He waited, but Laura remained stubbornly silent, barely hearing him as her brain worked furiously, searching for other means of escape. If not here, perhaps after they reached his carriage, or somewhere on the journey— at a posting inn—

Charleton's sigh rattled in her ear. "So inattentive, my dear wife. And we can't have that. Especially since while we wait for you to finish breeding—" he sucked her ear into his mouth, holding her rigid against him as she tried to jerk away, letting her pull free only after he'd left the hot drooling brand of his tongue around, inside it "—you're going to be a better wife to me, aren't you, Emily, darling?" He slid one hand from her shoulder down her chest, rubbing from her stomach down to the jointure of her thighs and back up, his palm coming to rest hard and flat on her belly. "Because we both know what might happen if I'm not satisfied, don't we?"

As she had so many times through the nightmares of the past, Laura clenched her teeth against the nausea rising in her throat and tried to make her mind float away, detached from the body Charleton controlled. Willing herself to reveal neither her revulsion nor her fear.

For the flicker of an instant her thoughts flew to desperate hope that Lord Beaulieu might come to her rescue. Had he somehow encountered Charleton, let slip her location? Oh, she had begged him not to intervene!

Whether he had or not didn't matter now. She was

alone, as she'd always been, and whatever the earl's feelings about them, he couldn't help her. The idea of failing to protect the child she had likely conceived during their precious night together was so horrifying all thoughts but the imperative of escape slipped away.

Somehow I'll get free, Jennie, she silently vowed as Charleton dragged her from the room. *I promise.*

Shortly after dawn the next morning Lord Beaulieu rode into Merriville. Pushing on by the light of a nearly full moon, he'd stopped for a few hours' rest only because otherwise he knew he'd likely have ridden to death the last job horse he'd hired. As soon as he'd obtained a suitable replacement this morning, he was back on the road, driven by a nameless imperative.

Though all his instincts screamed at him to ride directly to Laura's cottage, 'twas best to be more discreet. Accordingly, armed with the glib excuse of having broken his journey north to stop and again express his thanks for all the squire's assistance to him and his family, he headed for Everett Hall.

Enormous relief flooded him when the squire confirmed that everyone in the neighborhood—their exemplary Mrs. Martin included—was quite well. However, once the man imparted the disturbing news that, having been summoned to tend an ailing relation, she intended to soon depart, Beau quickly exhausted his small store of patience trading civilities before finding an excuse to break away. After casually mentioning he'd stop at her cottage to pay his respects before continuing his journey north, Beau finally managed to depart.

His smile died the moment he left the parlor. Why, after vigorously resisting every attempt on his part to relocate her, would Laura Martin suddenly want to leave Merriville?

Once beyond the gateposts of Everett Hall, he spurred his horse toward the one place he truly wished to be. The "ailing relative" he dismissed out of hand, knowing the fictitious Laura Martin had none. Had she been preparing the neighborhood with a story that would preserve her reputation when he returned to spirit her away?

That theory eased the irritation and vague hurt he'd initially felt, after the hell of worry and waiting she'd put him through this past month, upon hearing the squire's pronouncement. Still, he couldn't wait to have her confirm that comforting explanation with her own lips.

It would prove a useful story, he admitted. Today they could arrange a time and place to meet, perhaps at the first posting inn after the squire saw her safely on the next mail coach. Much as he'd prefer to stop the vehicle the second it left Merriville and carry her off forthwith.

Grinning at that indiscreet but vastly appealing prospect, he tied his horse in the barn and paced through the garden, breaking into a near run as he approached the house. Would her expressive face brighten with joy, her heart leap with gladness when they met, as he knew his would?

He let himself in the back door, calling her name so as not to startle her. And receiving no response. An impatient stroll through the silent rooms confirmed his first assessment. Laura Martin was not at home.

A niggle of foreboding underlay the vast disappointment that seeped up. He shrugged it off. She was out tending patients, no doubt. Too restless to simply sit and wait for her, he paced back to his horse. He would ride through the neighborhood and track her down.

Two hours later he returned to the silent cottage, worry

a cold lump in his stomach. He'd not found Laura Martin, nor encountered anyone who'd seen her today. The friendly postboy, when queried if he'd delivered to her a fictitious thank-you letter from Beau, cheerfully confirmed that Mrs. Martin hadn't received any mail in months. So much for the possibility that an urgent missive of some other sort had prompted her intention to depart.

The maid at the posting inn tossed him, along with a saucy look of invitation, the news that no passengers had embarked on the mail coach today or yesterday. Laura had not departed town by that means, then. So where was she?

He'd even, gritting his teeth, paid a short call to deliver his thanks to the vicar, ascertaining both that the man thought Mrs. Martin still in residence and that he strongly advised Beau not to call upon her unchaperoned.

As he entered the cottage this time Beau noticed immediately ominous signs he kicked himself for not having observed on his first visit. The stone-cold hearth in the parlor, where no fire had burned the night before. The full pot of cold tea left this morning by the squire's servant, the kitchen fire she'd kindled now reduced to a few glowing embers.

Alarm eating at him, he walked into the small room he'd entered only once before.

At the sight of the tidily made bed, a flood of rigidly suppressed memories broke free to engulf him. A vivid ballet of impressions danced through his senses—her silken hair against his chest, her arms urging his head to her breast, the soft sigh and fluid feel of her arching into him. He took a shuddering breath and forced them back. *Concentrate.*

The hearth in this room was cold, as well. Neatly

folded in a chest beside the single wardrobe lay a short stack of the hideous brown gowns he so detested, a few of her uncle's medicinal journals beside them.

She'd not spent the night here, of that he was almost certain. Where, then, had she fled yesterday without a word to anyone? And if she'd not spread news of her imminent departure to prepare for leaving with him when he returned for her, why *had* she gone?

As the short winter afternoon darkened to night, Beau sat in the cold parlor, disciplining his mind to consider only the facts. It now seemed obvious that Laura Martin had indeed left Merriville, taking with her not even her medicine chest, which he'd found behind the parlor door.

Why? he asked himself over and over, his mind struggling with that question like an animal caught in a poacher's trap. Only if she felt herself threatened would she have fled the home she'd clung to with such ferocity.

What, besides her husband, could have threatened her enough to force her departure did not take him long to determine. Only a scandal more lasting than rumors of dallying with a London lord, a scandal that would destroy both her reputation and her livelihood, could have sent her running from this haven, unwilling to let anyone know definitely where or for how long she'd gone. The scandal of bearing an out-of-wedlock child.

The stark realization that in the end she had not trusted him enough to send him word about it, stabbed in his gut. Staggering at the sharpness of the pain, he wrenched himself off the sofa and stumbled out to the deserted front porch.

In the darkness, silent snowflakes had begun to fall. Chill colder than their crystalline whiteness settled in his chest. Somewhere in that winter-barren wilderness, the woman he loved had fled, probably carrying his babe.

And the man she'd staged her own death to escape had a better idea how to find her than he did.

He'd simply have to work harder and faster, he concluded, thrusting the agony of his thoughts back into a tightly guarded corner. For there was no way under God's heaven a villainous bully like Exeter Charleton would outsmart that consummate puzzlebreaker Hugh Mannington Bradsleigh, Earl of Beaulieu.

A moment later Beau's whole body alerted to the sound of galloping hooves approaching out of the night. Bitter disappointment squashed a rising swell of elation as the horse neared and he recognized the rider. His secretary, James Maxwell.

"Thank God you're here, my lord," James gasped as he swung down from the spent beast. "I've just ridden over from Mernton Manner—home of Lady Charleton's old governess. Charleton was there before me. Beat the poor woman nearly to death—she's still unconscious. And I very much fear she may have revealed to him Lady Charleton's current location. You must remove her to safety at once!"

In one awful moment it all fell into place: the chest of folded clothing left open in the bedroom, the cold hearths and untasted tea, the medicine box abandoned behind the parlor door.

Terror he'd not experienced since he was a child paralyzed Beau. Unable to move, speak, even breathe, in his mind's eye he saw again the slow roll of the carriage, over and over down the long rocky slope into the ravine below, wood splintering and smashing at each contact. Saw himself awakening, after the final deafening crash, to a silence more frightening than his mother's screams. And heard again the sound that had haunted his nightmares for twenty years—his mother's dying gasp. "Help…me."

A jerk at his arm dragged Beau into the present. "What is it, my lord?" James demanded. "The lady is not—" he stopped in midsentence, suddenly able even in the meager light reflected by the swirling snowflakes to read the expression on Beau's face. "Merciful God," he whispered.

Pain mingled with raw fury rushed into the hollow the terror left in Beau's gut as it vanished, like a flashflood into a dry streambed. Beau gasped in a ragged breath, steadying himself, grabbing hold of the anger and welding it into iron purpose.

It was too late to agonize over decisions that might have been made differently. He needed all his wits and every bit of his experience to find Laura with all possible speed. "May God be merciful," he said starkly, "for Charleton will not be. And when I find him, neither will I."

Chapter Eighteen

Motioning for James to follow him, Beau strode into the dark house, turning up the lamp he'd lit earlier in the parlor. "Tell me everything else you've learned."

A few moments later, after his secretary had quickly outlined his most recent information—all of it confirming what he already knew, that Laura Martin was in fact Emily Marie Laura Trent Charleton—Beau issued his instructions, dousing the lamp and preparing to leave even as he spoke.

"Return to Merriville and hire every man who's willing. I want the whole village combed for evidence of a wealthy man passing by, probably in a closed carriage. Someone has to have seen them."

James glanced from the night lit by flickering snow back to Beau's face and swallowed the protest he'd probably intended to utter. "Yes, my lord. By the way, I had a message sent from Mernton to our people in London instructing them to determine the location of every property Charleton has owned or rented. The results will be sent, as fast as riders can proceed there and back, to your sister at Wentworth Hall. As that is not too distant, I thought if…events turned out to warrant the need, you might wish to set up a sort of headquarters there.''

Beau nodded his approval. "I'm off to enlist Squire Everett and Tom. They will know all the roads hereabouts that might support the passage of a carriage.''

Together the two men strode out the door. Before mounting his tired horse, James hesitated and looked over at Beau. "A carriage must travel more slowly than we can proceed on horseback. He has less than a day's march on us, and can't have taken her far. We *will* find them.''

"Oh, yes, we'll find them,'' Beau confirmed grimly. "But will we find them in time?''

A week later Beau rode up to the entryway of Wentworth Hall, his sister's country home. Legs numb from hours in the saddle, he fell more than dismounted from the exhausted mount a waiting groom led away. As he stumbled into the entry hall, mind bleary with fatigue, his sister rushed over to meet him. No doubt alerted by the outrider posted at the hall's gatehouse a half mile away to watch for him, James and his brother Kit already waited in the small parlor to which Ellie led him.

Inspecting him with a worried glance, Ellie dispensed a series of rapid-fire instructions to have food, clean clothes and warm grog brought immediately.

"Come now, Beau, you must go upstairs and rest this time, at least for a few hours. You won't be of any use to Laura when we find her if you're half dead and—'' she wrinkled her nose "—ripe as Stilton cheese.''

"I could ride a quadrant for you,'' Kit said. "I'm fully recovered now, and I know the roads in the county as well as you.''

"Nonsense, Kit, we can't have you bringing on another bout of pneumonia by riding out in this weather.

I'll stop long enough for grog and some stew. Then I must go out again. James, what is the latest news?''

''Nothing since yesterday, though I expect another dispatch momentarily.'' He hesitated, exchanging a glance with Ellie. ''Really, my lord, I must insist you accept your sister's advice and get some rest. You'll kill yourself at this pace.'' His secretary tapped Kit on the shoulder. ''Let's leave your brother to Lady Elspeth's care. I'll bring any new information as soon as it arrives.''

''Even the smallest bit,'' Beau called after him.

''Of course.'' Urging Kit along by the elbow, James led him out.

Beau inspected the food on the tray the butler had just placed in front of him. The smell of beefsteak and kidney pie nauseated him, and he pushed it away, choosing instead to spoon down a mouthful of stew, so hot it burned his tongue.

Ellie watched him in silence as, under her concerned gaze, he forced himself to consume several mouthfuls and drink half the spiced ale.

''James is right. Beau, I know you blame yourself for Charleton's finding Laura again! But you mustn't. You only did for her what you've done all these years for Kit and me. Tried to protect her by setting in motion the one thing that will free us *to* protect her—a divorce.''

''If I hadn't contacted him, he'd never have known she was still alive.''

''But you couldn't have predicted he would be able to trace her so quickly. And besides, nothing you said allowed him to—''

''Please, Ellie, don't!'' Beau cut her off. He tried to manufacture a smile to soften the harshness of his tone. ''Sweet sister, thank you for your care—even if I don't appear to appreciate it. And thank you for your concern for Laura. You will look after her if…when we find her.''

"Of course. I love her, too, you know. And stop driving yourself so hard. We must find her soon. You will rest—''

"Aye. In here, for an hour or so, although if you're worried about my dirtying the upholstery I can bed down in the stables.''

"Stables indeed!'' Ellie shook her head to dismiss so preposterous a notion. "Stay wherever you're most comfortable. But…do rest, won't you? Promise me?''

"Promise.'' He kissed her fingers. "Now go, and I'll try to make good on that pledge.''

His smile disappeared the moment she left the room. He knew Ellie, James, Kit—all of them were right. He was pushing himself—and everyone else—too hard. But he could not rest.

Not even to Ellie could he explain the demon that drove him, destroying his ability to swallow more than a mouthful, snatching him from fitful sleep. The sick despair that charged it was his own blind, arrogant belief in his ability to manage others like puppets on a string, a belief nourished by years of watching over his family and strengthened in a dozen successful missions for Lord Riverton, that had allowed Charlton to find the woman he had believed dead. Had Beau not convinced him otherwise, Charleton would never have set off after Laura with a ruthless efficiency Beau had been too stupidly overconfident to foresee.

For whatever she suffered at Charleton's hands, Beau held himself responsible.

Ah, yes, Beau Bradsleigh, brilliant mathematician, The Puzzlebreaker. The only thing that kept him from choking on his own bile was the meager fact that it was information gleaned from Laura's governess, not from Beau, that had led Charleton to her.

It didn't help much.

During the long hours in the saddle, he repeated endlessly one simple prayer. "Dear God, spare her life. Don't let the innocent suffer for my sins."

A single shred of information nourished the hope that his prayer might be answered, a hope that kept him still sane. James Maxwell's informants indicated Charleton was even more ill than he looked, with a heart complaint that had seen him bedridden twice this last year. As desperate as the viscount was for an heir, and knowing any child Laura bore would legally be his, her husband would, Beau prayed, treat her gently on account of the child she carried.

His child.

What he intended to do about that, Beau hadn't as yet devoted time or thought to determine. A future beyond locating and freeing Laura Martin did not exist.

A clatter of bootsteps on the marble floor interrupted his recriminations, and without even knocking, James burst through the door. "We've found them."

Beau was on his feet in an instant. "Where?"

"Not too distant from Merriville. Charleton's cousin owns a hunting lodge there, and our agents report that about a week ago a middle-aged gentleman of Charleton's description arrived in a closed carriage with his wife. The husband has been out riding, but the wife is reported to be ill. She's been confined in one of the upstairs chambers."

"How far?"

"Half a day's ride. Our man has rooms waiting at the closest inn. We can go in this afternoon, or hole up for the night to confer with the agents already in place, and strike in the morning.''

Beau was already ringing the bellpull to order a mount readied. "Today. I'll plan it out during the ride and confirm it with the agents when I arrive.''

He rode off thirty minutes later, both Kit and James insisting on coming along. Which was a good precaution, Beau had to admit. Without the restraining presence of cooler heads, when he caught up with them he'd likely kill Charleton on sight.

The plan they devised on the road required the rescuers to station themselves undetected around the perimeter of the hunting lodge, then storm it together at a prearranged signal. Beau would make for the upper room to free Laura; the others were to immobilize any opposition—and to find and restrain Charleton, well away from Beau. As he warned James, if Beau encountered the viscount he couldn't be responsible for his actions.

For the first time in his life Beau understood how a man could do murder. But he refused to let cold-blooded hatred or the heat of rage put such a blot on his own honor, however much the swine deserved to die. Besides, he couldn't very well later beg Laura Martin to grant her hand in marriage to the man who had killed her husband. As maddeningly slow as the legal route was, he would make himself wait for legal vengeance.

The information James had been steadily accumulating to implicate Charleton in his daughter's death was far too damning for the viscount to ignore it any longer. Should Charleton resist a divorce now, and Beau set his lawyers in motion, the viscount risked the noose. Though Beau was sorely tempted to turn the man over to the magistrates in any event, if Charleton proceeded swiftly with a bill of divorcement, Beau would honor the bargain he'd offered.

The delay until Laura won her freedom would be excruciating, but at least he would know she was safe. Beau had already cordoned off his London town house, put half a regiment's worth of guards in place, ready to keep a twenty-four-hour watch. He himself intended to sleep outside her door. If God granted his prayer, never again would he allow Laura Martin to come to harm.

But first, they had to rescue her from Charleton.

After a sullen-faced woman removed her luncheon tray, Laura rose to pace the small barred chamber in which Charleton had imprisoned her for the past week, wincing on her injured ankle. She'd not seen her husband since yesterday afternoon, a fact for which she'd be grateful under any circumstances, but the need to avoid or escape him now was imperative.

The lock on the door was too solid for her to attempt. Dread a tight knot in her stomach, she limped to the window. Taking a deep breath, she raised her bruised right hand to the shutter, tried to get her swollen fingers around the latch. A flash of pain so intense she gasped made her whole hand tremble. Tears starting in her eyes, she tried again, gritting her teeth against the agony.

It was no use—she couldn't make the fingers work. Cold sweat trickled down her unwashed back, between breasts that smelled of sweat and her husband. Sagging against the wall, she took deep breaths to still the rising panic, then clenched her jaw and tried the left hand, also swollen and badly bruised, but probably not broken.

The pain was less intense, but the seldom-used fingers didn't seem able to follow her brain's command to loosen the intricate loops of wire securing the latch. Fear rose in her throat again, a choking miasma, and with a little cry of frustration she dropped her hand.

Even had she succeeded in unfastening the shutters, this room was on the second floor, too high off the ground for her to jump down without injury, and her hands were in no condition to allow her to climb down the trellis. Charleton had done his work well.

Anger built at the conclusion, and with it a furious resolve. Charleton thought he had beaten her to his will, as he had so often before. He'd lamed one foot so she could not travel far, and rendered her fingers useless to master soap, buttons, or comb, so that even should she get away from him, the filthy, wild-haired creature she'd become would frighten off anyone she chanced to encounter. But she refused to let him cripple her spirit as he had her body.

She battled for herself now. Whether from distress, Charleton's hard use, or because they'd merely been delayed, her courses had begun this morning. With the agonizing slowness that was all her battered hands could manage, she'd fashioned some bed linen to use for the present, but her secret wouldn't last long after Charleton returned. If she didn't manage somehow to escape before he discovered she was not with child, he would kill her.

She'd cowered and endured to protect the babe she believed she was carrying, but she'd cower no more. If she were to die, she'd die fighting for every breath.

That, she suddenly realized, was her one hope. Charleton expected her to submit so as not to threaten the unborn child. Which meant she had perhaps one chance at surprise in which to use her remaining strength to break free from him.

A heavy tread of boots from the hallway penetrated her thoughts. Squelching a spurt of panic, she hobbled over and settled herself back in the chair in which she'd spent most of the past week, letting her head loll to one side as if sleeping. Perhaps Charleton would merely look in and leave her undisturbed.

But the footsteps continued through the door, up to her side. She remained silent and still, eyes closed.

Charleton shook her shoulder. "Wake up, my darling."

She stirred slowly. "T-tired," she mumbled, fluttering her eyes open groggily.

Charleton gave a snort of disgust. "You were always next to useless when breeding, sleeping away half the day. But now you must get up, my precious. We're going on a little journey."

A flash of excitement she took pains not to show sizzled through her. "J-journey?"

"Yes, we've been here a week. 'Tis time to move on. Can't have that clever lover of yours catching up to us, can we?"

Lord Beaulieu was looking for her? Incredulity and then joy swelled within her, nourishing the thin flicker of hope and strengthening her resolve. She let herself rouse, as surely Charleton would expect. "Catch us?"

Charleton "tsked" in mock-sympathy. "Sorry, my angel, but you shall not be here to welcome him if he comes. Though could he see you now I doubt he'd claim you." Charleton chuckled at his own joke, then reached over to wrench her up by her shoulder. "Come along. Beaulieu prides himself on his acumen, but he's not the only clever one. He'll not find you—unless I want him to." He threw a cloak around Laura and pushed her toward the door.

She stumbled along as slowly as she dared, moaning from time to time as they descended the stairs, and only increased her speed when Charleton threatened to throw her over his shoulder and carry her. All the while her mind worked feverishly.

Whether or not the earl was pursuing them, she blessed him for making Charleton suspicious enough to move her, for escaping this locked chamber had just multiplied her chances of evasion. There'd be no point trying to run off immediately as they exited the lodge; she wouldn't get far and doubtless none of the servants here would help her. But sometime during this journey, she must make an attempt.

How did the door on the carriage fasten? If it was a simple latch, she might be able, when the carriage slowed along a suitable stretch of road, to bang it open, throw herself out, and roll free. Charleton would not expect such a move, and by the time he got the driver to halt the carriage, she might be far enough away that he'd not be able to track her. Mercifully, the early snow of last week had already disappeared and her slight weight on the hard ground would leave no trace.

If she miscalculated and leaped out when the carriage was traveling too swiftly, she might break a limb—or kill herself. However, since it was unlikely she'd be able to hide her condition from Charleton once they reached their destination, she'd rather take her chances with the road.

In the meantime, as Charleton hustled her out to the carriage, she did her best to appear weak, pain-racked, and quiescent. He settled her in the corner of the vehicle opposite the door, pulling a carriage robe over her belly with teeth-gnashing solicitude. "Can't have my son taking a chill," he murmured.

After tapping on the roof to set the carriage in motion, Charleton began to tie down the windowshades, blocking her view of the countryside. Laura groaned and raised a swollen hand to her lips. "Don't!" she protested in a threadlike voice. "The movement makes me ill. I must have fresh air."

Charleton hesitated. Laura took a gasping breath, as if experiencing a wave of nausea. Frowning, Charleton threw the sash back open. "Very well," he rumbled. "Move by the window. If you cast up your accounts on my new boots, you'll be sorry."

A small flicker of satisfaction steadied her nerves. The flicker grew to a flame as she covertly examined the door latch and concluded that, despite her misshapen fingers, she should be able to bang it open with one quick blow—painful as that action would doubtless be. Now she just needed the right opportunity.

She'd hoped perhaps the motion of the carriage would make Charleton sleepy, but though he made no attempt to converse with her, neither did he nod off.

The short winter afternoon grew darker. Desperation and fear making her queasy in truth, Laura abandoned her covert watch over Charleton to lean her head against the window edge, drawing in deep breaths of cold air while she searched the passing countryside for the necessary thickness of woodland.

Then as the carriage lumbered slowly around a curve, she saw ahead a perfect stretch of road: tree-bordered to give her cover, the path ahead straight and slightly downhill so the coach would pick up speed, and narrow enough that turning the heavy vehicle would be time-consuming once Charleton got it to halt. They'd passed a cottage not far back, chimney smoking. If she succeeded in evading Charleton, there might be a barn she could hide in.

The coach began to accelerate. "Dear Lord, help me,"

she silently prayed. Then, pulse pounding so loudly in her ears she wondered Charleton could not hear it, she slammed her fist down on the latch, shouldered the door open, and launched herself out.

Chapter Nineteen

A starburst of pain, first in her fist, then in her shoulder shattered over her as she hit and rolled. For a moment dizzy blackness tried to claim her. She fought to stay conscious, knowing she had at best minutes to scrabble into the woods before Charleton came in pursuit.

Not pausing to see if the carriage had yet slowed, she clambered awkwardly to her feet and ran, ignoring the fire in her ankle and the agony in her hands as she struggled through a curtain of brush and trees at the road's edge to paw and drag herself up a small bluff. Once she reached level ground behind a thick screen of pine saplings she paused, sweat-soaked and gasping.

Pushing herself deep into their prickly embrace, she scrambled on her knees to the edge of the bluff where she could peer down at the roadway.

Her heart leaped as she watched the carriage bowling along toward the far curve. Had Charleton not ordered it to stop? Or had the driver been unable to halt the horses, in full gallop down the slope?

Dizzy hope bubbled through her. Keeping to the bluff's edge where she could watch the road, she fought her way along the pine thicket, intent on distancing herself as far as possible from the place where she'd leaped from the carriage. When the vehicle slowed, then rounded the far curve without halting, a rush of elation buoyed her spirits.

Grateful now for the cloak that had been a hindrance during her flight, she drew it around her against the chill that had begun to penetrate and settled herself in a thick patch of brush and pine, swiping up pine needles in painful scoops to cover her trail. Too clumsy in her condition to move quickly enough to evade Charleton when he returned to track her, she'd hide here until he gave up his search.

Gaze frozen on the far curve, she waited. Just as she'd begun to hope that perhaps Charleton had chosen to leave her by the side of the road to die, the carriage came into sight, approaching the curve at breakneck speed.

She held her breath as the vehicle began to swing into the turn, much faster than she would have thought safe. And then she realized it was not the coachman whipping the horses on, but Charleton himself on the box.

Obviously not used to driving a cumbersome conveyance at such speed, he was turning it too wide. The outside leader stumbled through the ditch at the road's edge, the carriage's right front wheel fell into it a second later, causing the vehicle to rock violently sideways. For an instant it teetered on two wheels, the screaming horses straining to right it. But though seconds later it finally settled back onto the roadbed, the momentum threw Charleton off the box and into the ditch beyond.

The driverless horses, panicked now, raced onward, passing by a moment later the bluff where she hid. Laura kept her eyes locked on the bulky figure in the caped driving coat lying motionless beside the road.

Minutes ticked away to the thudding beat of her heart. But the man in the ditch did not move.

A savage surge of joy rushed through her. Despite all that she'd suffered at his hands, a pang of guilt followed immediately after. He must be dead, or at the least badly hurt. But though she'd spent the last year giving succor to the ill and injured, she could not bring herself to approach her fallen husband and administer aid.

Someone was sure to come across the driverless team, or the coachman Charleton must have ejected from the carriage would walk back and find him. She'd limp to the cottage she'd seen, and if the occupants didn't drive her away, thinking her a madwoman escaped, she'd tell someone there of the accident.

Having salved her conscience, she struggled to her feet and picked her way through the underbrush, her wary glance still returning frequently to check Charleton's still figure. So deep was her fear and loathing, she could not yet trust he would not somehow manage to suddenly spring up and menace her again.

Hampered by her sodden cloak, her throbbing ankle and distracted by her watch over Charleton, while edging down the steep slope near the roadway Laura missed her step. Unable to grasp the saplings beside her to recover her balance, she fell.

Like a string of fireworks, pain exploded in her ankle, the hands that flailed uselessly at the nearby branches, her shoulder and then her head as she hit the ground hard and rolled downhill. This time, the blackness following the first white-hot bursts claimed her.

Out of a floating haze of cold and pain Laura heard someone calling her. No, she thought dully, better to die here rather than have Charleton seize her once more. Until the words themselves finally penetrated, and she realized the name being called was not "Emily" but "Laura."

She tried to open her eyes, but the world beyond her eyelids seemed formed from a shifting mélange of shapes and sounds that nauseated her. She'd almost drifted gratefully back into the blackness when the fragment of an image, a face too dearly loved and impossibly beyond reach to be real, shifted into focus.

Though the light as she opened her eyes wide sent a shaft of pain through her head, she held on to consciousness. "B-Beau?" she whispered.

She must have died. This must be heaven, for Lord Beaulieu's face loomed over her, then came closer as he dropped to his knees beside her. "Laura! You're alive, thank God!"

He seized one hand. The immediate burn of agony as he clutched her wrist wrenched a strangled shriek from her, confusing her. Surely one was beyond pain in heaven?

The pressure on her wrist vanished even as she cried out. Perhaps this *was* real, she thought, a bubble of wonder swelling her chest, for Lord Beaulieu did not look like the image of a peerless knight in some heavenly vision. Mud spattered up to his chin, his face was red-eyed, bewhiskered, and nearly as grimy as hers.

"Beau?" she whispered again.

Gently he eased her off the ground, leaned her against his chest. With infinite tenderness he carefully took each swollen hand in turn, examined it, then placed a whisper-light kiss on the gouged and purpled surface. Resting both her hands lightly in the warmth of his larger ones, he laid his cheek upon them.

"Forgive me, Sparrow," he murmured hoarsely. "Forgive me."

That seemed such a nonsensical thing for him to say, she smiled. But before she could tell him so, he lifted her. The dull smoldering in her shoulder ignited to a flame that sucked the breath from her and sent her reeling backward into the darkness.

Some indeterminate time later, the gray mists in which she'd been suspended slowly cleared. She was lying in a bed, on clean white linens that smelled faintly of roses, clothed in a long, cotton-soft night rail. Her body was clean, as well, her hair in a neat braid down her side, she realized with an enormous swell of gratitude to whomever had performed that kind service.

A flutter of gray fabric snagged her attention. She turned her head to follow it, and the jolt of pain through her neck and shoulder brought her fully awake.

"She's stirring, my lord!" a woman's voice said.

By the time the acid throb quieted once more to a dull ache, the space vacated by the gray cloth filled with the image of Lord Beaulieu's face. Dark hair combed, his neckcloth pristine white under a clean-shaven chin, his eyes clearer and less shadowed. Eyes that roved over her in intent examination.

"You're...not a dream?" she murmured.

His somber gaze softened in a smile. "No." He reached over, gently lifted her hand—swathed in bandages now, she noted—and brought it to his lips.

But if this wasn't heaven—where was Charleton?

She must have cried the name aloud, for the earl frowned. "Hush, sweeting, he can't hurt you. He's dead, Laura. The coachman told us after his master demanded that he stop the carriage and turn it around, Charleton kicked him off the box, grabbed the reins and sprung the horses. He may have thrown himself off going 'round the turn, or perhaps the excitement was too much for his failing heart. In any event, he fell, his head striking a rock when he landed. He's gone, Laura. You're free.''

Free. The precious word resonated through her, a word she still could barely trust herself to believe this side of heaven. Tears came to her eyes as she smiled at Beau. "Thank you," she whispered.

To her surprise, a muscle twitched as he clenched his jaw, his expression growing grim. Without replying, he laid her hand carefully back on the bed and turned to nod over his shoulder. "I've brought someone I thought you might wish to see," he said as he looked back at her.

She heard a rapid click of nails, then a familiar bark. A warm, wet nose pushed against her fingers.

"Misfit," she murmured.

"James found him in the garden behind your cottage, kicked bloody but still breathing. We brought him with us to my sister at Wentworth Hall, which is where you are now."

"How did you find—"

"Rest now. I'll explain everything later. There's someone else who's been waiting to see you."

Cautiously she angled her head up just a fraction to focus on the tall, vaguely familiar figure walking toward her. Then her eyes focused on a straight line of nose, the thick thatch of sandy hair going silver. Recognition, sharp and poignant, clogged her throat.

"P-papa!" she stuttered.

Lord Beaulieu stood aside as her father bent to kiss her forehead, his bright blue eyes glassy with tears. "My precious child," he said, his voice ragged, and gathered her in his arms.

* * *

In the afternoon of the next day, as golden sunlight filled her chamber, Lady Elspeth, Lord Beaulieu, his secretary, James Maxwell, Kit and Laura's father, Lord Farrington, stopped in for a visit. The earl allowed Mr. Maxwell, who, with her father, he credited for gathering the bulk of the clues that enabled them to track her, to narrate the story of how the rescue had taken place, Kit and Lady Elspeth inserting details along the way.

"You should have seen Beau when we reached the hunting lodge to discover Charleton had already taken Laura away," Kit broke in. "I swear, he was so angry I thought he would strangle the one groom we found still in the stables. But Charleton must have been one ruthless taskmaster. The fellow seemed only too happy to tell us in which direction the carriage had headed, even offering to ride along and point out the road."

"I'm just glad it all happened close to Wentworth Hall so that Beau could bring you to me," Lady Elspeth said. "We've discussed it, Laura, and your papa agrees that it would be best if we let it be known only that you and I came to be friends while you were nursing Kit, so that when the carriage in which you were traveling with your husband overturned, you asked to be brought here. Of course, the fact that you'd left Charleton can't be concealed, nor given his vicious behavior—" her voice took on a ferocious note "—should you be ashamed of doing so, but since it is everyone's desire that once you've recovered, you be restored to your place in society, we feel it best that the details of Charleton's death, and my brother's part in your rescue, not be revealed."

"As soon as you feel ready to travel," her father said, "I'm taking you home. Jack, Rob, Trent, Louisa, Charlotte and their families are all gathering at LeGrange to welcome you." His voice trembled. "I only wish your dear mama were still alive to see it."

Lady Elspeth patted Lord Farrington's hand. "Your father has agreed to let you come to London with me for the Season. My husband won't return from Vienna until mid-Spring, and I shall be desperately dull without him. Having you with me there will make the time fly so much faster."

After she'd thanked them for their help once again, asking the earl to also extend her gratitude to Squire Everett, Tom, the villagers of Merriville and all the men who had ridden quadrants across the countryside looking for them, she saw the earl give Ellie a nod.

Her hostess rose. "Come, everyone, let's let Laura rest. I've ordered tea sent to the winter parlor."

In a babble of voices, her visitors departed. All but Lord Beaulieu.

He hesitated by the doorway. "Do you mind if I remain for a few moments?"

"Please, stay." Even in her weakened condition, her pulse leaped at the prospect of being alone with him.

To her great disappointment, however, he did not seat himself beside her. "I must apologize once again for—"

"Oh, no you mustn't!" she protested, rising up to reach out a hand to him, then gasping at the pain.

"You mustn't distress yourself," he said, rapidly approaching her side and reaching tentatively to touch her bandaged hand. "I am so sorry for this."

"Were it not for you, I would have suffered much worse. Charleton only moved me because he feared you were in pursuit. And if you'd not been pursuing so closely, I would likely have died of injury and exposure before someone happened down that road."

The earl hesitated, stroking her clumsy hand gently. "Did he not have good reason to treat you kindly?"

"Charleton never saw reason to do that," Laura said flatly. She looked away, avoiding his gaze.

"And there's naught else you need to tell me?"

Once, she might have replied by confirming both she and her husband had believed she carried Beau's child, that Charleton had spared her because of it. But ironically, the marriage that had trapped her had also permitted her to speak freely. She might tell the earl the truth, knowing regardless of his response, he could do nothing.

But with her husband dead, she dared not admit the possibility. And she certainly couldn't confess that she loved the earl.

For if she did, the honorable, protective Lord Beaulieu would doubtless feel bound to ask for her hand.

She would not trap him in marriage with this oldest of tricks, nor did she wish to be tied once more to a man unless she were certain his feelings for her ran as deep as hers for him.

Of that, she had no assurance at all.

The earl stood beside her, patiently awaiting her reply. Laura sensed the questions still swirling in him, and knew she was too weary to evade them. Much as she hated to send him away, given how seldom she was likely to see him in future, she said, "Nothing of importance. I—I am rather tired. Could we speak again later?"

He hesitated, and for a moment Laura thought he might refuse. "I will leave you to your rest," he said at last.

But for another long moment he remained, studying her face before bending as if to kiss her. Instead, he merely touched his lips to her hand. Feeling bereft already, she closed eyes that stung with tears.

* * *

With a bow, Beau turned and left her room. Pensively he approached the stairs, but not yet ready for company, changed his mind and headed for his chamber instead.

Had Laura ever been with child? He'd given her a perfect opportunity to admit it, yet she had said nothing. If so, why had she not sent word to him in London? If not, then why had she spread that story about needing to leave Merriville? Had she been preparing the way for his return?

Before all that had transpired this past two weeks, he would have bluntly asked her those questions, demanded that she answer. But he no longer had the right to demand anything of her.

He'd hedged on his own promise to reveal everything, as well. Some facts he would never relate to her. The terror that sliced through his gladness as he carried her unconscious to the coach, cradled her in his arms for the endless drive to Wentworth Hall. His burn of anger mingled with shame after the doctor detailed her injuries, a sprain of her right ankle, broken bones in various fingers of both hands, a concussion from her fall onto the road way. Ellie sobbing against his chest in horror and anguish after she and her maids finished washing Laura's bruised, filthy body.

Only one other person had he ever failed as he had Laura. His mother's death he could not rectify. But Laura's injuries he could make right.

She'd been wed when barely out of the schoolroom to a man who abused her trust and forced her into a deception that had stolen two years from her life. Not until she had resumed her rightful place in the ton, respected, comfortable, and free to select the husband of her choice, would he feel the debt he owed her repaid.

Except for the harm she'd suffered, in the curious fashion of providence, the way things had worked out was probably better than the plan he'd initially devised. Being freed from Charleton by death avoided the scandal and possible social ruin a divorce would have entailed. The carefully edited facts they had all agreed to present to the world would allow Laura to reenter the society of her birth with a minimum of gossip and speculation. In a fitting twist of irony, Charlton's as yet unaltered will even left his former wife a rich woman.

Reestablished in society, as a lovely young widow of wit and considerable wealth, she would doubtless attract every unattached gentleman in London with any pretense to intelligence. Then after a suitable interval, when she'd been courted by enough suitors to decide the kind of man she truly wanted, only then would he permit himself to press his own suit.

The selfish, needy part of him that ached for her smile, her voice, her touch, urged him to beg for her hand now, before she was exposed to the practiced courtesies of a throng of other suitors. But though in his own mind, the injury he'd inadvertently allowed her to suffer outweighed any gratitude she might owe for her rescue, she seemed to feel indebted to him. Much as he longed to claim her for his wife, he'd not propose now and have her marry him out of gratitude. She deserved the time to learn her own mind and make a choice untainted by obligation.

After that proper interval, however, he intended to do everything in his power, perhaps even try to seduce her into a repetition of the glorious night they'd spent together, to insure *he* was her choice.

But for now, he must keep his distance. And wait.

He was much more successful at the last resolve than the first. Returning to London after escorting Laura and her father home to her family, he'd called immediately upon Lord Riverton and turned over the dossier on Lord Wolverton. That minister's subsequent resignation and Beau's behind-the-scenes maneuvering to help bring the lesser criminals to prosecution occupied a number of days.

But now that Ellie had come back to London, carrying Laura along as her guest, despite good intentions to the contrary he seemed nearly every day to find some compelling reason to call on them.

Of course, with Ellie's husband Lord Wentworth still abroad on his current diplomatic mission, it was only natural he should complete for her the small commissions Wentworth would normally have performed. Natural, as well, that he grant Ellie's request to escort them to the various social engagements at which Ellie was introducing Laura.

Like the musicale at Lady Harding's tonight. Having settled the ladies in chairs nearest the musicians, he was now procuring them some refreshment.

"I say, Beaulieu, 'tis a charming lady your sister's brought to town with her," Baron Brompton, an acquaintance from his Oxford days, said as they both obtained glasses of champagne from a passing footman. "Widow with a tidy fortune, I hear."

He'd never much liked Brompton, Beau concluded as he made a noncommittal murmur.

"Glorious auburn hair, too." Wexley, a tulip who prided himself on his discriminating taste in female beauty, inserted himself in the conversation. "Upon my word, a perfect foil for that alabaster skin."

"If you approve her, Wexley, she's bound to become the next Incomparable," Brompton said with a groan.

"I'd best try to work myself into her good graces before word gets around and every Pink and Tulip in the ton has a go at her. Does she like champagne, Beaulieu?"

"*I* am bringing my sister and Lady Charleton champagne," Beau informed him, finding Brompton more irritating by the minute.

"The next glass, then," Brompton said cheerfully. "Ah, the musicians are tuning up. I must find a seat."

After forcing himself to return Brompton's cordial bow, Beau hastened to bring the wine back to his ladies. For a moment he surrendered to the temptation to linger, but when Ellie invited him to take the chair next to Laura, Beau knew he must refuse.

There was no way he could sit close enough to feel the warmth of her body, breathe in the subtle rose scent of her perfume and maintain the semblance of detachment to which he'd pledged himself.

Mumbling an excuse, he walked to the far side of the room.

Of course, he knew his devious sister was doing all she could to encourage his constant attendance. But he couldn't bring himself to feel the irritation her well-intentioned meddling might have otherwise inspired in him.

It was too poignant a pleasure to gaze at Laura's beautiful face, admire the elegance of her figure clothed in a fashionable gown that emphasized her slender loveliness, enjoy the music of her voice, infinitely sweeter to his ears than the admittedly excellent fugue the well-trained performers were now playing.

Indeed, the chamber orchestra's melody scarcely registered in his senses. Freed by the concert from the need to make polite conversation or to control his constant, aching desire to be near Laura, he could simply stand and drink in the sight of her, observe the graceful line of her neck as she leaned to catch something Ellie was saying, the copper flash of her curls reflecting the massed light of the candelabra suspended above her.

Though he did retain enough self-control to refrain from engaging her in direct conversation. And he ruthlessly avoided the insanity of encountering her alone, knowing the temptation to speak with her, touch her, then would be far beyond his power to resist.

Still, his heart twisted with longing each time he saw her, his faltering resolve bargaining with the rigid sense of duty. After first vowing to hold himself aloof until the end of the Season, he'd reduced the waiting time to three months, then two.

Just two months. Surely he could last that long.

Surely in that time she wouldn't fall in love with any of the overly handsome, overdressed, overconfident Corinthians who hurried to surround her as the musicians took their break, as gentlemen had clustered around her at each social function to which he'd escorted her.

Yes, he'd survive two more months—but only, he decided, downing his glass, if he didn't have to torture himself watching other men court her. Feeling a pressing need for liberal quantities of the hard liquor available at his club, and afraid if he stayed a moment longer he would succumb to the urgent desire to wrench Baron Brompton's plump arm off the back of Laura's chair— and possibly out of its shoulder socket—Beau made himself cross to the landing. He'd summon James to escort the ladies home.

Sternly forbidding himself from gazing back for one last glimpse, he descended the stairs.

* * *

Laura looked over the shoulder of the pleasant young man offering her a glass of champagne to see Beau turn abruptly on his heel and exit the room.

He was leaving them again, she thought with a rush of dismay, as he had on each of the several occasions he had escorted them out. No doubt he'd send James or Kit or one of Ellie's friends to squire them home.

Her enjoyment of the frothy wine and frivolous conversation vanished. The first parties Ellie had taken her to upon their return to London had been amusing, even exciting. But to one who was shy by nature, and who had lived virtually without society for the past four years, the endless string of social engagements that made up the life of most ton ladies seemed to her like a steady diet of sweetmeats—overly sugared and ultimately unfulfilling.

She'd not yet determined what she meant to do. Ellie evidently hoped her friend would attract eligible suitors, one of whom might secure her a permanent place in society by inducing her to remarry.

But there was only one man for whom Laura would be willing to brave that institution again. And though she'd hoped Lord Beaulieu's devoting himself to her rescue meant he still harbored strong feelings for her, of late she'd seen no evidence whatsoever to support such a conclusion.

Perhaps he'd worked so tirelessly merely because he felt responsible for Charleton's finding her again. He'd hinted as much while she was under Ellie's care at Wentworth Hall. And now that she was safe, restored to health and society, he felt his obligation to her at an end.

Perhaps his strong preference for her company when he'd been in Merriville was simply the natural inclination of a healthy male to seek agreeable female companionship. Here in London, with ladies of much greater beauty and address available, she no longer merited his attention.

Her sagging spirits plummeted further.

None of the laughing compliments she received during the interlude—with a polite smile and a cynical ear—succeeded in reviving her interest in the evening's entertainment. With stoic calm, she waited for the party to end.

Her depressed spirits did not escape Ellie's sharp eye at breakfast the next morning.

"You look somber. Are you not feeling well?"

"No, my head is fully recovered and my hands are much better." Laura paused. "Please do not think I do not appreciate all you are doing by reintroducing me to society, but—"

"Nonsense," Ellie interrupted with a wave of her hand. "Your family was most eager to present you. They only permitted me to do it as a favor, to help take my mind off Wentworth's absence."

Laura felt a pang of envy at the obvious mutual affection her hostess was privileged to share with her husband. "You miss him very much."

"Dreadfully. And value your company immensely, as does Catherine. So let's have no more rubbish about gratitude."

"But you see, I—I just can't summon much enthusiasm for society. I never really had a place here, and in any event have occupied a different station for so long that it all seems—excuse me if this sounds offensive—rather frivolous. I know I cannot resume the work I did in Merriville, but I should like to do something useful."

Ellie gave her a knowing little smile. "When the right gentleman appears, you will know exactly what you wish to do. Unless I miss my guess, he already has. You have only to encourage him."

Laura stared at Ellie. Not bothering to pretend she did not understand her friend's inference, she instead blurted, "How can you know that?"

Ellie laughed. "Because my darling brother Beau can't seem to let a day pass without calling here. I assure you, he has not always been so assiduous in his attentions to his only sister."

"Your husband is away. He wants to assist you. And you've asked him to escort us to several parties."

"He's managed to delegate those duties before. Besides, when you enter the room, his eyes never leave you, whilst on his face there's such a look of yearning it fairly moves me to tears."

A wild hope soared and then plummeted. Shaking her head in denial, Laura said, "If he does care for me as you insist, why has he said nothing to me of his feelings?"

Ellie's teasing look faded. "Ah, Laura, you must understand Beau suffers from a nearly suffocating sense of duty. Though I can't imagine what he thinks a child of six could have done to rescue Mama after their carriage accident, I do know the tragedy still troubles him. As long as I can remember, he's been fanatical about safeguarding all those under his protection. As I imagine you realize, he holds himself responsible for the harm you suffered at Charleton's hands. In some perverse masculine way, I expect that makes him feel he has no right to ask for your love."

"Shouldn't that be my decision?"

"When has the male species ever asked a female's opinion on something they believe involves their precious honor?" Ellie replied with asperity. She leaned over to take Laura's hand. ''I'm nearly certain Beau loves you, but that for obscure reasons of his own, refuses to act upon it. If you do care for him, before he succeeds in mortaring that emotion behind a wall of new duties, I advise you to *make* him act.''

Uncertainty and longing tore at Laura's heart. But before she could fashion some reply, Ellie waved her to silence.

''You needn't say anything. Truly, I don't wish to interfere. But after all you've suffered, I do so want to see you happy. Both of you.'' Planting a quick kiss on Laura's cheek, she rose from the table and left Laura to her thoughts.

For a long time after Ellie's discreet departure, Laura sat at the table over her cold toast and cooling tea.

If Beau did feel something for her, it was hardly the gentleman who'd be considered unworthy.

Despite Ellie's grand plans, Laura had few illusions about her eventual place in society. Although for the moment, under the sponsorship of the well-respected Lady Elspeth, the ton seemed willing to accept her, Laura was quite certain not everyone would welcome her entry into that privileged circle. With a rueful smile she envisioned the reaction Lady Ardith Asquith would experience upon discovering her dowdy neighbor from Merriville was now the eligible widow Lady Charleton.

Laura expected the beauteous blonde would lose little time spreading throughout the ton as many salacious details as she could recall about the woman she'd known as Laura Martin, who expended herbal treatments to farmers and peasants and lived alone in a humble cottage. The elegant courtiers who now lisped praises about her shell-like ears would likely cease their versifying once Lady Ardith had done her work.

The mistreatment that had forced her to that deception would garner enough sympathy that she'd probably not be ostracized. But many in society might consider she'd failed in her duty by abandoning her husband and disgraced her class in her subsequent choice of employment. Though her tidy fortune would guarantee that not all her courtiers abandoned her, gentlemen of high birth and discrimination would probably conclude she was unworthy to be offered their hand and name.

Gentlemen of such rank and distinction as Lord Beaulieu. Even if he did still feel something for her, as Ellie seemed to believe, Laura was reasonably certain he did not view her as a potential wife. Mercifully, Ellie could not know they had already shared the greatest intimacy possible between a man and a woman.

Though she doubted she would ever marry again, she knew for a certainty that she loved Beau Bradsleigh. Whatever her new status, Lady Charleton would be more than happy to become what the earl had clearly wished to make Laura Martin during his sojourn in Merriville. His mistress.

Did he still desire her? If so, he would hardly, given Ellie's obvious belief that he intended to offer marriage, dare instead to offer her carte blanche while she was residing under his sister's roof.

Was that the reason he was so carefully maintaining his distance?

She did not know. But there was an easy way to find out, one that meshed with the vague plans she'd already been formulating for her future.

In the two weeks she'd spent becoming reacquainted with her family, she'd realized that, despite her papa's pleading that she come back to live in the home of her birth, she had been too long her own mistress to become permanently a dependent in his household or any other's.

Charleton's money, every farthing of it earned in blood, gave her the means to live on her own.

A glimmer of excitement penetrated the fog of depression that had settled over her last night. She would begin looking for a suitable house this very day. For the first time in her life, she would be mistress of a future free from fear and ripe with intriguing possibilities.

The most intriguing of which was divining the intentions of Lord Beaulieu.

Chapter Twenty

The next morning Beau received a highly unusual summons from his sister to attend her at breakfast on a matter of pressing importance. Intrigued, and drawn as always by the bittersweet possibility of seeing Laura, he presented himself in Curzon Street at the midmorning hour she considered appropriate for breakfast.

"Darling Beau, thank you for coming on such short notice!" She leaned up to take his kiss on her forehead, then waved him to the sideboard. "Please, fill a plate. The eggs are particularly fine this morning."

"Thank you, no." Beau refrained from mentioning he'd broken his fast an unfashionable several hours earlier. "So, dear sister, what is this matter that cannot wait?"

"Laura wants to leave me!" Ellie paused dramatically as a shaft of surprise and worry lanced through him. "She says though she's grateful for the hospitality I've extended, she's still most anxious to set up her own household. I tried to argue that a lady of gentle birth simply does not live alone, but she would not be dissuaded. She did agree to have her old governess come to bear her company, and to delay her departure until after Arthur returns next month. But the darling wretch hasn't wasted a moment. She told me last night she's arranged appointments to view houses for let this very morning!''

Beau's alarm eased. Laura wouldn't be leaving London. "'Tis not so surprising. She has been managing on her own for more than two years now. And she can certainly afford it.''

Ellie frowned at him. "If you're not going to support me, I wonder that I troubled to summon you. But there was another reason. Knowing so little of the city, Laura asked me to view the houses with her. But I'm feeling so vaporish this morning I dare not stir from the house. You must escort her for me.''

Beau inspected his sister with a raised eyebrow. Buttering her third slice of toast with an air of innocence, she looked hale enough to ride to the hounds.

Far be it for him, however, to question the veracity of a lady. Especially his sister.

He opened his lips to accept, and then hesitated.

To drive Laura in his curricle would be one thing. The side of his body tingled at the mere thought that she might be seated as close to him as the narrow vehicle demanded, but with the two of them out in plain view for any passerby to see, he felt reasonably sure he could maintain the required aloofness.

But alone with her, wandering through a deserted house? Through shuttered libraries like the squire's, where they'd spent long hours chatting, empty parlors like the snug room in her cottage where she'd invited him for tea, dustcover-shrouded bedchambers... Fire ignited in his belly and sweat broke out on his brow.

"Beau!" Ellie recalled his attention, her lips in a pout. "Surely you don't mean to refuse. You know the city as well as I, and certainly have a better grasp of the proper rents and such." She smiled sweetly. "I can't think of anyone better qualified to advise her. Ah, here she is now."

Wearing a carriage dress of deep cerulean blue nearly as brilliant as her luminous eyes, Laura walked in. The simple gown molded to her form, its color a perfect foil to her flawless skin and burnished auburn curls.

The unspoken connection that always linked them crackled anew, stronger than ever in the heat of his desire. He couldn't seem to take his eyes off her or to make his mouth produce syllables.

"Laura, dear, bid Beau good day," Ellie said. "I'm afraid I'm feeling too poorly to accompany you this morning, but Beau has agreed to escort you in my place."

At Ellie's words Laura halted and made him a curtsey. "Good morning, my lord." Her eyes when she looked back up were uncertain. "I—I could take a maid with me. I should hate to interrupt your busy schedule."

"Nonsense, I'm sure he can spare a few hours," Ellie replied. "And Beau is better able to advise you on the desirability of the locations, the suitability of the rent and such, even than I."

Laura's eyes fluttered back to his face. For a long moment she gazed at him, lips parted but saying nothing, as if she'd lost her train of thought.

Which was only fair. His had derailed the moment she entered the room.

"It's settled, then," Ellie said, turning to him with a mischievous look that had, during her growing-up years, always signaled trouble. "Unless you'd prefer me to send her with James?"

Send her with James? To prowl about deserted libraries, parlors and bedchambers unchaperoned? Not bloody likely!

"I'd be delighted to escort you, Lady Charleton," Beau said, finding his voice at last. "That is, if you are agreeable."

"Of course she is. Laura, I know you've already breakfasted, so you may leave at once. So as to take up as little as possible of Beau's valuable time. Brother dear, you must make sure my darling Laura accepts nothing less than a bargain she cannot resist. Now, off with you."

Grinning, she blew them both a kiss.

There seemed nothing to do but depart.

"Lady Charleton," he said, and offered her his arm.

She was silent as they walked out the entry, silent still as he helped her up into the curricle, not speaking until he'd clambered in himself and dismissed his tiger.

"The first house is on North Audley Street," she said.

Beau flicked the reins, acutely conscious of her beside him on the narrow seat. The rocking motion of the carriage jostled them together as he navigated the crowded street, his arms bumping hers as he worked the reins, his thigh pressing into her warmth as they rounded a curve. By the time they reached the Audley Street address his body was in flames, his oak-solid will reduced to splinters and his mind consumed, like a desert wanderer thirsting for water, with fighting the raging desire to touch her.

He secured the carriage and helped her down, keeping the touch that burned into his palms as brief as possible and praying the dwelling had a housekeeper in residence. Until from her reticule Laura produced a key, saying the estate agent had instructed her to let herself in, as the house was unstaffed.

His hands trembled from the force required to keep them at his sides. Desperately he searched through his mind for Latin verbs to decline, pausing halfway through the present tense of *venio* to unlock the front door.

How he was going to manage walking her unchaperoned through this deserted house?

Laura followed Beau through the door of the Audley Street dwelling, her heart thudding against her ribs.

Ellie, bless her, had presented Laura a perfect opportunity to determine whether or not the earl still harbored any desire for her. Now she just needed to summon up the courage to seize it.

He'd been so unencouraging when Ellie pressed him to drive Laura that she was on the point of declining his company when at last he offered his escort. Given his obvious reluctance, she probably should have declined it. But she'd not been able to bring herself to do so.

Just as she'd not been able to tear her eyes away from the virile face and form that dwarfed Ellie's small breakfast room, filled it with the vibrant aura of his compelling presence. She'd not been able, either, to dredge up a single shred of conversation during the drive here, so content was she to simply revel in the glorious, rare pleasure of his nearness.

On the other hand, a dispassionate review of his behavior thus far indicated that he didn't seem nearly as happy to be with her. He'd not troubled to initiate conversation, had handed her down with brusque efficiency and unlocked the door with jerky, almost angry motions. Her confidence, never high, wobbled further.

And yet. And yet she felt as strongly as ever that sense of spirits entwined, a bond that drew her to him at every meeting, brought her thoughts back to him even when they were apart. Did he feel it, too?

She'd promised herself when she embarked on her new life that she would never again be afraid or hang back in the shadows. Time to put that brave resolve to the test.

But nervousness made her palms damp, set her babbling nonsense about turnips while they viewed the kitchen, the price of ticking as they toured the parlor and dust on voile curtains as they climbed the stairs. Heart pounding at her ribs, she led the earl to the front bedchamber.

Which contained naught but a large, curtained bed.

Laura nearly giggled, giddy from nerves stretched taut—and remembered longing. *Now or never.*

"B-Beau," she said, her voice unsteady. "May I call you Beau, as I once did, even though we're now in London? It s-seems somehow too formal to refer to you as 'my lord' while we're inspecting bedchambers."

Was that a groan? No, she must be mistaken.

"As you wish," he replied, his voice tight.

"You may call me 'Laura,' of course. That's more suitable to the intimacy of the room, do you not think?"

He made no reply, halting in the doorway, fingers gripping the door frame as if he found the room too distasteful to enter.

"Come, you must see it from the inside," she urged. "Or do you not find the contents of the room pleasing?"

His knuckles were white, she noticed as, gathering her courage, she reached down to grasp his hand.

A shock seemed to ripple between them. For an instant he clutched her hand in a crushing grip, then batted it away. "You—ah, it appears... That is, the room is... fine."

He took a few stumbling steps away from her into the chamber and halted again, as if unsure where he should go. Her small store of confidence dwindled further.

Desperately she wished she had even a particle of experience at enticing a man. Why hadn't she watched more closely the behavior of the buxom upper housemaid all Charleton's staff had whispered was round-heeled?

She made herself walk away from him toward the bed in what she hoped was a slow, hip-swinging, sensual glide. Mercifully she reached it before her wobbly knees gave way.

Landing on the feather mattress with a thud more inelegant than seductive, she looked back at Beau and patted the spot beside her. "Come test it out with me."

His eyes widened and he swallowed hard. "T-test it?"

"Yes. After all, if I rent the house I shall be spending long hours in this bed. I should know if they are going to be…enjoyable. You can help me decide."

"A-about the bed?"

"Naturally. The floor appears a trifle too hard."

It's not the only thing, she thought he muttered.

"Please, Beau, I—"

"All right, I'm coming. That is, I'll help you…with the, um, bed." He lurched toward her to deposit himself on the edge as far from her as possible.

Before he could move away she scooted closer and seized his arm. The feather ticking obligingly bent to pinch them closer together.

"Oh, my, the mattress does sag…rather interestingly," she said, looking up into his face so tantalizingly close.

His eyes locked on hers, his labored breaths visible in the frosty room. Slowly he lowered his head toward her, his lips pursing deliciously.

Yes! she silently exulted, stretching up toward him, her eyelids fluttering shut.

Until two strong hands seized her shoulders.

"Laura, what in the world are you trying to do?"

Eyes snapping wide, she stared up at him. "S-seduce

you," she blurted a moment later, too rattled and mortified to dredge up a convincing lie.

To her enormous relief, he didn't laugh at her, though his lips did curve into a tender smile. "My rash sweetheart, a respectable matron just embarking on her first Season back among the ton needs to be much more careful of her reputation."

His hands had gentled, but they still grasped her shoulders. She lifted her own to cover his.

"Beau, I don't care about reputations and Seasons. All I want, the only thing I want, is what you and I shared in my cottage the night before you left for London. Please, tell me you still want that, too."

He exhaled a ragged breath, but twined his fingers with hers rather than brushing them away. "Sweeting, you were a child bride, an abused wife, a desperate runaway. You've never had the chance to experience what should have been yours by birthright—the opportunity to entertain a variety of suitors and make a real choice." His voice lowered. "Once you have, perhaps I can forgive myself."

"Forgive yourself?" she echoed, incredulous. "For what? Befriending a lonely woman who could hardly remember what it felt to have a friend? Caring enough for her to want her freed from the man who'd terrorized and abused her? Spending more than a week searching night and day to rescue her? No, I don't wish to forgive you all that! Oh, Beau, I know you blame yourself for Charleton's finding me again, but the fault was more mine than yours.

"No, hear me out." She put a finger to his lips as he started to speak. "If I had followed my heart and confessed the truth—all of it—if I'd not forced you to proceed in blind ignorance, none of that would have happened to me. It was so hard to trust again, Beau. But I do trust you now, absolutely. With my body and my love.''

He startled her by dropping to his knees before her in one fluid movement. ''I had intended to wait, not wanting to press you for fear you might come to me only out of gratitude. I still think you shouldn't give me an answer until you can be sure about your choice. But I can't hide any longer that it is my dearest wish that, once you've taken the time to truly know what you want, you'll accept my heart and hand.''

His heart and hand? ''D-do you mean you want to marry me?'' she asked incredulously.

''More than I have ever wanted anything.''

Shock, humility, and a deep sense of conviction filled her. ''Oh, Beau, I'm five-and-twenty. I've buried a child, survived illness, loss, isolation and pain. Do you really believe I don't know right now what I want?''

''Are you sure, my heart?''

''I want the man who taught me to trust again. Who gave me the most perfect night of my life, the only time I've ever felt desired and cherished. Were I to have as many suitors as the night sky has stars, my choice would always be you.''

She grasped his hands and stared down at him, willing him to believe. The lazy, wicked smile that slowly lit his face ignited a heat in her belly to match the conflagration burning in her heart.

''One perfect night, then,'' he agreed, rising from his knees to lean her back against the dustcloth-draped pillows. With hands as feverishly hot as hers, he helped her tug off his greatcoat, his vest, his shirt, unbutton her pelisse and slide up the skirt of her gown, seeming as desperate as she for the feel of her naked skin against his. "Starting right now, my greedy darling," he whispered, "one perfect night to last us the rest of our lives."

*   *   *   *   *

Be sure to look for
Julia's next book,
MY LADY'S PLEASURE,
coming from Harlequin Historicals
in the fall of 2002.
It's the story of a half-Irish rogue
who meets his match
in a young country widow.

Please turn the page for an exciting
preview!

Chapter One

If fornication were going to occur, it wouldn't be in her hayloft. That decided, Valeria Arnold frowned as she watched her maid, Sukey, loosen her bodice lacings to reveal more of her generous bosom, then turn the corner of the path leading to the barn, "assignation" written in every sway of her ample hips.

Now, how to enforce that resolution?

Valeria had been coming in for tea after her usual morning ride when she noticed Sukey, after a furtive backward glance, slip her sleeves off her shoulders and scurry out the kitchen door. Since the maid was now out of sight and well beyond hailing distance, if Valeria truly wished to stop her she'd have to follow the girl.

Well, if one must do something unpleasant, best to proceed quickly and be done with it.

Laying down her riding crop, Valeria lifted her chin and strode to the door. At the last moment she paused to pick up a stout walking stick from its stand beside the cupboard. In case her firmest governess's manner wasn't enough to dissuade the ardent youth awaiting Sukey, it wouldn't come amiss to be prepared.

Her courage nearly failed her when she reached the

barn. From within its stout walls emanated Sukey's high-pitched giggles interspersed with soft shufflings and low-toned masculine murmurs. Valeria took a deep breath and wiped nervous palms against the woolen skirt of her habit.

She'd call out a warning. No sense barging in unannounced and surprising them at...whatever they were now doing, she decided, her cheeks warming at the thought. The idea of viewing a man whose unclothed body was not in the last throes of deadly illness fired the warmth to flame.

Nonsense, she told herself, raising chilled hands to cool her hot cheeks. A respectable widow shouldn't be having such thoughts. Especially, honesty compelled her to add, when in this remote corner of Yorkshire there was so little opportunity for her to act upon them.

She pulled the barn door slightly ajar. "Sukey? Sukey Mae, are you in there? Cook needs you in the kitchen at once!"

At the sound of a gasp, followed by frantic rustlings, she entered.

Valeria saw Sukey first, hastily re-lacing her nearly bare bosom while her skirts, which must have snagged the edge of a nearby hay bale when she dropped them, were still hiked up to reveal a froth of white petticoat. Valeria's gaze moved to the man beside Sukey and stopped dead.

Tawny hair gleamed in the shaft of early morning sunlight, and the tall, well-muscled body that lazily rose to impressive full height was not that of the fumbling farm boy she'd expected. Golden cat eyes swept her with a glance from head to toe, their expression half annoyed, half amused, as finely chiseled lips curved into a smile.

"A ménage a trois? Who would have thought to find such delights in the wilds of Yorkshire?"

His voice whispered of Eton and Oxford, even as the fineness of the half unbuttoned linen shirt, the width of the cravat tossed on the hay and the expensive simplicity of the form-hugging buff breeches shouted "Bond Street."

The stranger's smile broadened, and Valeria realized she must have been staring with mouth agape. Though in truth, such a man was as out of place in this remote section of England as if he'd dropped from the moon. Wherever had Sukey stumbled across this London dandy?

Valeria shut her mouth with a snap. Before she remembered her purpose, though, she had to admit a certain sympathy for the susceptible Sukey. With his smiling eyes and rakish grin, the gentleman before her could tempt a saint to dalliance.

"Sukey Mae Gibson," Valeria said, her first attempt at a stern tone coming out more like a croak. "You will return to the kitchen immediately. We'll speak of this later."

Finishing the ties at her bodice with a jerk, Sukey gave her a sullen look. As she stepped past him, the unrepentant rogue had the audacity to wink at the girl. She halted, a foolish grin springing to her lips before she turned back to Valeria. "But Mistress—" she whined.

"At once, Sukey," Valeria interrupted. "Before I forget that it is a Christian virtue to forgive."

What no other housewife in the county would, Valeria added mentally, with a rueful sigh at the compromises poverty compelled.

Valeria kept her unflinching gaze locked on Sukey until the maid, with slow, reluctant steps, exited the barn.

Then she turned back to level the same stern look on her uninvited visitor.

"You, sirrah, will do me the favor of leaving my property by whatever means you came and returning to wherever it is you came from."

Apparently possessing not a particle of embarrassment, the man merely inspected her once more from head to toe, his gaze curious. "Will I now?"

He spoke the words with a slight lilt, whose origin her precise mind was distracted into trying to ascertain until she realized the rogue was approaching. Before she could move, with a smooth panther's gait he had reached her and seized a curling wisp of hair, escaped from its pins during her ride, between two tanned fingers.

"You so unkindly interrupted my morning's plans. Why should I not take you instead?"

Seen up close, the golden eyes mesmerized. For an instant, she couldn't seem to move—or breathe. Then she caught the odor of brandy, the lingering scent of cigar smoke. He was more than half disguised, she realized. Rather than rising early, he'd probably not yet been to bed. Her first thought—to wonder again where in the world he had sprung from—was rapidly swamped in acute awareness of the heat and scent of him hovering over her.

"You shall not," she said sharply, dragging herself back from lassitude to slap his hand away.

"And why is that, pray? You certainly look ready for kissing."

Since her rapt gaze *had* focused on his lips, she'd best not debate that. "You have the appearance of a gentleman, sir, and therefore would never take an unwilling lady," she pronounced.

To her surprise, the man threw back his head and

laughed. "Sure, and you're wrong on both counts! Shall I show you how much?" With the spurned hand, he reached out to tilt up her chin.

Valeria's gaze locked with his. She tightened her grip on her walking stick, though in truth, as the gentleman's height and reach far exceeded hers, should he really choose to attack her the wooden pole wouldn't prove much of a weapon. But despite his threat, she felt no fear.

"I'd prefer you didn't show me. I'd also prefer if you'd refrain from enticing my maid."

He released her chin, his glance sympathetic. "You waste your time there. The girl's as light-skirted as they come. If 'tis not me, 'twill be another lad she raises her petticoats for, sure as dawn follows the moonlight."

Valeria stifled a sigh. "Perhaps. But not in my barn."

With a lithe movement the man caught up his discarded jacket. "I wouldn't be too sure of that."

Nor was she, but she wasn't about to discuss with this bosky stranger what necessity forced her to tolerate. "I trust you can find your way out. Good day, sir."

She turned on her heel, but the man caught her shoulder. Startled, she looked back at him.

"Is it sure you are that you're unwilling?"

A shudder of heat radiated from his hand throughout her body. Something buried deep within her, a longing long denied, stirred in response.

Don't be a fool. Jerking her shoulder free, she stepped away. "Yes," she said crisply, and strode off.

His soft chuckle followed her. Just before the barn door closed, she heard him murmur, "Liar."

LINDSAY McKENNA

continues her popular series,

MORGAN'S MERCENARIES

with a brand-new, longer-length single title!

She had never needed anyone before. Never ached for a man before. Until her latest mission put Apache pilot Akiva Redtail in the hot seat next to army officer Joe Calhoun. And as they rode through the thunderous skies, dodging danger at every turn, Akiva discovered a strength in Joe's arms, a fiery passion she was powerless to battle against. For only with this rugged soldier by her side could this Native American beauty fulfill the destiny she was born to. Only with Joe did she dare open her heart to love....

"When it comes to action and romance, nobody does it better than Ms. McKenna."
—*Romantic Times Magazine*

Available in March from Silhouette Books!

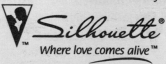

Where love comes alive™

Visit Silhouette at www.eHarlequin.com

PSDW

Silhouette Books invites you to cherish
a captivating keepsake collection by

DIANA PALMER

They're rugged and lean...and the best-looking, sweetest-talking men in the Lone Star State! CALHOUN, JUSTIN and TYLER—the three mesmerizing cowboys who started the legend. Now they're back by popular demand in one classic volume—ready to lasso your heart!

You won't want to miss this treasured collection from international bestselling author Diana Palmer!

LONG, TALL Texans

CALHOUN, JUSTIN & TYLER
(On sale March 2002)

Available at your favorite retail outlet.

Silhouette®

Where love comes alive™

Visit Silhouette at www.eHarlequin.com

PSLTT

Coming in February 2002

#1 *New York Times* bestselling author

NORA ROBERTS

brings you the newest book in her fabulously popular
Cordina's Royal Family series,

Cordina's Crown Jewel
(Silhouette Special Edition #1448)

Princess Camilla de Cordina runs away from royal
responsibility…and straight into the arms of a most unlikely
Prince Charming…cantankerous Delaney Caine.

Also available in July 2002

Read the stories where it all began in three
mesmerizing tales of palace intrigue and royal romance…

Cordina's Royal Family

containing AFFAIRE ROYALE, COMMAND PERFORMANCE
and THE PLAYBOY PRINCE

Available at your favorite retail outlet.

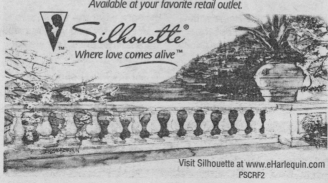

Silhouette®
Where love comes alive™

Visit Silhouette at www.eHarlequin.com
PSCRF2